Extraordinary Things

──────── ✶ ────────

Extraordinary Things

———— ✶ ————

A Novel

**Diana M. DeLuca
Director, Halifax Aircraft
Families Association**

iUniverse, Inc.
New York Lincoln Shanghai

Extraordinary Things

Copyright © 2007 by Diana M. DeLuca

All rights reserved. No part of this book may be used or reproduced by any means, graphic, electronic, or mechanical, including photocopying, recording, taping or by any information storage retrieval system without the written permission of the publisher except in the case of brief quotations embodied in critical articles and reviews.

iUniverse books may be ordered through booksellers or by contacting:

iUniverse
2021 Pine Lake Road, Suite 100
Lincoln, NE 68512
www.iuniverse.com
1-800-Authors (1-800-288-4677)

This is a work of fiction. All of the characters, names, incidents, organizations, and dialogue in this novel are either the products of the author's imagination or are used fictitiously.

ISBN-13: 978-0-595-41505-2 (pbk)
ISBN-13: 978-0-595-85854-5 (ebk)
ISBN-10: 0-595-41505-9 (pbk)
ISBN-10: 0-595-85854-6 (ebk)

Printed in the United States of America

For the men and women
Who volunteered to serve in the Air War

also

my dads with love and esteem:

Warrant Officer Sid Scott, 640 Squadron RAF
Squadron Commander George Sweanor, 419 Squadron RCAF

Acknowledgements

This book could not have been written without the generous support of those remaining gallant gentlemen who flew the Handley-Page Halifax bomber from airbases all over England and later in Africa and the East. They are scattered now, and each year sees fewer of them, but they gather round the two remaining examples of the "Halibag" at the York Air Museum and the Royal Canadian Air Force Memorial Museum in Trenton, Ontario. At both museums, I was given time to study the aircraft and to appreciate the danger and the importance of the aircrews' service to their countries. The Halifax bombers were miniature United Nations. While some squadrons were all RCAF, RAF, or RAAF, many might have three or more nations represented among the seven-member flight crews. The Halifax crew described in this book is authentic in this respect.

I want to acknowledge my first readers, Dr. Sidney Bronstein, Donald Plant, David DeLuca, Michelle McKeegan, and Kimi Mann. Also, the veterans themselves and squadron historians who shared their experiences with me and/or corrected early drafts: Louis Coleman, RCAF, bomb aimer, 35 Squadron, 77 Squadron (Pathfinders); W/C T. W. H (Howard) Hewer, CD, RCAF ret., wireless operator, 148 and 218 Squadrons, author of *In for a Penny, In for a Pound*; F/O F. E. "Jeff" Jeffery, DFC, RCAF ret., pilot, 432 Squadron, president, The Halifax Aircraft Association; Elaine Jeffery, RN, Jeff's adjutant, The Halifax Aircraft Association; Bill Norman, author of *Halifax Squadron: The Wartime Bombing Operations of No. 640 Squadron, Leconfield;* P/O, Fred Papple, RAAF, pilot, 640 Squadron, author of *Seventy Five Percent Luck*; Ann (Hebblewhite) Penny, Order of Australia Medal, LACW, Station Headquarters, Leconfield; F/L G. D. Perks, DFC, RAF ret., pilot, 420, 427, 434, and 571 (Pathfinders) Squadrons, flying instructor at No. 1669 HCU; F/L Sid Philp, RCAF, navigator, 434, 419, 426 Squadrons, memoirs published in "Observair," newsletter of the Ottawa Chapter of the Canadian Aviation Historical Society; F/O Doug Sample, CD, RCAF ret., rear gunner, 415 Squadron, President-Chairman, Yorkshire Air Museum, Canada Branch; L/C Bill Tytula, RCAF ret., Restoration Project Manager, Halifax Aircraft Association; and F/L D. Evans, DFC, Pilot 10 Squadron, 1658 HCU, RAF.

While I have benefited from the time, memory, and energy of these phenomenal people, any blunders and errors in this book are entirely my own. Also, while the events of the book are based on actual occurrences, I have taken many liberties with the story and with the experiences depicted. The characters are ultimately the author's own creation and should not be taken as depictions of specific people. A portion of the sales of this book will support Halifax NA337 at the Royal Canadian Air Force Memorial Museum and Friday the 13th at the York Air Museum.

1

An Operation to Hannover, September 1943

"G for George, M for Mother," the WAAF driver of the aircrew lorry calls out.

These are the letters assigned to two of the four-engine Handley-Page Halifax bombers assigned to Leaton, the Yorkshire home base for the RAF 958 "Long Shank" Squadron. Leaton houses two flights of nine aircraft each. Tonight, three hundred and twelve bombers have been called from airfields all over northern England. The battle order from Bomber Command calls for ten from 958 Squadron.

Two crews of seven men climb in to be driven out to frying-pan-shaped dispersal sites where their aircraft await them. They wear flying dress, fleece-lined boots with a hidden knife, and warm underwear, and carry Mae Wests, helmets, oxygen masks, gloves, and parachute packs. The RAF escape kits tucked into their battle dress include silk maps, Horlicks tablets, water-purifying equipment, fishing line and hooks, and Belgian, Dutch, French, and Danish currency as well as RAF identification. The two crews recognize each other from the socials, the local pubs, the NAAFI café on base, and the mess, but once they're formed, crews tend to keep to themselves. Other crews come and go. The casualty rate is so high that new crews are sometimes lost and replaced before anyone can learn their names.

The young woman driver swings slowly along the perimeter track and out to where the aircraft wait in the setting sun. It's as normal a September evening as wartime permits. The skies are darkening, a light ground fog hovers over the low spots, and a smoky burning-leaf smell clings to the damp air. The harvested fields next to the runway look black in the fading light. No one ever says anything on this ride. Everyone is apprehensive but will not admit it. If palms sweat or stomachs feel like lead, they are carefully hidden. Nevertheless, each crew believes itself the best on the squadron. And more, that it will be the other ones who buy it.

These feelings of immortality are needed for the crew to climb into the aircraft and fly it off into the dark.

The lorry stops first at the parking pan for M for Mother and then drives on. G for George looks like a frozen animal, nose twenty feet in the air, sniffing and peering into the distance. Many crews believe the aircraft have lives and characters all their own. They describe some of them as bad actors, but they rub their good luck charms all the more fiercely and fly them anyway. The crew jump down from the lorry and throw their gear into the aircraft. They've flown G for George before. On their first Operation, or "Op" as they call them, they went to France. A "milk run" given to new crews to make them think that perhaps they can do this and perhaps they even might survive. A "piece of cake" the squadron calls them. It was the same for their second Op. Tonight, though, is their first Op to Germany. There will be aircraft bunched up over the target, flak is projected to be heavy, and German night fighters are expected to be out in force.

They sit on a bomb trolley while the pilot does a slow external inspection of the aircraft. The composition of the crew of G for George is typical for the squadron. Four are British, two are Canadian, and one is Australian. Through training and camaraderie they have become a brotherhood and do most things together. Five of them have been together since the Operational Training Unit. The engineer and the second gunner joined them at the Heavy Conversion Unit where they learned to fly the Halifax. But it's the pilot who's in charge. Even if someone on the crew outranks him, he's the skipper.

The skipper walks round the outside of the aircraft to inspect tail, trim tabs, and wing flaps. He doesn't expect to find anything wrong that the erks, the dedicated ground crew, would not have noticed. But it is his job. Finding everything operational, he nods to the ground-crew sergeant and signs the Form 700 to accept the aircraft. He fingers his lucky coin. His wife gave it to him and he always carries it. He knows that the others all have something—keepsakes, or medals, or even toys. If someone loses his lucky bit, everyone breaks out to help him find it. It's that serious.

"Getting to be time," the skipper says. The crew stand up from the bomb trolley. Cigarettes hiss in puddles. They line up along the grass perimeter and relieve themselves on the grass for luck. Some of the rear gunners pee on the tail wheel, but the skipper doesn't think it's good for the rubber. Aircrews are superstitious and once something has become established, like this ritual pee, breaking routine is bad luck. Anyway, no one wants to use the Elsen toilet on board. It's almost impossible to get out of the flying gear, the temperature may be well below zero, and ground crews don't like cleaning up the aftermath. Crews quickly learn to control their bladders.

They climb in through the aircraft's entrance hatch in their usual order. The wireless operator goes in first and down the steps to his place under the pilot. The engineer goes to his panel on the bulkhead behind the pilot. The bomb aimer climbs down into his cramped position in the nose. When he is lying prone on his mattress looking into the bombsight, his feet will be under the navigator's table. The navigator follows and spreads out his maps on his table. Then the gunners go one to the mid-upper position and one to the Boulton Paul turret at the rear. The skipper follows last. Even if they must climb off the aircraft to wait, they will follow this order for re-entry. This skipper wants to be the last one in, the one who secures the entrance hatch. They have to be careful with that. It opens in and up. Somebody can hit his head and get a nasty cut. Not much sympathy if he does. "Bloody careless," the medical orderly calls it.

The skipper crawls into the pilot's seat. The seat is small for him in his bulky flying suit. But he'll need all the clothes he's wearing in the mostly unheated aircraft. Once they're at their assigned altitude, it's so cold that they can get immediate frostbite if they remove their gloves and touch anything metal.

In the wireless compartment beneath the pilot, the wireless operator sets the frequencies and listens for updates on the weather and wind. Once when they were all aboard, the message came that the Op was scrubbed. They hate that when it happens. It means they have to go through the mental preparation again the following night and it's too late to go into town and let off steam.

"Engineer?" the skipper asks.

"Roger," comes the reply. "Ready for start-up."

The skipper gives the thumbs up to the ground crew who have pulled the trolley/accumulator up to the Halifax. It looks like a large vacuum cleaner and when attached to G-George's port side it powers the start-up. By custom the inner engines will be first as these engines power the hydraulic and electrical systems.

"Contact," comes a yell through the growing dark from beneath the aircraft.

The skipper adjusts the throttle for the port inner engine. The engineer pushes the starter button and the engine sputters into life and then emits a steady, tractor-roar. One by one, the other three engines come to life in order. The plane vibrates as each engine crackles in sequence and the plane shakes as the engines warm up at 1000 rpm. The altimeter and gyrocompass are set.

"Checking mags port inner," the skipper calls out.

The engine roars to 1500 rpm in answer to the forward thrust of the throttle. The other engines are tested. The ground crew detach the trolley and wheel it away.

The skipper concentrates on the preflight checks of the instruments and the gauges in front of him. He goes through the regular routine: hood latched, harness fastened, elevator trim tabs set 2 degrees tail heavy, aileron and rudder trim tabs neutral, tension on, suction on, oxygen on, brakes on, controls full and free movement, bomb door closed, each engine connected to its appropriate main fuel tank, call light system on, and propeller fully fine. He then checks the intercom communication with all crew stations. He is already feeling hot in his flying clothes.

"Wireless?"

"Reading," comes the reply. The wireless operator has the emergency frequencies and the colours of the day in case they need to signal who they are. Once they get over the enemy coast, he will drop bundles of foil called Window through the flare chute in the aircraft floor. This is to confuse the enemy radar.

"Rear gunner?"

"Heading to take-off position."

"Mid-upper here. Going to take-off position."

"Navigator set. Going up to take-off position."

The bomb aimer comes up the steps and pulls down the dickey chair that swings out from the aircraft wall. He snaps it into place over the steps. This puts him right next to the pilot. The bomb aimer has had previous flight training and during take-off will help hold the four throttles at full power against the gate. A couple of others can fly the plane straight and level if they have to. That was something that the skipper insisted on teaching them when he had time. On the ground, he also made them practice escaping through the hatches in the dark.

The skipper and engineer continue their checklists.

"Flaps serviceable. Hydraulic pressure. Landing lamp retracted. All trim controls set for full travel."

The trim tab lever is moved to its halfway position.

"Undercarriage lever down. Check auto controls. Heater on. Full fuel mixture for take-off. Oil pressure?"

"85 lbs," the engineer reports.

The ground crew pull away the chocks and stand by to wave the crew on their way. Everyone on the station always turns out for this. It can be a crowd.

"Weather?"

"Reporting winds 270, 30 knots," the wireless operator replies.

"Should get us there in good shape," the skipper comments. "If it holds, we'll have a headwind coming back."

The control tower gives them permission to enter the taxiway. The skipper releases the brakes and moves the throttles forward. G for George moves toward the perimeter track guided by the ground crew. M for Mother is already in line.

Evening is settling into the airfield now but the navigation lights of the aircraft ahead tell the skipper where they are in the line. They are to take off in one-minute intervals, signaled by an Aldis lamp operated by the duty pilot in a van parked by the end of the runway. Red to wait, green to go.

The Halifax turns 90 degrees onto the runway. The skipper applies the brakes. Together he and the bomb aimer push the throttles forward. The engines rev up to 3000 rpm. The aircraft shakes and shudders in response. In the take-off position behind the pilot and engineer, the safest part of the aircraft in case there's a crash, the rest of the crew listen to the creaking of the seams.

The Halifax's engines continue to roar with full power and the interior of the aircraft bounces. The light flashes green. The skipper grips the control column tightly and releases the brakes. He applies starboard rudder to counter the aircraft's tendency to swing. Then the Halifax roars down the runway, 70, 80, 90 knots until they gain the speed to rise over the end of the field. The brakes are then applied to stop the wheels rotating.

"Retract undercarriage," the skipper says. When the undercarriage is back in place, the engineer engages the manual undercarriage lock.

They continue to climb and make a slow turn to port to follow the others ahead of them. The bomb aimer unstraps himself, snaps the folding chair back into position, and goes down into the bomb aimer's area. It will be his job to assist with navigation until they get close to the target area. The navigator follows and clicks on his light over the chart-filled table. This will be the only light, except for dials and switches, on board. The gunners head to their turrets.

"Navigator, confirm course please."

The navigator has fixed his position as they flew over the airfield.

"Steer 101. Assigned altitude 1000 feet. At speed of 170 knots."

"Roger. Steer 101."

The aircraft continues across Yorkshire, across Flamborough Head, and out over the dark North Sea. All navigational lamps have been turned off, and G for George enters the darkened bomber stream. Outside it is soon completely dark. They fly on their assigned route at their assigned altitude and at their assigned time, knowing that there are aircraft in front and behind, all invisible in the night, and all headed to the same target. The bombing will commence at H-hour, and all have been assigned a time of H-hour plus to indicate their position in the bombing order.

"Rear gunner requesting permission to test guns."

They are now over the North Sea and it is time for the gunners to check their equipment.

"Go ahead," the skipper replies.

The rattle of the four .303 machineguns from the rear is silenced by the sound of the engines. The rear turret is the most isolated part of the Halifax. Sometimes a badly damaged aircraft returns missing the turret and its occupant.

The mid-upper gunner asks for and receives permission to do the same.

"Skipper, prepare to alter course starboard onto 110, five minutes. Speed 155. Climb to 18,000."

The navigator spends the entire flight continually calculating their position. Each aircraft navigates independently. Each navigator is responsible for getting the plane to its target and back.

"Turn now," the navigator says when the time comes.

"Roger steer 110."

The skipper begins the process of automatic checks of the crew to make sure they are all right. He will also regularly raise and lower the wing tips and weave the aircraft to allow the gunners to see enemy aircraft below them. Chatter is not permitted, particularly not once they are over the enemy coast.

"Eight thousand feet. Check oxygen," the skipper tells the engineer as the Halifax gains altitude. It is the engineer's job to turn the oxygen valve on.

"Reporting variable winds of 50-60 knots over target." The wireless operator has disconnected his headset from the intercom system to save the rest of the crew from listening to Morse code signals. He rejoins them as needed or when they need to hear the Master Bomber in the target area. His job is to help with radio fixes when he can and to listen for recalls and for the weather forecasts sent back by the Pathfinders. The Pathfinders fly Mosquitos to drop initial markers on the target and follow up in Lancasters and Halifaxes to drop more.

"Preparing to switch fuel tanks," the engineer says.

They cross over the enemy coast and see flashes of guns and flak from the shore batteries. The explosions are like deadly fireworks.

"Gunners, keep your eyes peeled for night fighters," the skipper says.

"Skipper, third turn point in five minutes," the navigator breaks in. Then when the moment comes. "Alter course to 135."

Thirty minutes to target and an explosion ahead. A Halifax spirals down in front of them in flames. Then another. The night fighters are active.

"Fighter, fighter, prepare to corkscrew port. *Go!*" The rear gunner's voice tears across the intercom.

Without waiting, the skipper lowers the left wing and pushes the control column forward. He makes a steep diving turn using the rudder to balance the aircraft. The Halifax's guns blaze. A night fighter has come up from below where it couldn't be seen. The night fighter's cannon strafe the plane but mostly miss because of the aircraft's twisting. Still, bullet holes tear through the forward part of the Halifax and rake across the port wing. The plane jumps in the air like a wounded animal. Through the window, a burst of flames indicates that the port inner engine is on fire. The controls have become heavy and sluggish.

"Turn off fuel to port inner." The skipper sounds frustrated but calm.

The engineer turns off the fuel and sets the fire extinguisher for the engine. The propeller is feathered.

"Still on fire," the engineer says. "Fuel tank's ruptured."

"I'll dive to put it out."

The skipper puts the aircraft's nose sharply down, but even after a drop of several thousand feet, the flames persist. Fuel from the damaged engine hits against the side of the aircraft and runs in black streaks up the fuselage. The smell of the petrol comes into the aircraft.

"Corkscrew starboard. *Go!*"

The skipper doesn't know whether the aircraft can sustain another violent manoeuvre. He puts the nose down and turns it anyway. By now they have lost a lot of altitude.

The mid-upper gunner can feel sweat trickle down his face. Cannon shells hit against the aircraft in a sickening rattle. They rip holes down the side of the aircraft and shatter the perspex bubble in front of him. He isn't hit, but he feels an icy blast of air in his face.

The shells have also hit the starboard outer engine. It bursts into flames and the wing vibrates violently. The aircraft keeps slipping to port and wants to turn over. The skipper fights to keep it level, but the second attack has blown away more of the controls. The altimeter shows it to be a losing battle. He raises the bomb-release lever beside his seat and jettisons the bombs. The aircraft leaps upward.

"We're done for. Bale out, bale out," he yells into his face mask. "I'll hold as long as I can. Good luck."

The crew moves quickly, a tribute to their training and the skipper's insistence that they practice. The navigator clips on his parachute and opens the escape hatch in the floor at the foot of the steps. Opening that hatch is his job because he's the closest to it. He sits for only a moment on the side of the small hole. The wind tears off his flying boots as he pitches himself forward. The bomb aimer follows. The engineer comes down the steps and goes out next. The rear gunner turns his turret and goes out the back.

The mid-upper gunner drops out of the turret and clips on his parachute. But when he tries to open the entrance hatch he finds it won't budge. He climbs back up through the fuselage holding on to whatever he can find in the dark. He forces his way over the rear spar of the rest area and falls heavily. Then he struggles to his feet and lurches over the front spar. Time seems to be on hold for him, but it has been only a few seconds. He hangs on to the wall by the empty engineer's position and throws himself toward the steps. He glances briefly toward the pilot's seat. The skipper points down the steps and gives him a thumbs up. Then a moment's recheck of his parachute at the open escape hatch, and the gunner is gone into the bitter cold of the night.

The aircraft holds on for a couple of minutes more and then noses down sharply to port and goes into a twisting dive. Both engines are blazing. With the torque of the dive, the port wing tears off and falls to earth on a parallel course with the rest of the aircraft. The Halifax finally crashes far below, somewhere north of Hannover. The engines explode on contact and the fuselage breaks violently apart. Burning petrol streams out of the tanks and billows thick smoke into the sky. Ammunition explodes like fireworks. Then another, larger explosion reduces what is left of the Halifax into a jumbled heap of black, twisted metal. Very little remains recognizable. The charred ground is littered with metal pieces, burned wires, and mangled bits of the fuselage. The fire stops when there is no more fuel to feed the flames. Then there is only an occasional flicker until everything flammable on board is consumed, including the two crewmembers that did not get out.

2

Nothing Will Ever be Same, London, June 1980

"How was the show last night?"

Marilyn MacDonald stirs the leaves in the familiar brown teapot, puts on the cracked lid, and pulls down the quilted cat-shaped cozy. She and her daughter, Barbara, are both night people. Barbara is an actress appearing as second lead in *Yesterday's Lies* on the West End. Marilyn is a private night nurse who falls into bed as soon as she gets through the front door in the morning. When they both wake up about midday, Marilyn loves to sit at their kitchen table and insists on being told stories about her daughter's life. It's her substitute for the hopes she once had for her own.

"Not bad, Mum," Barbara replies. "They say Maggie's thinking about concentrating on films after her contract is up. Oh and they laughed where they ought to at my 'limp dreams' line."

Barbara is aware that her mother is consumed with her acting career and tries to share the gossip with her. The theatre, though, is both a bond and a barrier between them. Marilyn believes in the power of personal will. In her view, Barbara is not the lead actress only because she lacks the drive to insist on it. Barbara finds this vehemence draining. She tries to discourage her mother's lectures, but every so often something comes up to make that impossible. Then they play out a well-established pattern of thrust and parry.

Marilyn pulls her pink flannel dressing gown tightly across her ample chest and looks intently across the table. She is an imposing woman. Her eyes are a smoky grey and although her face has softened, her chiseled profile is a reminder of her once considerable beauty.

"Any chance of you getting it?"

"Getting what?"

"The lead when Maggie leaves."

Marilyn's voice is exasperated and a little defensive. What else could she mean? Who else is in line to replace Maggie Carpenter as the star of the play? She's always expected that Barbara would have an important career. She's known that ever since Barbara came close to winning a speech competition for children in the south of England. She can deliver Shakespearean lines with warmth and understanding, and Marilyn loves to listen to her.

Barbara pulls her own dressing gown tightly around her in her turn. She is much taller than her mother and more slender than her mother ever was, but when faced with her mother's eager and depressing encouragement, she feels like a small child again. She frowns.

"Not much. I don't think they'll consider me. Not big enough name recognition." Barbara shrugs. The gesture and its implied indifference are practiced.

The teacups clatter as Marilyn studiedly fills them and pushes one and the milk across the table. Her mouth is pressed into a firm line. She cannot believe the world to be so blind that it cannot see her daughter's talent, intelligence, and worthiness.

"Aren't you even going to ask? Babs, it's 1980 and you're a grown woman. When are you going to stop letting other people decide what's right for you? It doesn't matter what they think or say. There's no one more experienced or funnier than you. You need to go down and insist on being considered. You've paid your dues."

Barbara sighs with the familiarity of the conversation. She finds it difficult enough to live for one person, almost impossible to live for two. Of course she's thought about the role when Maggie leaves. But if she admits it, she has to deal with her mother's disappointment as well as her own. She's come close several times to what might have been a breakthrough, but she always ended up with a secondary role and as understudy to the star. In each case, her mother said outright that Barbara had been cheated.

"How many times do we have to go through this, Mum? It doesn't work that way."

"What doesn't work that way? Are you afraid of being turned down? You can't let that stop you."

Marilyn puts her hands emphatically on the table on either side of her teacup. She wants to will Barbara to seize the things that should be hers. But instead of breathing in this formidable encouragement, it seems to Marilyn that her daughter seems to shrink before her eyes. What will it take, she wonders, to make her daughter demand what by right belongs to her?

"If I'm afraid of rejection, then I'm in the wrong business. You know I've wanted to be an actor all my life. But I could see who was going to succeed in my first RADA class. They told me then that I was too restrained."

"And you accepted that?"

"Mum, I'm doing the best I can. Let's leave it at that, all right?"

Barbara tries to smile ingratiatingly while Marilyn frowns and stirs her tea. Marilyn always stirs it even though she doesn't use milk or sugar. She soon dashes Barbara's hope that she has given up. She has been regrouping.

"Bickie?" she says after a few moments of the considered silence and pushes a plate of digestive biscuits across the table. "You'll get stomach noise on stage if you don't eat something."

"Ta everso," Barbara says carelessly, echoing her mother's baby talk. She wishes she had a newspaper or something to distract her from her mother's questions.

"Will you be late tonight?"

Marilyn's inquiry is both expected and unwelcome. Barbara controls yet another flash of annoyance.

"No, Mum, I am not going out after the performance."

Marilyn affects an air of injured innocence. She raises her eyebrows and looks offended. Her chair creaks as she leans back in it.

"You don't have to get on your high horse with me, young woman. I was only asking about your plans."

"No you're not. You're saying I'm 36. That I should get on with finding someone, get married, and have children. That question is fraught."

Marilyn's eyes become moist and Barbara feels guilty. This is the way it always seems to go between them.

"You don't have to always be after me like that. I can't say anything to you any more. I didn't mean to upset you. I only asked if I should leave something for you to eat. You'll be hungry. You always are."

Barbara shakes her head in frustration and takes a large swallow of tea. As usual, she is in the wrong.

"A meat pie is fine."

"That's not healthy."

"Make whatever you want, Mum. Anything's fine."

"You don't have to be like that. You know I want to please you."

"Whatever, Mum. Do whatever."

More moments of silence. Marilyn looks up at Barbara from lowered, red-rimmed eyes.

"We can't talk anymore," she says softly. "You've changed. All I've ever wanted was a loving daughter. You're all I've got in the world. You know I want the top brick off the chimney pot for you."

Barbara looks at her mother with resignation. Her mother's motives have never been in question. It's always been how she puts them into action. Her mother's words, though, are an accusation. Has she changed? All Barbara can think is that lately the frustrations of living together may have changed them both. Yet neither of them can nor wants to change their lives. They know they are better off together.

"Why is it, Mum, that my life is like some open story? Why can we talk about my life and my disappointments but not about yours?"

Marilyn catches her breath in surprise and lets her eyes slip sideways. She had not expected the challenge. It is out of the order of their usual disagreements. She takes some time to study the red-checked tablecloth and smooth down an imaginary wrinkle. Then she gazes round the compact kitchen of their little flat and then at her daughter's tiny hands. Doll's hands she'd called them once when the little girl was small.

"I tell you things," Marilyn says evasively. "You can't say that I don't. I'm your biggest admirer. You know you'll feel the draft when I've gone. Believe me. I know. Once you've lost your mother, you've lost your best friend."

"Whatever you say, Mum."

Barbara has lost the momentum of the argument. Marilyn regained it when she changed the subject. A new battleground has opened and Barbara feels too listless to engage it. She simply slides her cup across the table be refilled. The best she can hope for is that the conversation is over.

Marilyn fills the cup and then sits quietly looking at her daughter. She marvels at her daughter's turquoise eyes with their dark ring of lashes, her dark wavy hair, and her lovely, clear complexion. She's never understood why a girl as beautiful as Barbara hasn't found someone. She is worried for her. She shakes her head irresolutely leaving her daughter to dread what might be coming next. She keeps silent for several more moments and then starts to twist her wedding band. Barbara knows it's not a good sign. It always precedes some terrible moment of retribution when Barbara has done something close to unforgivable. The ring belonged to Marilyn's mother and it means recollection, connection, comfort, and authority to her. To Barbara it is a talisman of the crushing power of the past, invoked when Marilyn wishes to speak for generations of farmers, artisans, and military officers who would all join with Marilyn in disapproving of her daughter.

But Marilyn does not look angry. Instead, she stares out of the kitchen window with its view into the laundry room in the building next door. Her thoughts are somewhere else. She is remembering how excited they were when could finally afford a two-bedroom flat in the London suburbs. It was small and in a nondescript building but so much better than the two unconnected rooms they'd lived in after the war. They'd even had to use the public baths down the road then. They didn't have much. Just some bits of second-hand furniture and a few family things. But they'd done all right, hadn't they? She'd paid for Barbara's private school and its uniforms. They'd had their holidays on the continent, even if she had to pay off on them. Barbara had her party frocks. She'd raised her daughter properly, hadn't she? She looks at Barbara with an expression almost of defiance.

"I went to see the doctor yesterday." Marilyn lets the words hang in the air and waits for Barbara's reaction.

"What ever for?" Barbara has been caught completely by surprise. But she has enough presence of mind to realize that her mother would not have told her if it wasn't serious.

"I went to see Fairbrooks."

Barbara now looks confounded, and Marilyn seems pleased with her reaction. She has her daughter's full attention and she likes it. Barbara looks as if she is trying to connect two ends of a cord that are not long enough to reach. Something isn't adding up.

"But you hate him. Why did you go to see him?"

"He's all right. I might try someone else and dislike them more."

Marilyn's airy tone implies that she makes her own decisions and doesn't care to have them questioned. The implication set Barbara's teeth on edge. But Marilyn's mood passes quickly. Whatever is pressing on her mind reasserts itself. She doesn't like what she is about to share, so she lets it come out with a burst of words.

"That bastard thinks I have a tumour."

Barbara looks at her mother with wide, stunned eyes. Somewhere a clock ticks and the sound fills the room.

"What the hell does he know?" Marilyn adds.

"Why does he think so?" Barbara's voice sounds raspy. She is having trouble connecting her words to her thoughts.

"I found blood in the toilet."

Barbara feels rooted to her chair in shock. Marilyn's short sentences remind her of a child standing in front of a broken window. The evidence is there. There is no other option to confessing. But the child doesn't like it and would like to find someone else to blame.

"You didn't say anything about that," she says accusingly.

"Yes, well I don't have to tell you everything, do I?"

Marilyn puts her cup down rebelliously and lets her voice rise in pitch and volume. She doesn't care to discuss her motives. She's Mother, after all.

"What does he think it is?"

"He thinks I have something in my colon. Maybe cancer. Can you believe it? He thinks I may have cancer. Cancer? Me?"

Marilyn wrinkles her upper lip, shudders, and looks down at her hands as if she can see something growing under the skin. She doesn't see what right he had to tell her that. It's his job to tell her that she is immortal and that the rules of aging don't apply to her. She picks up her teacup with two hands and takes another swallow.

"What does he want you to do?"

"He wants me to have a barium swallow and enema. But I'm not going to do it. He doesn't know what he's doing, the little twerp. *I don't have cancer.*"

Marilyn sets down her teacup with too much force. The china rings across the room.

"But you're going to have it done, aren't you?"

"He doesn't know what he's talking about."

"Mum, maybe it would be a good thing to have it done and find out for sure. You'd enjoy proving him wrong, wouldn't you?"

Barbara looks anxiously at her mother. The older woman looks pale but she has never aged. Her forehead is furrowed but otherwise her face is unlined. She's picked up some weight over the years, but her skin is soft and her grey eyes are clear. In fact, Barbara thinks, she has remained a beautiful woman who doesn't look ill like the other people Barbara's known who have had cancer.

"I'm not going to go there and have it done. They're wasting their time if they think I'll show up," Marilyn says with finality.

"Did he make an appointment for you? Where is it supposed to be done?"

Marilyn looks away with a sneer. "Some clinic next Friday."

Barbara's shock is now turning into panic. She needs to find something hopeful. Surely, if they do exactly what the doctor says then maybe this thing can be beaten. She wants to urge her mother to fight this enemy. She survived the war. She can survive anything. But Barbara knows that her need for her mother to fight the cancer comes from her own fear of losing the one person in the world who cares for her. What will it take to convince her fiercely independent mother to admit that she has the disease and, more, that she needs to do what others are asking her to? She has never responded to pleas to take care of herself. The only argument that has ever worked is an appeal to her sense of duty.

"Look, Mum, I'll go with you. This is serious stuff. Two musketeers, right? Us against London?"

Marilyn looks contemptuous, but she inclines her head slightly. She has to concede some part of her daughter's observation since she's been the one who has maintained the power of their partnership. But it's her body not her daughter's. She doesn't like the feeling of being pressured into something that will tell her what she doesn't want to hear.

"I'll think about it."

"Mum, how am I supposed to go to the theatre tonight and play a silly comedy when all I can think about is that you have something wrong with you and you won't do anything about it?"

Marilyn looks cornered and unhappy. She doesn't like the suggestion that she is standing in her daughter's way. But she also feels angry that her body has let her down.

"I knew you were going to carry on like this. That's why I didn't tell you in the first place."

"Mum, I can't go on like this. Do you want me to fall flat on my face?"

"That's not fair. I want the best for you. You know that."

"Well, what's it going to be, Mum?"

"I'll think about it. I don't like being rushed like this."

"Mum, there obviously isn't time. There might have been if you'd told me about it. You spring it on me now, and I don't even have time to get used to the idea of it. This is serious. It's no time for secrets."

Marilyn recoils at the direction in her daughter's tone. Barbara sits back waiting for the inevitable outburst. God forbid that Barbara should tell her mother what to do, but Barbara is frightened. The clock ticks while Marilyn considers. The anger Barbara has expected doesn't come. Instead, Marilyn pours another cup of tea and looks thoughtful.

"There's always time for secrets. It's what life's all about. You can't expect to know everything."

"What are you talking about, Mum?" Barbara is puzzled and impatient. She suspects that her mother is playing with her.

"I could tell you a few things if I wanted to. Maybe I will." Marilyn smiles almost gleefully. She looks at her daughter though lowered eyelids.

Barbara sighs. All she wants to hear is that her mother plans to have the tests. Marilyn seems surprised that her comment has not had the impact she hoped for. She adds another clue as enticement. "It's about Gran and your brother—and about you."

"Mum I've got to go to the theatre and I'm going to arrange for the understudy. Let's both accept that as settled. If you don't do this for me, I'm going to give a rotten performance."

"Don't you want to know?"

"I have no idea what you're talking about, Mum. If I've gone this long without knowing, maybe I don't need to."

Marilyn leans forward in her chair and puts down her cup. She seems disappointed. Since she has not regained her authority, she shrugs her shoulders in resignation.

"If I go, you can come with me, but don't let the understudy go on. There may be someone in the audience who is meant to see you and your understudy will get it."

Barbara sighs again. This line of argument has seen her go to the theatre feeling like something the cat killed and refused to eat.

"You know, Mum. You're the one who should have been an actor. Your timing would have been perfect. You would have polished each word until it shone. I can even picture you sweeping through the theatre with your silver cigarette case with your initials in diamonds, your hair swept up into a pile of curls, and reeking of perfume."

"You think so?" Marilyn likes the idea and brightens. It has occurred to her from time to time. She knows what roles she'd have liked. She'd play royalty, someone with noblesse to her oblige. Someone romantic and passionate. Not the pinched, suffering characters her daughter seems to play. She'd want to be someone reckless who risks everything for love. Someone like Mary, Queen of Scots. Yes, she'd have made a powerful Mary. She'd have done the role better than the real queen. She wouldn't have taken on such a weakling husband. Her face takes on hauteur.

"Well, Mum, if you want me to go on tonight," Barbara says stubbornly, "you're going to have to get your x-ray."

"That's blackmail."

Barbara smiles and the argument is over.

3

Yesterday's Lies

The theatre is dim with the lowered house lights when Barbara gets there. The curtain is suspended a few feet above the stage to allow the cleaners to work on the heavy gold fringe. She watches them for a moment and smells the dust of the velvet curtain they are disturbing.

She stopped at the library on the way to work and copied pages from a medical encyclopedia on the subject of barium swallows and enemas. It didn't sound good. She knew right away that there was no way that she could let her mother be by herself after having them done. She looks for Joe, the stage manager, to tell him that she is going to need the next night off. That means that there will be no understudy for Maggie Carpenter, the star of the show. That shouldn't be a problem, though, because Maggie's work ethic is as strong as Barbara's. Neither has missed a performance since the show opened.

Barbara likes Maggie. Everyone does. She is generous and funny and loves jokes and pranks. She comes from the West Country. "Land of the Marcher Lords," she says as she refers to both the area and its history. "Right on the border of Wales. Gloriously, unrepentantly, rebellious to anyone from outside trying to impose order on them. Never tamed. It's in the blood." She is tiny and Barbara thinks she must wear about a size four dress. Her shoes can't be that much bigger. Barbara once heard a stage worker comment that if he were going to screw Maggie, he wouldn't know where to start. But Maggie can reach the upper dress circle without a microphone, and she plays her voice like a fine violin. When she sits beside her former lover in the play and tells him how she plans to have revenge, Barbara finds her both repelling and seductive.

Maggie is theatre royalty. She's married to the president of Calloram Computers, which has been phenomenally successful in the UK, and has a daughter at Roedean and a little boy of five. As soon as she's done in the evening, she hurries home to them. But when she's on stage, she's what they call "there." Every muscle in her body is barbed and eloquent. Barbara often stands in the wings to watch her. Maggie never seems to play Lily quite the same way. Some new gesture will emerge, some new inflection to her voice, and some new way of communicating with the audience. The audience can't get enough of her. She has somehow managed to make Lily human where others have played her as a monster. Maggie's Lily is a woman betrayed who sets out to destroy her former lover—and the town—who cast her out. Barbara plays the lover's wife who has to face his hypocrisy and deceit. Lily succeeds in her revenge, but as Maggie plays her, she is sadly fulfilling a destiny. If she must destroy a town and its inhabitants, she is just the instrument of the Furies, who must be served. But regret or not, she does it, and it's funny to watch her control the stage. That is if you like Black Comedy.

Barbara gets through the show and takes her bow in the usual order. The audience seems pleased and there are several curtain calls. Maggie takes a couple of solo bows and then calls the other actors forward to share the applause. This evening the bows seems overly orchestrated to Barbara, although they look spontaneous. Barbara wonders to herself about her new cynicism, but then Maggie and the others in the cast aren't going to be taking their mothers in for tests tomorrow.

"Great show, Miss Carpenter," Joe says as usual as the star of the show sweeps through the wings after the final curtain. She acknowledges him with a chuckle and a nod of her head before she disappears into her stage-side dressing room. Barbara's dressing room is almost directly over hers. People have to pass Barbara's door to get to the stage, so there is always movement and people coming and going. Barbara likes the activity and bustle.

"Good going, Barbara," Joe says.

Joe's been stage manager for ages and his deeply lined face seems etched by the theatre's dust. The years have only added headphones and a microphone. Joe loves to talk about theatre people—he's worked with them all—and particularly about Sheridan Mann, the director of the current show. Barbara loves to listen. Many of his stories have made their way home to Marilyn.

One of his tales involves the time when the male lead took a bet that he could play his role drunk and that no one would notice. He won the bet but Joe said you could have got drunk off the fumes. Sheridan was unflappable: "If you are going to support a distillery single-handed, then let me know which one so I can invest. Otherwise, I expect you to support this company."

Another was when Sheridan was doing a rare musical, and one of the chorus forgot to put on underwear beneath her tights. Mashed pubic hair cast obvious shadows. Sheridan again when he caught up with her after she came off stage:

"Ladies generally receive a lot more money for showing cunt than you are getting in this chorus. Now go put on your drawers."

Barbara loves to hear these stories. In fact, in her more honest moments, she can trace the budding of an infatuation with Sheridan that over time has become something far more serious. She's never told anyone. She knows that if it were Marilyn in love with Sheridan, she would have sailed into his life and made off with him. But Barbara is reticent. She doesn't like the idea of competing with the rest of London. She knows that every woman in London would like to brush back the lock of light brown hair that falls perpetually across Sheridan's forehead.

So instead of doing anything, she watches him. She sees how he helps actors centre into their roles by making spot-on observations. How he makes everyone feel special and how his presence fills a room. How his sensitivity is unforced and effortless. How he shows the same easy charm whether he's talking with working people or with aristocrats. Barbara heard him tell an off-colour joke to the Prince of Wales during a backstage visit. The prince roared with laughter. Barbara has never told Marilyn about her feelings. Marilyn has him down as a good-looking man who reminds her of David Niven. High praise indeed. She once asked Barbara about him. When she learned he was married, she had asked. "Happily?" Neither one of his marriages lasted more than two years, and there were no children. His wives were models and all he ever said about them was that they ate like birds even though the London tabloids were full of the addiction problems of the last one.

Barbara goes to her dressing room and sits down at the make-up table, glancing briefly up at the bank of lights above the mirror. The bulbs seem to have a life of their own. They flicker uncertainly from time to time. Barbara likes to pretend it's the theatre's resident ghost. Usually there's one burned out, as there is tonight. She slathers on cold cream and starts removing Max Factor pancake with steady wipes of tissue. She's sitting there in her robe and a towel around her shoulders, one half of her face streaked with melting mascara when there's a knock at the door.

"It's open."

"May I come in?"

Sheridan's voice makes her self-conscious. She wonders if she's done something wrong, missed a cue or something. He sits down on the one somewhat rickety chair beside the make-up table and looks for a moment at the messy array of makeup, cold cream, sticks brushes, and pots. Then he bends down and picks up a small brush and places it thoughtfully back on the table. She hadn't even known it was on the floor.

"I hear that you've asked for tomorrow night off. That's not like you, and I wanted to ask if everything's all right."

"It's my mother. She has to have a barium x-ray tomorrow and I don't want her to be alone. I've read about them and it sounds awful." Barbara is aware that half of her face is melting and the rest is greasy. But in that small moment, it doesn't seem to matter. She listens to herself trying to remain calm.

Sheridan nods thoughtfully. "I had one not too long ago, myself. Thought I had an ulcer. Turned out not to be, but everything inside seemed to work much better afterwards. I take it though that they aren't looking for an ulcer?"

Barbara shakes her head and looks down.

"I'm sorry to hear that." His voice is soft and his concern seems real. "You know, I'm sure she will be fine. That generation of women is almost indestructible. They came through the war, worked full time, and raised their families. Remarkable women. My family gave my mother a seventieth birthday party a few years back. We gave her a soft warm-up suit that she could get on and off easily because she's got a spot of arthritis. I'll be damned if she didn't put in on and turn a somersault right in the restaurant. I'm not even sure I could do one. Truly amazing women"

Barbara smiles and looks up. She could imagine Marilyn doing something like that. She swipes off some more makeup and throws the tissue into the wastepaper basket.

"Right now, I'd rather not say anything about this. I don't want to get people unnecessarily worried about things when it may turn out to be nothing."

"Of course," he nods. "Keep us posted how things are going."

"It will be this one performance."

"Let's keep that open. By the way, you need to get that bulb changed." He gestures at the lights at the top of her make-up table, stands up, pats her shoulder, and is gone in what seems like one continuous movement. Barbara is left staring at the shut door and feeling the aura of his presence.

Barbara finishes out the evening and rushes home. Marilyn has arranged for the night off and has sat up waiting. She offers Barbara a plate of baked beans on toast with custard over a jam roll for dessert. She's put out the good tablecloth. The knife and fork and spoon are wrapped up in a napkin as if they are in a restaurant. Marilyn's always had a streak of formality, perhaps because she has nursed all those rich people and, in her own words, "seen how it's done." She sits down across the table from Barbara and has a cup of tea while she watches her daughter eat.

"How are you feeling?" Barbara asks.

"Now don't you worry about me. I'm going to be fine. It's the bloody medical profession. And what do they know? I've seen what they do. I've worked in a hospital."

"Mum, you're in the profession yourself. How can you be so negative when you need care?"

"It's because I'm in the profession and I see what the doctors do. I've been the Lord Mayor's Cart nursing the aftermath. Ask any nurse and you'll hear her say 'I wouldn't let them do that to me'."

Barbara can see that Marilyn has used her time alone to regroup. She is head nurse again, back in control, back in charge of her life.

"So you wait until you're in real trouble before you go to see a doctor?" Barbara feels again the insecurities of her childhood. Her adolescent strategy was always to try to show her mother the inconsistencies of her positions. But Marilyn never cared about being consistent.

"Now don't you start. I've known many a person who was in good health until they went to see a doctor. Then all of a sudden, they're dead. It's all very well for you young ones to go because you don't expect to hear that anything's wrong. Wait until you're older and they go looking for things. Not much fun, I assure you."

Barbara can see Marilyn's knuckles turn white as she grasps her cup far too tightly. She needs to find a way to change the subject and soothe her mother's agitation. But it is a new role for her, calming her mother down, and she doesn't have a developed formula to rely on. She has to think rapidly about what might distract her mother.

"Tell me again about your training."

Marilyn stiffens and looks suspicious. The change of subject has been too rapid for her. Why does Barbara want her to go over the old stories? She stares at her daughter but finds no immediate answer. Barbara is occupying herself with the soggy toast left after the beans are gone.

"What do you want to know about that for?"

"You were up in Berkshire, weren't you? And Gran was with you."

"You're changing the subject. Don't think I don't know what you're doing."

Barbara tries to look innocent and interested. It doesn't matter if her mother sees through the ruse as long as it works. The stories of her mother's family are all she's ever had. After her grandmother died, there were the two of them, mother and daughter. If she ever inquired about other family, Marilyn deflected her by asking weren't they all right on their own? Barbara had her own reasons for not asking more. She remembers once shaking hands with a tall, gaunt man whom she was told was her father. His indifference was obvious even to a child.

For a few moments the room is silent. Marilyn still can't make out why her daughter suddenly wants to hear about her training. She doesn't want her daughter's pity or her condescension. But Barbara was right in choosing this topic. Talking about the past is like a comforting drug to Marilyn, always rewarding as long as she controls what they discuss. In the end, Marilyn decides that revisiting her training is better than talking about what's going to happen tomorrow. She takes a swallow of tea and starts to reminisce.

"I trained up in Berkshire, near Pangbourne on the Thames. Lovely country. Swans on the river. I chose that hospital because I could live at home while I trained. That way I could take care of Gran. She wasn't so well after her stroke and my father left us. I used to ride my bike to work. The milkman would give me a ride now and then but I had to find another way to get there when he left a box of chocolates on my doorstep and said he was sweet on me. And he was married. Just what I needed. It was difficult work and the training staff were hard on us. Had to be, I suppose, to get us tough enough. We had twenty ladies on the ward, all certified by the local board. Some had attacked people, some were delusional, and some were senile. We had to make the beds, clean the ward, serve the food, and do little projects with the ladies all the while we were attending lectures on mental illness, sanitation, and health. There were no drugs then and there wasn't much we could do for the patients except keep them secure and safe. And if they hit us—and they did—it was our hard luck. I remember once that I fell off my bike on the way to work—skidded on gravel. My face was badly cut. Matron gave me some iodine and bandages and told me that it couldn't hurt beauty that wasn't there. That's how they treated us. But hard as it was for us, it was the hardest on the young female patients because we had to keep them away from the male patients. Couldn't take chances with pregnancies. It was sad for the young women who were about the same age as we students were. The men would throw little messages wrapped around stones over the fence. They'd show them to us. Those messages never said much. I remember one said, 'You're the girl of my dreams.' The girl that got that note treasured it. It was sad."

Marilyn shakes her head at the memory. She can't forget the young women she nursed, locked away until they became old without ever knowing what life was about. How little hope they could give them once they'd been committed, and how easy it was for that to happen. That's why she had hidden her mother. She wants her daughter to understand that.

"They used to call people "insufficient" then. A receiving officer and his wife used to go around and find people who were behaving strangely. Neighbours might report them or the police. This couple had the authority to arrest someone and force that person in for observation. They'd testify at the hearing and it took only a doctor's signature to commit someone. Once committed, they never got out. That's why I had to hide Gran. She was never the same after her stroke."

Barbara remembers her grandmother. Gran waved her hand incessantly to drive away demons and yelled, "I believe in Jesus Christ" out of the window. They moved a lot. She was seven when the old woman died

"I wasn't well liked there," Marilyn continues with a grin. "They said I thought I was superior to everyone else. They were probably right. They might have liked to get rid of me, but I worked harder than anyone else, and they grudgingly said I had a gift for managing the ladies. I went up to London for the certification exams, passed them, and became a Royal Mental Nurse. Then I went to Guildford, married Horace MacDonald, and had your brother. And then the war came."

"What was it like during the war?" Barbara has become absorbed by her mother's story and is no longer asking questions for their own sake. She wants her mother to continue.

"I'll never forget when we nurses went down to Guildford Station to meet the hospital train bringing in the burn victims from Dunkirk. There was a big to-do. The mayor was there. A band struck up when the train pulled into the station. People cheered the men and gave them chocolate bars. Matron was done up as usual: blue dress, dark stockings, stiff corset, starched cap like a sail out behind her, and her blue and silver SRN badge shining on her apron. When they started bringing the men off on stretchers, Matron wept openly and called the men my darlings as they were put into ambulances. I'm not judging her. The war affected us all that way. It was personal."

"Did you think about leaving Guildford?"

"I did once the bombing started and Horace left for a medical unit. I thought it would be better for your brother."

"What was Horace MacDonald like?"

Barbara is amazed by her own audacity. She's never asked about him so directly before. Her mother usually dismisses him by saying their marriage was a terrible mistake. But things are different now. Barbara may not have the chance to ask again. She is surprised when Marilyn seems willing to continue.

"He was all right in his own way, I suppose."

Marilyn's face hardens. She stops but not in a way that suggests she is through with her thoughts. Barbara waits until she continues.

"We weren't suited to one another. Should never have married. But it was wartime and you grabbed at things or you might never have another chance. We tried to make a go of it. But there was his mother always interfering. I didn't clean the house properly. I didn't polish his shoes and press his trousers under the mattress. Then there was my mother to worry about. We couldn't have a normal life with your brother sick as well. We never had a chance. I tried to make a home for us. We had a nice detached house in Guildford and we made enough to be comfortable, but when I look back on it, I think he was ashamed of being a nurse."

"Ashamed?"

"Not manly enough for him. At least that's what he said the day he left."

"Were you in love with him?"

Marilyn looks strangely at Barbara. She looks as if she wants to know the answer to that herself. "I was fond of him initially. I don't know what it had become by the time he left. By then we were arguing all the time, and he was spending more and more time out of the house. He'd go to the pub or his mother's. He even put her in charge of his bank account. I learned that after he left. He was a better son than ever he was a husband."

Marilyn looks irresolute and tired, and Barbara is amazed that she has said as much as she has. Those days she's talking about in Guildford were the terrible times before Barbara's brother, Marilyn's first child, died of pneumonia. When they get to that point, Marilyn usually changes the subject. Now it is Barbara's turn to do it.

"So you'll be back among the medical profession again tomorrow," Barbara says.

Marilyn bristles immediately. "I'll thank you not to rub that point home."

Barbara relaxes. Marilyn has finally acknowledged that she will be there and the test will be done. Barbara hadn't been sure of her mother's intention until now.

"Well, we need to get some sleep so you'll be ready."

"I'll do what I think fit," Marilyn says crossly and slightly off the topic. "We all have to live as we think best."

That night, Barbara does not sleep well and, judging from the light and rustling coming from Marilyn's room, her mother doesn't sleep at all. When Barbara does drift into fitful sleep, she dreams about her dead brother and Guildford and what happened there to smash her mother's marriage into pieces.

4
The Purple is Up, Guildford, June 1942

"Watch your lights, little girl. The yellow is up."

George's voice was calm but he hung up quickly. As the hospital porter, he had other staff to warn that German aircraft were approaching the coast. The mental wards where Marilyn worked were separate from the hospital's main brick buildings. They were flimsy by comparison, but the main buildings weren't safer. Everyone believed that the hospital's laundry with its high chimneystack made the buildings look like a factory. Everyone also believed that enemy bombs were directed to where they fell. "Must have been trying for the town hall or the gas works," they'd say if a bomb hit within a mile of the main street.

Moaning Millie, the siren housed next door to Marilyn's ward, wailed its warning a few minutes later. Marilyn ran to the windows and checked the black-out curtains. Another call from George. Red up: ten minutes warning. Then one more. Purple. Bombing is imminent. The ack-ack guns at the top of the hill started up.

"Stay under your beds," she yelled. She ran down the ward and checked each room. The women were housed in six rooms, three on each side with the office and lounge at the end. They had gone under their beds when Marilyn called out the red. The aircraft engines came nearer, sounding like angry lions. Marilyn had a moment's fear. Maybe it wasn't the usual. Maybe they weren't after London this time. Maybe they wanted Guildford instead. The whistle of a falling bomb confirmed it. Marilyn ran up the corridor, her starched nurse's cap bouncing on her black curls. She ducked under the lounge table in the room at the end. Six women in various stages of mental derangement waited with her for the bombs to fall.

The first bomb dropped some distance away. The ground shook and the impact knocked books off the shelf in the lounge area. One fell on the table where Marilyn was hiding and knocked over a small vase containing a single red rose. Marilyn had pinched it from the supervising doctor's garden on her way to work. The water from the upturned vase dripped down the table and onto Marilyn's black shoes and stockings. The next bomb fell a couple of seconds later. They could hear the whistle and the shock of the impact. It was closer this time, almost on top of them. Marilyn could hear the contents of the medicine cabinet fall on the floor in the surgery, and the rattle of the windows behind the blackout curtains. Another shrill whine and a third bomb made the ground jump. The explosion was deafening. It sounded as if it was right outside the window. Marilyn put her hands over her ears and clenched her teeth. Then four more bombs fell. Each seemed further away. The first plane had moved on. But others were following. Marilyn held her head tightly down to her knees and wished she could yell another reminder to her patients. She knew there was no way they could hear her. She closed her eyes and braced for another impact. One-two-three coming closer to them with the fourth impact seemingly right outside. Then two more planes with the same pattern of bombs. The lights went off on the ward and somebody screamed.

"It's all right," Marilyn yelled. "We're all right. It'll be over in a few minutes."

She didn't know if she had been heard, but the screaming stopped.

"It's all right," Marilyn yelled again into the ward as the sounds of the engines faded away. "They're going. Stay down."

Then the guns became silent. After a few moments the All Clear sounded. Ambulance bells began ringing and screams filtered their way onto the ward. Marilyn got out from under the table. She couldn't look outside. Any staff member leaving a ward was sacked immediately. She knew the hillside around the hospital was full of houses, many of them belonging to the staff. Marilyn didn't. She lived up near the cathedral because it was cheaper. She bicycled to work each day. But that didn't mean where she lived was safer. She was terrified for her mother and son at home, but she could do nothing. She found her torch and looked into each of the rooms. The narrow beam threw large jagged shadows and emphasized the white faces of her patients. They were slowly climbing out from under the beds. No one seemed hurt. Just pale and shaken.

"Who's ready for a cup of tea?" she called out when she saw they were safe. "The lights will be on in a minute." Sure enough, the lights flickered back on as the auxiliary system took over. Marilyn went into the ward office and filled the kettle noisily. She spooned the tea leaves into the pot and clattered the cups to give the sense of the ward returning to normal.

The door opened with a noisy turn of keys.

"Everything all right here, Nurse MacDonald?"

Matron and three of the Barts interns came onto the ward. The Barts doctors were billeted in Guildford, sent down when the hospital transferred non-critical patients out of St Bartholomew's Hospital in London. The beds were needed there for the city's casualties. They had got to the ward quickly, before Marilyn had time to clean anything up.

"Yes, Matron," Marilyn replied.

"Are the patients all right?" Matron's first concern was always the patients. The staff could fend for themselves.

"Yes, Matron." Marilyn was shaky herself but not about to let the patients, the doctors, or particularly Matron know it. The patients were gathering at the ward office with its possibility of tea. Matron nodded in approval.

"Very well, Nurse, carry on," Matron didn't say much. Her small smile suggested her pride in the way her staff had dealt with the emergency. Particularly in front of the doctors. She wanted her wards efficient, and she ordered the doctors off them if she thought they weren't treating the patients properly. Some of them, even including Dr. Ross-Davies the supervising doctor, would duck into cupboards and lavatories to avoid her.

"Did the hospital get hit?"

Marilyn whispered her question to one of the doctors as Matron swept out of the room. He looked at Matron's departing back and replied softly. Hospital regulations said that no one was to discuss possible damage, particularly if it might affect staff homes.

"Don't think so," he replied. "The residential area around the hospital got it. We'll have to see in the daylight."

Through the open ward door Marilyn could hear the ring of the bells on rescue lorries and fire engines. There were shouts of "Over here!" and the smell of dust and explosives. She knew the surgical wings would be busy throughout the day.

"By the way," he added before he shut the door to the outside world, "we found Horace hiding under a sink in the men's ward. We told him that if the sink had shattered, the porcelain fragments would have slashed his jugular. He might have been the sole hospital casualty of the night."

Marilyn shut and locked the ward door behind the doctor and then went back to making the tea for the patients. The kettle was emitting a comforting whistle. They would be all right after they'd had their tea. She poured the water into the pot and left it to steep. Then she started to put the things back into the medicine cabinet. One more stir of the leaves and then she sat down and had a cup of tea with the women. Each of them had private thoughts. Marilyn did not share hers: how could she admit that she felt indifferent about whether the sink might have shattered and taken the life of her husband?

If she felt that way, she wondered, why had she married him? She supposed it was the heartless glamour of war that made people seem more than they were. More than they ever might have become without it. That's what it was, she finally decided as she sat there. He had seemed more than he was. When she had met him, he had been a gangling, good-natured young man, a nurse on the men's ward. She had liked him. She remembered how generous he was with his smokes in the staff room. He was sweet on her, she knew that. She liked him well enough but had she loved him? She's not sure about that. When he asked her to marry him, she said she needed time to think about it. If it hadn't been for the war, she wouldn't have. But there didn't seem to be time for life unless you grabbed it. She hadn't worn her wedding ring for months after their brief civil ceremony. One day, Matron told her kindly that she should because she had a right to. Was she embarrassed about marrying him? Even though she had found out that she was pregnant and soon everyone would know?

"Nurse, may I have some more tea?"

"Of course, dear."

Marilyn reached out to refill the cup. Jenny's thin fragile face reflected the depression she experienced after the birth of her child. She was one of the few who were going home. "Give her two weeks," Dr. Ross-Davies had said. Then two weeks more. He knew once someone was committed to a mental hospital, they didn't get out. Finally, a week ago, Jenny started to recover.

Marilyn looked around the room.

"Any one else?"

"Yes, Nurse." Mildred was a beefy woman with a florid face and wild grey hair. The constable had brought her in for stripping off her clothes under the clock in Guildford High Street. On the ward she was all right until a man came near her. She could throw punches, but never at Marilyn.

"Yes." A quiet whisper from Margaret. She was in her teens, a shy young woman who wouldn't talk to anyone. The staff suspected that her father had abused her, but she didn't trust them enough to tell them.

Marilyn refilled the cups of the two women who hadn't said anything. They were elderly and going to be committed so someone could care for them.

The last one pushed her cup forward silently. Lizzie's husband was lost at sea when his ship was torpedoed. On the ward she was simply withdrawn—except when the bombs were falling. Marilyn knew that she was the one who had screamed.

The telephone rang. It was George again. George loved to gossip. This was an important part of his function because it kept people informed and together. George's voice was excited this time. The gossip must be good.

"My God, Marilyn," George almost shouted. "Did you know that Michael has the biggest prong in Guildford?" Michael was one of the male nurses who worked with Horace on the men's side. His wife, Eileen, worked with Marilyn.

"How do you know that?" Marilyn giggled.

"An incendiary landed in his front yard. He ran out in his all together to douse it. You could see him plain as day. Everybody saw him, including the wardens, and the story's going round Guildford."

Marilyn laughed. It was good to laugh at anything. There would be little to even smile about once she got outside the hospital. She went back to the ladies and started making up their beds. It was protocol that the ward be clean and picked up by the time the breakfast trays arrived. She had just finished picking up the things from the floor when she heard the rattle of keys in the door.

Eileen came on the ward. She was full of the devastation around the hospital. "It's terrible out there, Marilyn. A whole row of houses is gone right across the road from the hospital. The wardens kept challenging me despite my uniform, and I had to show identification and keep explaining I was coming to work. They had to help me climb over rubble, and they've still not cleared the road into the hospital. George was outside at the porter's cottage picking up bricks one at a time and throwing them off to side. I've never seen anything like it."

"Were you all right?" Marilyn asked quickly.

"Yes. The house is all right. Our side of the hill didn't get it except for an incendiary in the garden. Michael got that out. But this side is awful. Roofs are gone and all you see are rafters. There are huge holes in the ground. Lots of people were hurt. You'll have to carry your bicycle down most of the hill."

"They were close," Marilyn admitted. "A few seconds either way and it would have been us."

"How were the patients?"

Marilyn looked at the ladies sitting around the lounge table eating their breakfast. "They understood what was happening and got under their beds. We were all right."

Marilyn went into the office to sign off on the night nurse's report. This was her last duty. She then walked over to the locked men's ward and knocked loudly. She and Horace were supposed to go home together. She hoped he was ready to leave because she wouldn't be at peace until she was sure their house was all right. Horace didn't smile when he opened the door and saw who it was. He asked her to wait inside and said he had to talk to the charge nurse. Marilyn was annoyed. Why hadn't he done this before? Didn't he know she would want to get home? Then he came back and suggested that they go out to the garden in back as he needed to talk with her.

Despite the continuing shouts and alarms going on outside the hospital, the garden was quiet. She noticed that some more of Dr. Ross-Davies' roses had opened. They sat down on a wooden bench. She looked at his clipped orange hair and the almost adolescent cast of his face. He had never looked his age.

Horace squirmed, looked at her sideways and took a deep breath. "I'm not going back with you. Some of the staff called in because their houses were hit. I said I'd work the double shift and sleep in the hospital tonight."

Marilyn frowned. Why use up precious time for this when she should be on her way home? She'd worked double shifts herself when the hospital was short. It took a terrible toll to work doubles, so staff would often find a place to sleep if they didn't live close. She kept it to a minimum though because of her mother and son.

"Do you want me to bring you extra clothes when I come back tonight?" The hospital laundered their uniforms but *not* their personal items.

He shook his head and said nothing for a moment. His hesitation made Marilyn suspicious. Had he known he was going to do this earlier and not said anything?

"I brought everything in with me last night."

Marilyn had wondered why he'd insisted on following later when she left for work last night. "Go ahead," he'd said as she set off on her bicycle. "I've asked the charge for a lift." She'd thought it strange but said nothing.

Finally he looked straight at her and the words came out in a rush. "I've signed up for a medical unit in the army and I'm leaving in a couple of days."

Marilyn was confused. He had signed up? He was leaving? Then a new thought occurred to her. He must have been planning this for some time. He'd given up his status in a reserved occupation to enlist. It took time to sign up, to be examined and passed by the Selection Board. Also, the hospital had to release him. She felt a pang of realization that no one at the hospital had said anything to her.

"And when did you make this decision?"

He had known this was going to be her first question. He answered her carefully. "Several weeks ago. I went down to the recruiting centre in Guildford on my day off. They needed medical staff and were glad to have me. I asked the hospital not to say anything about it. I said that you knew and we wanted to keep it a secret for now."

"And what did the hospital say about it?"

"They wished me luck."

Marilyn's eyes slid away from his face to focus on the stones of the pathway. She tried to sort out her feelings. She knew she felt indignant. Why wasn't she part of the decision? But she was also worried. What was this going to mean for them all? How could he have done this with no discussion? She looked back at him sharply. "Shouldn't you have discussed this with me before you did it?"

Horace had also anticipated this question. Because he didn't think she would understand, he wanted to reduce her objections to something he could deal with.

"I didn't think it concerned you that much. You'll get a family allowance."

Marilyn's mouth opened involuntarily. He couldn't believe what he was saying. There had to be more. She wasn't about to be fobbed off with no real explanation.

"I thought," she said icily, "that married people made decisions together."

She paused. He said nothing. Marilyn knew he was struggling. He had never been an imaginative man. He wanted things done the way his family had done them. He wanted to conform as his family had. Marilyn knew that about him. She also hated it about him.

"I want to feel like a man again," he finally said. "I don't like their pity and I feel their contempt."

"Who in God's name are you talking about?"

"The men down at the pub. They come in for a drink. They're on leave or in for the day. They ask me where I'm from. I have to say I'm a nurse at the hospital."

"What's wrong with that?"

"I want to feel like a man."

Marilyn's eyes opened wide. This was not what she'd expected to hear. But she had no reason to doubt it. She tried to think who might have shaped his idea of manhood. His mother was a tiny, disapproving woman who wore a high-necked blouse with a silver and amethyst thistle pin at the neck. His father didn't say much. He sat in a corner with his newspaper. Marilyn found little guidance in the memory.

"And you've let some drips down at the pub decide your life for you? That's being a man?"

He shook his head. "I'm not doing any good here."

Marilyn laughed bitterly. Her voice was tinged with sarcasm. "So what will it take for you to feel that you are doing good? If it's having responsibility, you've got responsibilities here in the hospital. And there's your family."

"Other men have families and are doing their duty."

"I assume then that doing good is going somewhere with the other men and getting shot at?"

Horace had expected this. He knew that Marilyn would make his intentions sound absurd. That's why he hadn't told her. He felt he was doing his duty to his country. If he could see that, why couldn't she? Yet he knew she wouldn't. It had to be the money. That's what they said down at the pub. All women want is your money. They're all the same.

"You'll get your money," he said condescendingly.

"That's nonsense," she said coldly. "Do you realize what the family allowance is for privates? I assume that's what you'll be. It's twenty-five shillings a week. I wouldn't have taken this large house if I hadn't thought you would be here. What do I do now to keep a roof over the head of the baby?"

Horace's shoulders slumped. He'd never believed that talking to her would be easy. How could he explain to her that he was caught between two forms of duty? The way was clear to him. Why couldn't she see that?

"I didn't expect that you'd understand," he said lamely.

"You bet I don't. Nursing is a reserved occupation. You're needed here and not only by your family. Last night there were casualties here in Guildford. Isn't that important too?"

Horace finally looked squarely at Marilyn. "I have to do a man's work."

"You've already said that."

"Well it's true. I feel no man in a household with you. You go your own way. You don't give me respect."

"I do when you make sense."

"That's what I'm talking about," he snapped. "You've set yourself up as some idol of purity. How many times have you done something without asking me?"

"You want me to respect you when you do something like this without even discussing it first? You'd ruin us and put us all in the poor house."

Marilyn's voice had gone dangerously quiet. Horace didn't seem to notice. He warmed to his list of grievances. "You never have time for me. It's always the child. And the child's always ill. And then there's your mother."

"What about my mother?" Marilyn's voice now was a deadly hiss. She could not dispute their son's needs. The night air and air raid shelters gave him constant colds. He was always desperately ill. Her mother was another matter.

Horace stood up from the bench and moved slightly away. His momentary self-indulgence had put him on dangerous ground. But he was too far down the road of self-righteousness to turn back now. "She belongs in a mental hospital," he said nastily. "Our tenants, the policeman and his family, said something about her the other day. They asked if she was all right."

"And what did you say?" Marilyn sprang to her feet with her fists clenched. Her face was contorted with fear and anger. Horace took another step back.

"I didn't say anything."

"Did they say anything about calling for the receiving officer to examine her?"

Horace shook his head dumbly. He'd said nothing. "She's old," he'd said. "She's all right."

Marilyn did not trust him. Now she was glad he was going. But now she had to get away. Guildford was no longer safe. "Right," she said finally as they stood frozen, glaring at one another. "You can go. Go do whatever you have to. I'm going too. I can run away like you. The policeman offered me money to let them have the house. But, oh no, I said. I thought we needed a roof over our heads. And now you do this. Yes, you go off and be a man. And don't you come back, do you hear? Don't you come back because I'm not taking you back."

Marilyn tasted hate and fear at that moment. She twisted her panic into a powerful coil and spat out the last words venomously. Horace stretched his long, lanky body to its full height in an attempt to intimidate her. It didn't work. Marilyn had lost all capacity for fear in her desperate need to protect her family. Deep down, Marilyn suspected that he hadn't meant to threaten her mother. It was another wedge in their private war. But it was one she had to win decisively.

"And what right do you have to leave here?" he sneered back, echoing her words. "Aren't you supposed to discuss this with me. It's my house."

"The hell it is. I've got receipts for the furniture. I paid for it myself and nearly all of it long before I married you."

"Maybe if you're lucky," he retorted, "I'll get killed and you'll get a widow's benefit for the rest of your life. That'd suit you, wouldn't it?"

Horace knew he was feeling sorry for himself. But he couldn't stop.

"Self pity is it?" she sneered right back. "You bastard. You sorry sack of shit." She enjoyed his look of shock. She knew that his mother had told him that common women, coarse women from the streets, used strong language. It was a pleasure to throw it at him.

Horace knew then that he had lost more than the argument with her. He had wanted to be noble and admired. He had wanted her to see him as a man of principle and duty, one who was ready to sacrifice himself for his country and for his family. Instead, she was now dragging them both through the gutter. He felt his self-respect ooze away.

"I'll give you grounds for a divorce if that's what you want. I'll get a hotel receipt." He blustered from wounded pride. He wanted her to see the depths of degradation to which she had reduced him.

"Grounds?" Marilyn's voice rose from a low-pitched growl to a roar of accusation. "Grounds?" she repeated with a scornful laugh. "One breath of scandal and neither of us works in nursing again. Is that what you want? To ruin us both?"

Horace said nothing. She was right. They could both be struck from the Nursing Register, which indeed meant ruin. Marilyn had scored a major point. They might not hold his adultery against her, but they would against him. They stood facing one another at an impasse. *This isn't nobility on his part*, she thought. *It's madness. This isn't how a wife should behave*, he thought. *It's sinful*.

"All right," she said finally in a deadly calm tone. "You can have your divorce. But my way. You make no claims on my son. You say not one word about my mother. I'll charge you with desertion. Then you're out of our lives."

Horace felt a pang of regret. He loved the little boy. His family did too and would be angry that they couldn't see him. Why did she have to be so absolute about everything?

"He's my son too. The boy's going to need a father," he objected.

"Not like you he doesn't."

Horace didn't want to argue with her any more. She had an answer for everything. It was too undignified. It was something that he couldn't win. His mother had been right. She'd predicted that Marilyn wouldn't be a good wife. Now thanks to Marilyn, the boy might not know his own family. The idea pained him. But then he rationalized that the army would send him abroad. He wouldn't see him anyway. Later, when she calmed down she'd be more reasonable. Give her time and let the boy grow up and have a mind of his own. Then he could come back into his life. Horace justified his actions to his own advantage. If he had to give up his son for the moment, then that's the price that would have to be paid for getting rid of her.

Marilyn turned away from him abruptly and walked back toward the hospital doors. When she got there, she stopped and looked back at him. She wanted a parting shot. She wanted him to know he had never had never earned her respect. She wanted him to feel the utter insult of what he had proposed.

"Yes, do get yourself fucking killed. Do us all a favour." Then she went inside and let the door bang noisily shut behind her.

5
Nothing's Going to Happen to Me

Barbara waits two hours in the outer office of the clinic while her mother has her tests. Marilyn looks tired when the nurse brings her out and will say only that it was difficult to suck the stuff out of the tube. They wait another half hour before they are given a large brown envelope closed with a string tie to take to Fairbrooks' office. Once they are in his waiting area, with its brown chairs and reproduction Turner landscapes, Marilyn keeps going to the bathroom and passing what she describes as grey, silvery muck.

It's another hour before Fairbrooks can see them. He is a flat-faced man with bubble-gum pink skin showing through sparse blonde hair. He's what Marilyn snobbily might describe as a clever boy who got scholarships.

"There's a large mass in the upper right quadrant of the large intestine," he says briskly as if he were holding up some organ during a forensic autopsy.

Marilyn says nothing but belches as quietly as she can into a tissue she is clutching.

"What does that mean?" Barbara asks, breaking the silence that has enveloped the room.

"It has to come out," he replies in a slightly surprised tone, as if the x-ray needs no explanation.

Barbara stares at the grey mass he is tapping with a pen on the x-ray film. She feels an irrational annoyance. She wants Fairbrooks to offer hope. She wants him to assure them that everything will be all right. Clearly, he isn't about to. "That sounds bleak," she says in a dejected tone.

"I didn't mean it to sound like that," he says quickly. "There's a good chance we can get it all. Intestinal cancer usually grows slowly. It all depends on what type it is. Once we're in there, we can see whether the lymph nodes are involved. If so, we will need to take them too. But we need to be optimistic."

"Then what would a positive outcome be?" Barbara's voice is cold in her effort to hide her fear.

Fairbrooks glances quickly at the strangely quiet Marilyn. He seems to be waiting for her to join in, but she remains silent. Barbara has the sudden impression that he may be a little afraid of her mother.

"Cancer is serious. There's no way around that, and you can't do half-measures in treating it. But the survival rates are getting better every day as long as we catch it early. Right now, we don't know how long this cancer has been there. From what we can tell, we think we can remove the growth completely. With chemotherapy afterwards, there's a good chance that any loose cells can be destroyed."

That information seems to wake Marilyn up. "What's the worst I'm looking at?" She arches her eyebrows, purses her lips, and manages to look down her nose.

"Let's not talk about that yet," Fairbrooks replies.

"On the contrary, I'd like to know. How long might I have?" Marilyn squares her shoulders and faces her doctor down. She is not to be put off by platitudes. Fairbrooks looks cornered. Don't play god with her, Barbara thinks to herself. He doesn't.

"The average survival rate for gastro-intestinal cancer is one to three years, depending on when it is diagnosed and whether it has metastasized. But at the same time, the remission rate is getting better, and I've known patients who have lived much longer."

"Thank you, doctor," Marilyn says coolly. "When exactly will this surgery take place? I have my work to think about."

"I've asked my staff to make the necessary appointments. Because this is classified as urgent, we should have you in there on Monday. If all goes as I expect, you will be out the following Friday. But you will have to take it easy for a couple of weeks."

"What about afterwards?" Barbara asks.

"We'll have to see what type of cancer it is. It may be chemotherapy or radiation, but let's leave that for now."

"Are you absolutely certain it's cancer?" Marilyn's voice betrays a mixture of hope and resignation. She would love to prove him wrong. But even in her most overbearing moments, she realizes how slim the chances of that must be.

"No one can be sure of anything until we operate and get the reports, unless of course we do a biopsy. But I don't think we should wait for that. Of course it could be benign, but we need to be ready to move quickly to the next step."

Marilyn's fragile bravado crumbles at that point. She clutches her daughter's arm and leans forward. "What about my work? I've got a living to earn. I can't be living off my daughter."

"I'm going to be honest with you," Fairbrooks replies. "This is going to take a lot out of you even without chemotherapy. If you need that, I'd say that you are going to need rest for several months."

Marilyn releases her daughter's arm and sits back, holding the tissue tightly against her mouth. Her eyes dart round the room. Barbara is grateful that he made the need for rest clear to her mother. She didn't think that her mother would have listened to her.

"It'll be all right, Mum. We can make it."

"But what if the show folds? What then?"

"That isn't going to happen. We'll be all right." Barbara speaks her words definitely and stands up. Her mother has had enough for today. She intends to put her arm around her and guide her out of the door.

"My staff will call you with the arrangements," Fairbrooks says as they leave.

They go home on the underground in silence. Marilyn stares at the black outsides of the tunnels and the flashes of light in the stations. People press on an off, but she doesn't notice. Barbara is glad that they don't have to change stations. All they have to contend with is a long ride up the moving staircase to the surface. On the way up, they pass a framed poster for *Yesterday's Lies* with a large picture of Maggie. Barbara's name is half way down on the right. It's the sort of thing that Marilyn would point out to the world. But if Marilyn sees it, she doesn't say anything. Barbara picks up some sliced chicken, bread, and a quarter of butter at Bradshaw's at the end of the road, but she doesn't expect that Marilyn will want to eat anything.

The next days are anxious. Marilyn finishes up her private case and turns it over to another nurse. Once the distraction of work is gone, she is more unpredictable than ever. Sometimes she wants to talk about her surgery, but at other times she becomes upset if Barbara mentions it. For the first time she admits she can feel the mass when she presses hard. Barbara does the evening shows and the matinee and somehow gets through them. Sheridan has been good to his word and no one else seems to know.

They get to the hospital before dawn on Monday. Over Marilyn's protests, Barbara insists on splurging on a taxi. Marilyn's taken most of the preparatory laxative drink until she started to gag and couldn't get the rest down. She's been told it's all right as long as she's passing clear fluid. They paint Marilyn's stomach where they are going to make the incision. When they put her in what looks like a shower cap and remove the last vestiges of nail polish, she looks pathetically vulnerable. Barbara's fear swells.

"It's the anaesthesia," Marilyn says suddenly.

"What's that, Mum?"

"It's the anaesthesia," she repeats.

Barbara frowns in confusion. Marilyn hasn't had any yet.

"That's what will get me. I may not wake up from it. Take care of Gran's things, won't you? And your brother's." Marilyn's lips tremble.

"Mum, you'll be fine. You won't feel a thing. I had this done a couple of years ago. Remember? When they went in and took out a cyst. It was fine. Sore afterwards, but I'm still here."

Marilyn settles. "That's right. You did, didn't you? I was terrified for you. But you were all right. I'll be all right."

The curtains swish open and there is the nurse and an orderly. The brake release snaps on the bed. Marilyn starts at the vibration from it.

"All ready now, Mrs. MacDonald?" the nurse says brightly. "They're waiting for you."

Marilyn reaches out and clutches Barbara's hand before the forward motion of the bed breaks her hold.

"You can wait for her at the surgery waiting room on the first floor," the orderly tells Barbara as he hands her the bag of her mother's belongings.

"I'll be here when you get out," Barbara calls to the departing bed.

The waiting room is full of strange magazines. Barbara can't concentrate enough for them to make sense. Besides she's not interested in golf and yacht racing. She walks to the machines in the foyer and puts in some coins for a cup of tea. It tastes metallic but she drinks it. She keeps looking at the clock: one hour, two hours, three hours.

She does one more run on the tea machine. Doctors come in and talk to the families. Four hours pass and she's one of three families left in the waiting room. She tries to watch the television. It's repeats, and the monotonous drone drops her off to sleep. Then she is being shaken awake. A surgeon is bending over her still in his scrubs with his facemask hanging around his neck. She snaps her dry mouth shut. Marilyn went in five hours ago.

"Miss MacDonald?" he asks. "Sorry to wake you, but there's no one else here who answered to that name."

Barbara nods and gulps.

"She came through fine," he continues. "There was more than we expected, but we think we got it all." He places his hand reassuringly on her shoulder. She can see flecks of something on his smudged glasses. Then he sits down beside her.

"Was it cancer?"

"We'll know more when we get the final pathology report, but yes the preliminary test shows that it was malignant."

"What happens next?"

"She's going to need rest but things did go well so we're expecting she'll be discharged on Friday. The medical team will meet this afternoon to talk about what's best for her. There was lymph node involvement so we have to plan the next steps. Dr. Fairbrooks will be part of the discussion. He'll be talking with your mother about it. I'm sure your mother will share it with you. I want to stress to you that she came through beautifully. She's a gallant lady. I enjoyed meeting her."

Barbara nods disjointedly at this compliment to her mother.

"If you have questions, don't hesitate to call my office. I'll be checking on her while she's in the hospital and then she'll be having follow-up office visits with Dr Fairbrooks."

"Thank you, Doctor," Barbara whispers.

He stands up to leave but then turns around and smiles at her. "My wife and I saw *Yesterday's Lies* the other night. We liked it very much and enjoyed your performance."

Barbara smiles uncertainly and nods. She wonders if he recognized her or if her mother has boasted about her. Marilyn tells everyone she meets about her daughter who is starring in the West End. Barbara swallows hard to quell her queasy stomach. If her mother dies she will be on her own, as Marilyn has always predicted.

Marilyn comes out of recovery and is taken back to her room. She's cold and grey, but when she sees Barbara she groggily says hello. The orderlies move her onto her bed and she goes off to sleep. Barbara kisses her cold cheek and then goes to the theatre, where she falls asleep with her head on the makeup table and nearly falls out of the chair. The indented ring on her cheek where her head rested on a cosmetic jar lid doesn't fade until the end of the evening.

Next day, Barbara gets to the hospital at the start of visiting hours. She finds Marilyn resting against the pillows on her bed looking proud of herself.

"I'd go in for an operation any time," she says as she lifts her gown to show the row of metal staples holding her incision together. It stretches from beneath her chest to below her navel. "It wasn't anything like I thought it would be. They even made me get up today for a little while."

"She's doing well," the nurse confirms as she refills Marilyn's water pitcher and leaves the room.

"They've been wonderful to me," Marilyn says. "It's like being on a ward again. They come down and chat about their problems. Once you're a nurse, things don't ever change."

"Have you seen the doctor?"

Marilyn's face falls. She looks as if she is thinking of something disagreeable. "Fairbrooks came by briefly. He's still a little shit. He said he was on his way to confer with the surgeon. He said they'd let me know sometime later today about how many treatments and when they start. I like my surgeon. He's good looking. Too bad he's married."

"Mum! You didn't ask him, did you?"

"Well, I'm not dead yet, am I? I'm allowed to look. He'd have been nice for you."

"What did they say about the growth?"

Marilyn pouts and looks out the window. "It's cancer, that's all. Intestinal cancer grows slowly you know. They got it all."

"Did they say what kind of cancer it is?"

"He said he wasn't sure yet. There were two types of cancer growing together. They have to sort it out. So how did it go last night?" Marilyn looks like a child anticipating a present. She wants the reassurance of life continuing on track.

"All right, I suppose," Barbara replies. "Sheridan asked after you."

"Now there's a good-looking man."

"Don't you start on that subject," Barbara laughs. "You think all the men on the stage are good looking."

"Well, they are, aren't they?" Marilyn gives her daughter a look that says you little cluck, couldn't you have found yourself something good? Barbara does not reply. Marilyn finally breaks the silence by describing a visit she had that morning.

"You'll never guess who came to see me," she says with a tinge of smugness. "Someone from the Cancer Society. Sits on that chair, large as life, and starts to talk about having had colon cancer. Just what I needed to hear, mind you. She'd had a bout of it five years ago and comes to the hospital to volunteer. I didn't want to be impolite, but I said I didn't need help. Told her so, nice and sweet as can be. 'No thank you, I say, I don't plan to lose my hair. I won't need the wig you're offering me'. I don't want to be part of a bloody cancer-survivor group. I nurse cancer patients. I'm not one myself. Finally, she gets up to go but she says let me leave you some pamphlets on what to eat while you get chemo. People get put off by the food they eat on the day, she says. If you eat a banana that day, chances are you'll never eat one again. Now that was interesting, so I took her pamphlets."

She points to a small pile of paper booklets on her side table. Barbara looks at them. They have titles like *Surviving Cancer* and *What to Expect When You Have Chemotherapy*. She shudders with resentment and fear. Marilyn notices her daughter's reaction and smiles resolutely. She's proud of how she drove away the woman and told her to take the cancer with her. "Now don't you worry about me," she tells Barbara. "I'll be all right. You'll see. Nothing's going to happen to me."

She wants her daughter to understand that this is nothing to what she's already been through. She can survive this. She reaches for Barbara's hand to give it a squeeze. But the comfort she offers is elusive. All her frightened and disillusioned daughter can think is that something already has happened to her mother and that there is worse to come.

6

The Madness of It All

"How's your mother doing?" Sheridan sits down beside her make-up table one night and isn't about to leave until she gives him some information.

"About as well as can be expected."

Marilyn has not been doing well. She's been losing weight rapidly in the two months since her surgery, and Barbara has had to find ways to deflect well-meaning questions about her mother's condition. She has discovered that she can modify how much she reveals by the tone of her voice and the expression on her face. But Sheridan seems to regard the question and its answer as a mere preliminary to what's on his mind.

"There's an edge to your acting that wasn't there before. It fits the role and is adding depth to your portrayal. No one else might notice it as much, but it tells me that something's not right."

Sheridan has cut to the heart of the matter. By now Barbara is tired of evasion, and she sees no purpose in not answering. She has known for some time what has to be faced. She takes a deep breath and blurts out the truth.

"My mother is dying."

Sheridan does not seem surprised. Perhaps he has expected this and felt he needed to ask. "Do you need some time off?"

She shakes her head. "I need to work. Mum would be furious if I don't. Perhaps later."

"Let me know if we can do anything to help."

"I need time to sort out my emotions right now."

"I understand."

"Mum's brave. But I'm not sure the chemotherapy's helping her. I asked the doctor if we should stop it, but he says she has to be the one who decides that."

"They do decide at some point," Sheridan says. "She'll let you know when she's ready."

That night when Barbara comes home, Marilyn is in bed, groaning in pain. The drugs have lost their ability to work, and Barbara knows that no amount of anticipation has prepared her for this moment. She has to make the decision that's she dreaded.

"I'm going to call the ambulance, Mum. You need to be in the hospital where they can give you something stronger for the pain."

"No," Marilyn shouts in a growling, anguished voice. "I'll never come back if you do."

Barbara trembles and feels hot tears on her cheeks. "Mum, I can't let you be like this. I've got to call them. I'm sorry." Marilyn lets out a terrible groan as Barbara makes the call.

"The tumour has grown back and caused a blockage," the emergency room doctor tells Barbara. "She's throwing up intestinal juices because there's nowhere for them to go. All we can do is make her comfortable and call her doctor."

Marilyn is in a heavily drugged sleep when Fairbrooks arrives. He reads her chart carefully and then gestures for Barbara to go out into the hallway with him.

"I thought you had got it all. That's what you all told her."

"We hoped so, too. But one of the two cancers was a very aggressive strain and has not responded to the chemotherapy."

"What's the prognosis? Can you do further surgery?"

He looks at Barbara sympathetically. "Her surgeon and the oncologist and I discussed this after the first surgery. We felt then that the best chance was chemotherapy. We agreed that there was nothing more to be gained by surgery. What we can do now is to keep her comfortable. As the pain gets more intense, we'll give her increased morphine. But I do have to ask you whether you want us to use extraordinary means."

"Extraordinary means?"

"If her heart stops, do you want us to restart it? Do you want her to be on a respirator?"

"No," Barbara says emphatically. "But has she said what she wants?"

"Your mother signed papers indicating that she didn't want to be kept alive artificially. We have that record. But we have to check with you also. The family may not always go along with it."

"I'm not ready to lose her," she whispers. "I'm just not ready."

"That's the hardest part—letting go."

Marilyn has woken up when Barbara goes into her room. She looks white and waxy. She is breathing oxygen and has a white plastic kidney-shaped bowl on her night table. It has something in it that she covers with a towel.

"Hello, darling," she says and puts out her hand. Barbara grasps it anxiously. It is cold and dry. Her skin looks transparent.

"How are you feeling, Mum?"

"It's all right, darling. I'm ready to go. I've had a good innings."

"Oh, Mum." Now the tears are out of Barbara's control. "Has any of this been worth it? The loss of your son, your mother, now this."

She smiles. "For the privilege of knowing you and your brother, a thousand times yes."

Barbara sits down heavily beside the bed and lets her mother wipe the tears away with a tissue.

"I need to tell you some things," Marilyn says as she caresses her face. "I want to tell you about your father."

Barbara's head jerks up involuntarily. "What about him? That son of a bitch."

"What are you talking about?"

"Horace MacDonald. The man at the station."

Marilyn is taken aback at her daughter's reaction. She had almost forgotten about that meeting. "You remember that?"

"I've never forgotten it. You don't forget things like that. One look at me and he went. I get angry at the thought of him."

Marilyn leans back in the bed and looks stunned. "I never thought it would affect you like that. It was all those years ago."

"Well, there it is. How can a man reject his child? I must have been pretty bad."

"You mustn't make those assumptions."

Barbara shakes her head. She is surprised by the vehemence of her own feelings. Years of carefully cultivated indifference have collapsed in the face of her mother's impending death. The newly emerging resentment forces itself into her stiff body and quavering voice.

Marilyn can feel Barbara's anger. She moves her hands irresolutely and looks at the clouds barely visible out of the ward windows. She speaks her next words deliberately, wanting to release her daughter's pain but also shocked at what she put in place all those years ago.

"That man at the station was not your father."

Barbara is not sure at first that she has heard correctly. She fixes her eyes on her mother. Her stomach churns. She loses all sense of space and cannot feel the chair she is sitting on. All she can do is stare. Marilyn smiles slightly, a little self-consciously but also sympathetically. She apparently understands the whirlpool of feelings into which she has thrust her daughter.

"Not my father?" Barbara's voice is breathless and every word has to be forced into coherence.

"That was Horace MacDonald and you have his name. He was my husband but he wasn't your father. You saw him only because he'd asked me to meet him."

Barbara sits mutely. Confusion replaces shock as she tries to deal with the situation. With horror, she understands that her mother has lied to her and done so all her life.

"Then why did you tell me to shake hands with him? You told me to shake hands with my father."

"Because if anyone ever asked you if you'd met him, I wanted you to be able to say that you had."

Now Barbara feels betrayed. "You thought that was important? That it was better to appear conventional and let me believe the man had abandoned me. Did you think you were protecting me?"

"I *was* protecting you," Marilyn says forcefully. "And don't you dare judge me."

For several moments there is silence in the room as the two women glare at one another. Marilyn is tired, though, and when she speaks again her voice is weak.

"I made sure that you had a legal, full birth certificate that named a father. That was the price of his freedom. I said he could go but that he was never to question you. I gave him his divorce by claiming desertion. I took no alimony and child support so he wasn't hurt."

"In other words, you used him to cover your tracks. I can't be illegitimate because I have a birth certificate that names a father? Now I understand why he had no time for me, the living evidence of his wife's adultery."

"Don't ever use those words. I paid dearly for your birth certificate. And don't feel too sorry for him. After he went in the army he had a string of affairs. His mother made sure I knew about them. She didn't want us to get back together. I protected you. No one could say anything about you. And a short while after I filed for divorce the silly blighter said he wanted to meet me and talk about starting fresh. That's why you and I went up there. So he didn't think he had it so bad. He'd have done a damned sight better if I'd taken him back, but by that time I'd had enough of him, so I told him no."

"Didn't you think this might have some effect on me?"

"Would you prefer not have been born?"

There is silence for some further moments. Barbara is aghast and Marilyn is defensive. The atmosphere takes several minutes to settle. Marilyn recovers first.

"Do you want to know about your father?"

"My *real* father?"

"Yes. His name was Jimmy Baldock. He was in the RAF. I met him in Cornwall. He told me he'd lost his family—his wife and his father—in the London bombing. He was killed about the time that you were born."

"What were you doing in Cornwall?"

A tear trickles down Marilyn's face and she looks away. "I was there because of your brother."

Barbara sits mutely while her mother weeps. Barbara has never been included in this part of her mother's life. Always before, she has accepted her exclusion. But this time she is not willing to. She wants an explanation.

"Jimmy was younger than I was, and I knew he was sweet on me. I was good looking then. I was on my own. Horace was gone. Your brother seemed to be getting better."

"Were you in love with him?"

"We were friends. We talked about things. Talking was all you had during the war. You'd talk about how things were going and what they might be like after it was all over. He'd talk about his dead wife and his father and how much he missed them. He used to play with your brother. Maybe would have liked a child himself. He'd talk about his crew but never much. I'd taken a job as a cocktail waitress in a hotel taken over by the RAF because there weren't any nursing jobs. He'd come in, usually by himself. He'd sit quietly and nurse a beer. He had such a lovely smile. He was handsome in his RAF uniform."

"Did he know about me?"

"He knew I was expecting you. The arrangement was that I would get settled, have you, and let him know where we were. Gran and I moved to Brighton. The night you were born, I was watching a Betty Davis film at the Curzon. I wanted to see the end so I stayed and then had to rush to get the midwife. We'd just made it to the flat when you were born and then a few minutes afterwards there was an air raid. So all four of us, me, you, Gran, and the midwife wound up under the bed. 'It's a little girl,' the midwife said. 'You will love her as much as a boy, won't you?' Was there ever any doubt of that? When the alert was over, we looked at you for the first time. 'She's got blue eyes,' Gran said. After a few months, I got a job with a nursing co-op and the head of it used to put me to the top of the list because she knew I had you to support. When you were a few months old, I wrote to tell him where I was in case he wanted to know. His commanding officer wrote back and told me he'd been killed."

"Did you keep that letter?"

"Yes."

"Why didn't you tell me?"

"I couldn't take the chance on someone finding out. In those days I could have been struck from the Nursing Register, which meant I'd be without work. But you did all right, didn't you? Brighton was a good place to grow up. I chose it carefully after we left Cornwall. You had to be there to understand the madness of it all. Any life you had was stolen from the war. People went to cinemas because they said Hitler wasn't going to steal their youth, and sometimes they died there. You began to think that today was all there was. I wasn't going to tell you. But then I thought why should that bastard MacDonald have any claim on you? I know you. You might have tried to track him down. Well now you know. And I've left something for you to read."

Marilyn's words tumble about in disorder. It's difficult for her to admit the past. It makes her vulnerable, and she hates the feeling.

"What was he like?"

Barbara's shock has yielded to curiosity. She wonders what kind of story her mother can weave around the fact of her affair.

"He was kind. He told me that when he interviewed with the RAF they asked him to indicate his choice for aircrew. He put down pilot, pilot, pilot. They all wanted that. I think it was the sadness drew me to him. I could sense it. We'd sit with your brother and feed the ducks and talk. He said he loved flying but it scared him. Do you know that you have your father's same thick black hair and blue eyes? Same turquoise blue exactly. Even your hands are small like his."

Marilyn closes her eyes for a moment. She takes a deep breath and rubs the skin where the oxygen tube feeds into her nose. "I told him about Gran's illness. How Horace was gone. How I was frightened. When I lost your brother, I went and asked him to help me. I said I couldn't live unless I had another child. He understood."

Marilyn doesn't seem able to talk much more. She looks tired and frail, so Barbara leaves her to rest. Next day, Barbara finds that her eyes have taken on a curious purplish cast. She looks as if she is somewhere else and must make a great effort to come back. Barbara is frightened and calls the nurse who is able to get a distant mumble from Marilyn. The nurse says she's all right. It's the morphine.

"You can stay here with her tonight," she tells Barbara.

"I need to arrange for my understudy," Barbara says and goes to use the ward phone. She has to dial twice because her hands are shaking. "Come on, come on," she growls urgently into the telephone receiver. "Pick it up, damn you." The box office clerk's familiar voice finally sounds on the other end and she asks for Joe. They have to go find him. It takes a few minutes but it seems like forever. Joe doesn't ask questions. He says he'll take care of things. But short as the time was, Barbara rushes back to the room with a sense of foreboding. When she comes back the nurse is wiping spittle from her mother's lips.

"She's gone," the nurse says simply.

"But I was only a few minutes."

"They choose their time," the nurse says. "She probably didn't want you to see her leave. I've seen this happen many times before. The family waits all night and then the person slips out with the dawn when no one is watching."

Barbara sits down heavily beside the bed and takes Marilyn's hand. It feels warm. The nurse bustles around disconnecting lines and turning off the equipment. A small bubble forms on the corner of Marilyn's mouth and the nurse wipes it away. "Stay as long as you want," she says quietly and closes the door as she leaves the room.

Barbara watches as the pain and worry lines seem to relax from her mother's face. She looks at rest and even happy. Barbara hopes that she has found her son and mother. Then she leaves. She spends the rest of the day mechanically arranging for someone to collect Marilyn's body. She takes Marilyn's favourite dress, a pale blue evening gown, down to the mortuary for the cremation. The undertakers seem taken aback by it.

She doesn't sleep that night and next day takes the train down to the seashore at Brighton to be where she grew up. She sits on a bench inside a salt-etched glass shelter on the promenade and lets the tears come. No one comes near her. After a while, she walks back up Queens Road to the station. They call her when the ashes are ready. The brass box they give her seems little to show for her mother's life. She puts it in the now empty flat, knowing that she has neither the will nor ability yet to part with it. She sits and talks to it and runs her hand over its burnished surface. It says loss and loneliness. So after three days, she goes back to the only thing she knows, her work.

When she returns to the theatre, her dressing room is alive with flowers. The costume assistant has brought roses from her garden. The cast has chipped in on a basket. The largest arrangement is from Sheridan, expressing his deepest sympathy and welcoming her back. He ends his message by saying that the cast has missed her. She gathers the little notes and put them in her bag to read later. That night she plays the downtrodden wife with a mixture of the black comedy of life and the pain of existence. She finally knows what the woman feels.

7

Don't Mind if I Do, May 1941

Jimmy Baldock waited impatiently to be called once he volunteered for the RAF reserve. They all wanted to wear the blue uniform, but it wasn't so easy. Everyone knew that the RAF took only the best. Finally, the letter came and told him to report to the Oxford Recruiting Centre. He was told to set aside three days for his interviews and testing. The manager at the bank where he worked wished him luck.

Many other men in the train up to Oxford were undoubtedly headed to the same place. There were sporadic conversations in the carriage about the latest reports. The war had made people more willing to talk with one another rather than be shy in the English custom, but the woman next to him was more concerned with a colicky baby and the man across from him was stolidly reading a newspaper. This left Jimmy time to think as the train ploughed through the sodden countryside, often stopping on the tracks until a train from the opposite direction sucked out the air and shot by with an unexpected bang. He hadn't brought anything to read, a mistake he wouldn't repeat. Finally, he closed his eyes and tried to nap. At the station, the young men piling off the train from London might have been university students arriving for a new term. But there were no tennis racquets and trunks, and no porters to help with their luggage. Just a sergeant who yelled down the platform for men going to the reception centre to form up outside the station. They then walked briskly to keep warm in a cold drizzle.

Oxford was curiously undamaged and seemed to be in a different country from the pockmarked and missing buildings of London. Jimmy had with him a small bag with the papers and personal items he'd been told to bring. There was anticipation in the air. If the RAF didn't accept them, it meant the army.

"Line up here," bellowed another sergeant when they reached the centre and entered into a large hallway. "Double file. Have your papers ready." Jimmy was in the middle of a line that ended at a couple of desks. There were twenty men ahead, and the rear snaked back toward the doors they had come through. No one jostled. Everyone stood in polite patience until his turn was called.

"Next."

Jimmy approached the desk with his papers ready. The clerk reached for them without looking up.

"Name, Sir?"

"James Baldock."

The clerk looked for his name on a roster and handed him a sheet. One box had already been ticked.

"Take this into the next room, Sir."

In the next room, he gave the sheet to another clerk and was directed to sit in the waiting area until his name was called. He sat down next to a man who smiled ruefully at him. The man had fine, chiseled features and a lock of auburn hair that fell across his forehead. His smile folded his green eyes into an infectious boyishness. He emanated the warmth that women love and men respect. You could like him without even knowing him.

"Hurry up and wait, isn't it?" the young man said as he brushed back his wet lock of hair.

"So far, it seems to be."

Jimmy brushed his sleeve, aware that it was shedding raindrops on the floor. He was also aware that his wavy hair had swirled over his face as it always did when it was wet. Jimmy tried to push it down, but his hair sprang right back up.

"Where are you from?"

"London," Jimmy replied without further explanation as to which part he had in mind. "You?"

"Tunbridge Wells."

Jimmy was impressed. Tunbridge Wells was a fashionable city like Bath, packed with genteel history. Its name implied fashion and country estates. Jimmy was silent, but the young man seemed determined to continue the conversation. "What are you trying for?"

"Pilot." Jimmy announced his choice flatly. It was his first and only choice. He didn't fancy doing things like repairing engines. He'd done enough fixing his friends' motorcycles and—later—cars. He didn't know much about the other jobs, but he knew what pilots did.

"Me too. That's what everyone wants to be. It's the glamour job. I watch the girls smile at my brother. He's a Spitfire pilot. That's for me, I said. But my brother says you get to be a pilot only if they need you. They can change you if they need more gunners or more navigators. You never know."

"Well, I'll keep my fingers crossed." Jimmy hadn't known that. He wasn't sure that he wanted to.

"Name's Nigel Broadbent." He extended his hand out to Jimmy.

"Jimmy Baldock." Jimmy took the proffered hand and shook it solemnly.

"Pleased to meet you, Jimmy. And the best of luck to you."

"Broadbent," called the clerk.

"Good luck to you, too," Jimmy said as Nigel got up and then disappeared into one of the doorways leading from the hall.

"Baldock," called the clerk.

"Here," said Jimmy out of habit because they always answered that way when their names were called at school. The clerk gave him his billet for the next two nights. Then he was directed to a small side room where his eyes were tested in the dark as well as in the light and for colour blindness. Another stamp was put on his sheet and he was told to take it with him to yet another room where he was told to strip. The doctor listened to his heart and lungs, told him to bend over, and carefully inspected his genitals. He was asked to cough. He was prodded and poked. He was instructed to indicate whether he had ever suffered from a long list of illnesses or disabilities. Some he'd never heard before. While he dressed, his sheet was stamped again. Then he was told to go to his billet and that testing would resume first thing in the morning.

There were six bunks in the room, five already spoken for. Jimmy took the last upper. They must have assigned the rooms alphabetically for Nigel was sitting on a lower one, grinning broadly. Judging from the list on the door outside everyone had a last name that started with the same letter.

"Hello, again, Old Sport. Seems we're meant to keep running across each other."

Jimmy nodded and threw his bag up on the bunk. He glanced at the others sharing the room. They had the slightly lost look of young men away from home for the first time.

"What's next?" Jimmy directed this question to no one in particular and to make conversation.

"We eat at 6 o'clock, or I suppose we should say 1800. After that I assume it will be lights out and rise in the morning around 5:00." Nigel had obviously been doing some reconnoitering.

"Supper" a loud female voice shouted from below.

They got in line and served themselves to chips and sausage with beans. Then it was back to their room and lights out. Next day after breakfast they all filed into a large room set up with desks. They were directed to take whatever one was unoccupied. Nigel sat several rows down from Jimmy and gave him a grin. The test was in several parts that took the whole day except for the break for lunch. By the time they were done with the required reading, calculating, counting, mapping, and thinking, they were spent. They fell into their bunks and spoke very little.

On the third day and final day, they were interviewed by the selection board and then told to wait. One by one they were called into a side office and given the results. The clerk reviewing Jimmy's papers wore sergeant's stripes. Jimmy thought they looked good on his sleeve.

"Mr. Baldock, congratulations, the board has recommended you as fit for aircrew duty. We have reviewed your tests and are recommending you for training as a wireless operator and gunner."

"Is it possible to review and change that?" Jimmy asked in a disappointed tone.

"You mean, train for another position in the crew?"

"I wanted to be a pilot."

The sergeant smiled slightly. "Everyone does. These assignments depend on current RAF service needs, which may change by the time you are ready. Why don't you ask again when you've completed basic training and see where things are? In the meantime, go home and wait until you are called to report. You'll also need to sign up with the local air cadets to start learning Morse code."

Jimmy nodded and got up to leave. At least he had been accepted. He would get to wear the RAF uniform. In the hallway, he ran into Nigel who was emerging from another room. Both men headed out the door together.

"What say we stop at the pub and get something to eat, if there's anything available. You're old enough, right?" Nigel winked at Jimmy to show he was jesting.

Jimmy smiled a little grimly. This wasn't the first time he'd been gassed about looking younger than his age. You'll like it when you're older, his dad had said. But then his dad was nearly fifty when his son was born, and his dad still had thick, wavy black hair with little grey. Jimmy had inherited that black hair as well as his eyes that were a curious blue.

"All right by me," Jimmy said.

They ducked into the public area of the next pub they saw. It was a long room with a bar down one side and tables down the other. They could hear a female voice on the saloon side separated from them by panels of frosted glass. A sporadically noisy game of darts was going on in the back on their side. A large red and turquoise parrot walked down the bar sipping anything that hadn't been wiped up.

"What's on today, Harry?" Nigel called to the bartender.

"I can let you gents have a half-pint each, that's it. Don't get the next allotment until tomorrow."

"That's fine. Anything to eat?"

"I can do some bread, a bit of cheese and pickle. Or some chips and mushy peas."

"The bread and cheese for me. That all right with you Jimmy?"

"Don't mind if I do."

The bartender laughed. "You're not from the Ministry of Aggravation and Twerps, are you?"

"More like Colonel Chin Strap," replied Nigel. "We've joined the RAF."

"Well, good for you, Boys. We'll be counting on you. I'll see if we can do better than half a pint for our flyers."

They sat down at a dark, water-ringed table in the front corner by the blacked-in window. The front door was open and through it they could see what was happening in the street. Several horse-drawn carts went by, the horses' heads buried in black leather feedbags, women went by pushing prams loaded with blankets to protect the occupants from the wet, a bus passed and splashed up a puddle; otherwise, there were young men coming and going.

Jimmy gave Nigel his share of the bill and let him pick up the glasses and plates at the bar and bring them over. The beer was warm and tasted malty. You never knew what you were going to get, and the alcohol content had been reduced. But it was wet.

"Do you know when the next train goes back to London?" Jimmy asked.

"They go every two to three hours now," Nigel replied. "Used to be much more, but what with it all, the service is down. One went half-an-hour ago so you've got time."

"Sounds good to me."

"Did you get your post?" Nigel asked.

"Wireless operator. But he says I can ask to be reassigned after initial training. You?"

"Pilot. But they didn't say what. Don't know if it's fighters or bombers."

Jimmy said nothing in reply and Nigel changed the subject. "What are you going to do until they call us up?"

"What I've been doing so far. I have a job with a bank," replied Jimmy. "It's a good job, and it has a future, so they tell me. Of course, that was before all this started. I have to sign up to learn Morse code before we get called up. What about you?"

"Nothing much, I suppose. I can finish off the term at the university, but after that I'll probably work for my father. He goes around buying dead people's furniture. He has people restore it if needed and then sells it other people. It's an endless cycle. Lately, though, all his craftsmen have signed up and people aren't as interested in buying things as they used to be. But he does all right."

"You're at university?"

Jimmy was impressed. Going to university was reserved for the privileged few and the very brilliant. It had never been suggested for the likes of him. It was get through school and get out and work.

"Just the first term. It was hard to take it seriously when I knew I was going to volunteer."

Jimmy had a sudden insight. There was a reason that Nigel knew the train schedules and knew the pub.

"Are you here at Oxford?"

Nigel nodded. Apparently it seemed unremarkable to him.

"What are you reading?"

"I was interested in international affairs. Maybe the foreign office later. But then I found I was more interested in history and maybe should see if I can get into Cambridge. Bit hard though since my father and brother are Oxford men, both sculled on the Thames and all. My father wants me to be practical and be sure to get a job later. I think he wanted to look on it all as an investment with some profit at the end. Bit boring."

"My dad's always talking about the same thing. Find a job with a future is what he always says."

"Well, now we're in the RAF. Wonder what that future is."

"Won't be forever," Jimmy said practically.

"I wonder."

"We'll be all right."

Nigel smiled. "Of course, we will. Nobody needs to worry about us."

Jimmy sipped his beer. He was used to nursing a drink along, and one beer could last him an evening. It was a good trick to have when you didn't have much money. "Do you like working with your dad in the furniture business?"

"No."

There was silence for a few seconds. Jimmy felt self-conscious at the finality of Nigel's statement. Jimmy had meant to change the subject not introduce a controversy. "Sorry if I shouldn't have asked," he managed to say with embarrassment.

Nigel could see his companion's discomfort. He smiled but his eyes were unreadable. "I don't get on much with dad. We're either too alike or too different. Don't know. My brother—he's the Spitfire pilot—is the golden one. He's two years older. The sun rises and sets on him. He's good at everything. Great at sports, great at school, girls love him, dad dotes on him. Trouble is it's impossible not to love him. He's also a great brother. It's difficult to have dad tell me how much better my brother is at the business when I can't dislike him. So I suppose I dislike my dad instead."

Jimmy was feeling slight warmth, all that was possible with the diluted beer. He wasn't much for self-analysis. This all sounded too deep for him and he looked blank. Nigel quickly caught and assessed the look.

'You're right, old sport. We've all got our crosses. Tell me about your family."

"My dad's in his seventies. Mum died two years ago. Irony was that Mum was dad's second wife and much younger. But she's the one who died." Jimmy didn't like talking about himself, but he felt obliged to respond since his companion had been so open.

"And you were the dutiful son and brother?"

"Not on your life," Jimmy said. "I was a scrapper. Gave my dad a turn about it. I've got scars to prove it. But then I settled down. No future to it, as my dad would say."

"Somehow, I can't picture that. You seem quiet, reserved even."

"Well, it was true enough. I volunteered because I'm glad to do my bit and the war has given me some direction."

"Ha!" said Nigel, "I knew it. A romantic. That's why I thought you looked like a likely someone to talk to."

"Romantic?" Jimmy had no idea what Nigel was talking about. He associated the word with the cinema and things that the girls read.

"Yes," laughed Nigel. "Romantics believe in duty and sacrifice."

Jimmy shook his head slowly. This was a new idea. "Don't know about the sacrifice part," he said cautiously. "I'm not planning on dying if I don't have to."

"If you don't mind me asking," Nigel said with a laugh, "what did you tell the selection board when they asked why you wanted to be in the RAF?"

"I said I wouldn't feel right if everyone else was going and I didn't do my bit. Isn't that what everyone said? What did you tell them?"

"I said that we hadn't had much success with the army's expeditionary forces and that unless we wanted to be sitting ducks for the Germans, then bombing was all we had. We had a taste in World War I when London got bombed, but I said it would be worse this time."

Jimmy nodded. Nigel obviously had a way with words.

"Did they ask you if you would have a problem with bombing?" Nigel asked.

"I didn't know what they were talking about, so I said I would do whatever was asked."

"Good answer. What they were asking, though, was whether you would have a problem dropping bombs on cities and people rather than on military targets."

"But the Germans started it," Jimmy replied. "They blitzed London. Why shouldn't we get some of our own back?"

"I fully agree with you, Old Chap. That's what I told the board. I said I doubted that I'd have time to think much about it, the anonymity of machinery and all that. Bombs are going to fall where they may. Even fighters are anonymous. You don't usually see the enemy pilots."

Jimmy sat for a few minutes absorbing the complexities of the situations he might face as a crewmember. Then he dismissed them characteristically with a shrug. Nigel obviously thought about these things more than he did. "I'll do what's asked," he said finally.

"We all will, Old Chap, and that's how we'll survive, by taking care of one another. I respect your faith in the power of ideas such as duty and responsibility and patriotism. We're going to get on fine."

"Why's that?"

"Because I'm not sure I believe it. There are ideas and banners that we have to stand behind if the country is to get through this. But I distrust how they can be used. I'm not even sure if I can believe in a Church that preaches the national purpose of killing our fellow human beings. Once this is all over, we'll have to look carefully at where the country's headed. So, if I am cynical, you can keep me honest. If you ever get recklessly committed, I'll keep you safe. The point is to survive because the country will need men to rebuild it. You won't be volunteering for suicide missions while I'm around. And I know that you'll try to convince me that there's some reason for all this."

"You need convincing?"

"One lunatic German and all our youth and futures are gone. Tell me that makes sense."

"Well," said Jimmy, "I can't plan for anything so I intend to enjoy the day. Seems to me that's all we have so we might as well hold onto that." Jimmy was already picturing his dad holding a grandson—Jimmy was sure it was a boy—while Rose looked on with the sweet smile of a new mother. That would be the day that he lived for, the thing that kept him going.

"I'll accept that," Nigel said, "and perhaps I'll even come to agree with it. It saddens me to think about the wonderful inventions we've made and the terrible uses that we put them to. Look at the motorcar. It carries people all around the country all right, but it also carries soldiers to the front. Look at the airplane. We can go around the world with it, but we can also fight and bomb. The airplane means that everyone at home, mums and dads, little children—everyone is part of the war. But right now I wonder in the scale of things what difference you and I will make."

"I'll try not to think about it and do what I have to," Jimmy replied.

Jimmy had not thought much about the future or the past. He had found through his life that the less he said about himself, the better off he was. Close behind his sense of duty, though, came a thirst for adventure. The RAF recruitment posters had been a siren call for him. Nigel exuded that sense of adventure. Jimmy had never met anyone like him before. On his part, Nigel wasn't in the least disturbed by Jimmy's reticence, perhaps he had not even noticed it in his eager delight to play with ideas and try to understand. He liked the steadiness of this man from London. He reached out his hand enthusiastically.

"Let's shake to that—to surviving and not thinking about the future."

If anyone had asked Jimmy what Nigel was talking about, he would have shaken his head. But the Baldock men were intelligent in their own way, hard-working, and not inclined to waste time in debate, so he shook the outstretched hand over the beer glasses. The warmth of their handshake cemented a friendship between two completely different men.

Back at the bar, someone shouted at the parrot to get out of his drink. The parrot spread its wings and raised its crest at the owner of the beer.

"Stoppit, you soppy bugger," said the bartender affectionately as he walked down to flick the parrot on the tail. The bird squawked before it folded its wings and waddled back down the bar away from the offended patron.

"Sorry, Mate," said the bartender. "But nobody's been poisoned yet by sharing with him."

"Bloody bird," laughed the patron.

"Where did you get him?" Nigel asked the bartender.

"Belonged to a mate of mine, a merchant sailor. Got him in South America somewhere and asked me to keep him for a while. Heard later that a sub sunk his boat in a convoy, so Davey Jones here will be staying with us permanent like. Wouldn't part with him now. Although you're a destructive bugger aren't you?

He's eaten all my cupboard doors back here. Good thing I like you, you pest. Anything happens to you and we'll all have had it."

He gave his arm to the parrot, which used its beak and claws to climb onto the new perch. When the bartender scratched the parrot's head, the bird closed its eyes.

"He's a beauty," said Nigel. "He's a splash of colour when everything else is so dreary these days."

"You've got that right, Mate," said the bartender, putting the bird back down on the bar. "Let's hope they get that bloody German battleship they're chasing in the channel. We'll lose more good sailors if it gets away."

"Has there been word?" Nigel asked.

"They're saying they got some hits on the bastard but the weather's bad."

"Well, let's wish them luck with it. We can always use good news."

Nigel turned back to their table. "You've heard about the Germans in the channel, haven't you? It's depressing the news about Singapore. And then a neutral Turkey will unsettle the Middle East and North Africa."

Jimmy's head spun. He knew about the battleship because it had been the headline on the boards outside the newsagents' shops. In the past these boards had provided a running tally of how many German planes the Spitfire boys had shot down and how many the RAF had lost. It was like the cricket scores. The battleship was like the shoot-down scores—real and tangible. Singapore and Turkey, it seemed to him, were much further away both in distance and danger. When he didn't respond, Nigel changed the subject.

"So you're going back to the bank," Nigel said. "What do you do there?"

"I work in the property management department."

"What's that?"

"People ask the bank to handle rentals and subleases for them, and I keep the books when the collectors go out."

"It sounds like a perfectly good way to make a living."

"But it's not what I want to do for the rest of my life, even if my dad thinks it is. I'd like to design a high-speed motor car and race it around the world."

"You know about motors? I'm impressed."

"I've been taking things apart since I was ten. Once I took apart a clock to see how it worked. Of course, I couldn't get it back together so my old dad said I had better learn how to do it properly. Then I started on motors. Loved motorcycles. Then cars. I can keep them running, and I've worked out a few improvements. I know I can do a much better job designing electrical systems."

"Say, Old Chap, I've got a Morris that has been giving me hell. If we wind up somewhere together—and we might since we've signed up at the same time and place—do you suppose you could give it a look-over and see if you can set it right?"

"What's wrong with it?"

"God knows. Sometimes it goes all right. Then it won't start and once I had to have it pulled into the garage because it stopped right in the middle of the road. They get it running and it behaves for a time and then it all starts again. Damned annoying."

"You supply the petrol and a worthwhile place to go, and I'll keep it running."

"That's a plan, and we'll make it a place where there are some girls."

"Afternoon closing time coming up, gents," interrupted the bartender loudly. "Have to ask you all to finish up."

The darts' players counted up their points and the loser came up to the bar to pay the bill. It wasn't much. The two men had nursed a beer apiece for several hours. They shuffled out, their clothes patched here and there and darkly stained from railway work.

"Cheerio, Harry," said the man who passed over the money. "We'll see you next day off, whenever that is."

The man at the bar drained his glass and made a pretend pull at the parrot's tail as he walked by it. The parrot spread its wings again and made to lunge at him with an open beak.

"Steady on there, you daft bird," the man laughed. "I wasn't going to hurt you."

"He gets offended now and then," said the bartender. "He gets on his high horse when it comes to his tail." He hoisted the bird over to its perch behind the bar. The bird then hung upside down and began shredding the half-eaten stump of wood. It gave a loud wolf whistle as a large chunk fell to the floor.

"Well, Old Man," Nigel said as he turned up his collar against the cold drizzle, "if you get out to Kent look up Broadbent's Estate Removal and Antiques. I'll be there after the end of the term if they don't call us up first."

Jimmy took his proffered hand and shook it. "I'll look for you at the camp, you and that Morris."

"That's a plan. You keep it running, and I'll find us girls. Watch out for yourself. It's near the time when Jerry likes to come calling."

8

The Key to the Lock

The month after Marilyn's death passes in a blur for Barbara. She eats as badly as before, sandwiches in the train station and cans of soup taken on the run. She puts in a token appearance at the cast party when the London show reaches its six-month anniversary. She leaves Marilyn's clothes in her cupboard as they were although she often stands in the doorway to her room, breathing in her scent. Marilyn always loved gardenia. Barbara had known for some time that it was going to take forceful self-discipline to go through her mother's things. Once she circled a date on the calendar, a day when she didn't have to do a matinee. But when that day came, she stepped into the room and then beat a hasty and guilty retreat. She simply wasn't ready. Then one day the rumour starts that planning has begun for a touring company. Several names are said to be under consideration for the lead. There are also rumours about who is being considered for the lead in the London production after Maggie leaves. Barbara can hear Marilyn saying, "Babs, don't talk yourself out of any chances at it."

One night Sheridan asks her to have dinner with him. He says that he has several things he wants to discuss. He takes her to an old pub on the Thames where the river is calm and swans glide among the trailing willows. The dining room has dark wood panelling, highly polished tables, gleaming brass and glassware, and windows that look out on the water.

"It's about the lead in the touring company of *Yesterday's Lies*," he says after they've ordered. "We're considering you for that. I personally know you can do it well, but there are some concerns about your strength in the role. You've understudied Maggie and moving you into the role would be logical. It's not decided, but I wanted you to hear about it from me, not from the theatre gossip."

"What about the London show after Maggie leaves?"

"Chandler Taylor is going to take it."

"I thought she did only films."

"This will be her first stage production. But she's eager and available for six months between movies. It gets us over the hump, and people know who she is."

"And will it open sometime in New York?"

"We don't know about that yet. Probably we'll use an American actress since the actors' union over there allows only name stars to transfer with UK shows."

"I see," she says quietly.

"Barbara, I want you to know that you're a great trooper. We rely on you to be professional, and you've never let us down. In fact, you're so important to the cast that there was some feeling that you should stay with the London production and not tour at all. Chandler's going to need a strong second. In the end, we came to the conclusion that you deserved a chance at the lead, and name recognition isn't going to be a problem in Birmingham or Manchester. The play itself will be the draw."

"When does this all happen?" Barbara takes a big swallow of wine. Name recognition again.

"Chandler arrives in March for rehearsals. You'll be an important part of getting her ready. We'll be putting together the touring company using a mix of the West End cast and newcomers some time next summer. Some preparation has already been done, so we hope things will be smooth. The bookings are currently being put in place and we'll let you know well before then."

Barbara nods. At least she has a job. She plays with the stem of her glass and then swallows down the rest of the wine. Sheridan refills their glasses. Barbara's head starts to buzz.

"May I ask you a personal question?" Sheridan tilts his head slightly and gives her a quizzical look.

Barbara nods and hopes she appears more sober than she feels.

"You seem dedicated to your work and I don't sense that you have much life outside the theatre. Or am I completely wrong?"

"I'll answer that if I can ask you something personal in return." Barbara keeps her voice steady, but she feels daring. She assumes it's the wine.

"A bargain."

She swirls her wine slowly so she doesn't sling it onto the tablecloth.

"I suppose I could say that I've been too tied up with my mother to venture out much. If you mean seeing someone, I could say that I've been waiting for the right somebody—that's what one would expect me to say, isn't it? But the truth is I have been so busy fending off my mother from asking that same question, only a little more bluntly, that I haven't been willing to get involved with anyone.

Doesn't that sound childish? I don't have a life because my mother wanted me to have one so badly."

"So there's not been anyone serious?"

"Oh there was once. But he told me that he didn't want to share his wife—his possession—with the theatre. Mum liked him because he used to bring her little presents and drop by after work to have tea. I sent him on his way without telling her why. It's just been in the last few years or so when I didn't bring anybody home that Mum got concerned. Otherwise, they were threats to her."

Sheridan smiles and looks reflective. "Parenting is hard. My parents and I worked out all right except that I wasn't close to my father. My sister had more trouble. She and Dad had their run-ins. Too much alike. Both stubborn. He was old fashioned and wanted to keep her under wraps. You can't do that with young people these days. She married young to get away and then divorced. That set Dad off again as he was funny about marriage. He wanted her to come home as if nothing had happened. She wanted to catch up on the youth she'd given up to marry. Then he insisted. She refused and went to work. She and Dad hardly talked until he got sick. Dad didn't understand why she was angry. From his perspective, he had done what fathers were supposed to. He thought he was watching out for her. She felt he was smothering and interfering. They were both right, and that's what made it so hard. She didn't come home again until just before he died."

Sheridan offers a refill, but Barbara waves him off. Tipsily she remembers a French actress who told her that two drinks she was under the table, three and she was under her host.

"Have you always lived with your mother?" he asks.

"It worked out," she says vaguely. In reality, she can't remember a time when she wasn't living with Marilyn, but she doesn't want to admit that. It makes her feel dependent and unadventurous, particularly in comparison with his sister. "It didn't leave much room for anything else. I think Mum had me so she wouldn't be on her own. I guess it worked."

"And now she's gone."

"And now she's gone." Barbara's voice sounds hollow as if she is in a tunnel down which the words "what's next?" keep sliding along the walls.

"What does that mean for you now?"

He asks the question casually, as if it is the most normal thing in the world to ask a young, well youngish, unmarried woman.

Barbara drinks some water. She'd read somewhere that alcohol dehydrates the brain so it's a good thing to drink water. It gives her a moment to think.

"I don't know yet," she says thickly. "I haven't had time to think."

"So what did you want to ask me? My life's an open book—almost. At least the gossip columns seem to think so."

She considers her question carefully. It's been the subject of endless speculation in the Green Room. "All right," she says, "Here goes. Why don't you date women who are older than 24?"

She takes a deep breath and waits for the evasion or even annoyance. Instead he bursts out laughing. He doesn't seem offended at all.

"Other than the fact they are available everywhere and look good on my arm? But let's get this straight, my lady. It's not that I don't date women older than 24. It's that I don't end up marrying them. At least so far."

"But," she protests, "you can't marry them if you don't date them."

"True. But it's the twenty somethings who make themselves available. I like a forthright woman who lets it be known what she wants. I was hopeful that this last one was really the last one."

"Are you telling me that you don't have a choice when one approaches you?"

"If a determined woman drenched in expensive French perfume appears on the horizon, my defences may indeed be down." Sheridan's eyes shine with amusement, and his moustache hikes at a rakish angle.

"That's all it takes?"

"Well," he smiles roguishly. "That's all as long as she is intelligent, witty, mischievous, and sophisticated."

"And looks good on your arm?"

"That certainly doesn't hurt."

"I'll have to keep all that in mind," she finally says.

That night, she has a vivid dream. It might have been the unaccustomed wine or the kiss on the cheek that Sheridan gave her at the entry door to her building. For the first time since her death, she sees Marilyn. She is standing in her bedroom doorway as she used to every morning. She looks as she did in her hospital bed, with the gown tied tightly around her. "Babs, you have got to get on with your life," she says in her most authoritative tone. The one she always used when her daughter perplexed her.

Barbara startles herself awake and looks at the door. But there is nothing there. She gets up and realizes that she has a hangover. She drinks a large glass of water and takes two aspirins. Then a strong cup of tea. She knows it's time and what she has to do.

She takes her tea into Marilyn's room and sits down in her chair. She can see that dust has layered the top of the chest of drawers. Marilyn's carpet slippers, the fabric worn down at the heels, are under the bed. Her clothes are hanging in the closet, still smelling faintly of gardenia. Everything's the same. But there are no clues to finding whatever it is that Marilyn wants her to see.

She takes another swallow of tea, gets up and goes to Marilyn's chest of drawers. Her reading glasses, wallet, keys, and underwear are in the top drawer. Her wallet has her identification card and a few pounds. The second drawer down has her woollies. The third, her scarves and gloves. No messages there.

The desk and her cupboard have nothing. There's nothing in her coat pockets. Barbara finally pulls everything out of her chest of drawers. She even searches the cupboards in the bathroom and the kitchen. Still nothing. She is starting to wonder if she should start tapping the walls and floor for hollow spaces when she finds a suitcase hidden under the bed behind Marilyn's slippers and a box of Christmas wrap. It is locked, of course, and the key is not on her key ring.

"Come on, Mum," she says out loud. I'm tired of these games." She shakes her head in vexation because she'd wanted to settle things but now has to leave for the theatre. Trust her mother not to make things easy.

The play goes well that night and the house is full. It's the Americans coming over, Sheridan claims. They fly over for a couple of days to do the shows. The overseas reviews are good, so it's getting to be time to think about opening the show over there. Barbara notices that there are some shouts of bravo for her. It is a heady feeling and Sheridan seems pleased that the play is what he calls evolving.

She grabs a Cornish pastie on the way home and once there lays out every key she can find on the kitchen table. There are fifteen keys. They are all shapes and sizes including the four on Marilyn's key ring. She starts trying them one by one in various combinations of up and down in the suitcase lock. None fits. All right, she thinks to herself, where would her mother hide something that she didn't want found? She looks through the storage box where Marilyn kept Gran's things. She finds a brittle black leather handbag with dried licorice gums that look like little beehives, a bun of grey hair, and some desiccated Ponds cold cream. Nothing like a key. Certainly not in the shrivelled white leather gloves, faded pink silk blouse, or pair of old-fashioned black shoes. Then she goes to the box where Marilyn kept her son's things. Inside there's his christening gown and his baby book. Barbara opens the book reverently and looks through the pictures and birthday cards. One catches her eye: Happy Birthday from your father, Horace MacDonald. Just as Barbara is thinking how strangely this man has signed his name, a small object drops from the album, and there's the key, small and silver and very real.

It's a moment's work to insert it in the suitcase lock and turn it. Then the suitcase lid comes wobbling up. Inside are velvet boxes containing Marilyn's jewellery. There are Gran's pearl strand, a little brownish from lack of wearing, a silver cigarette case with Marilyn's initials set in diamond chips, a gift from her father, and a gold chain Barbara had given her. And then underneath it all is a thick envelope with Marilyn's distinctive handwriting: "Babs, to be opened in case of my death. With all my love, Mum." It is closed with bright red sealing wax with the letter M impressed into it. The wax crumbles apart as Barbara runs her finger under the envelope's flap. She pulls out a sheaf of papers held together with a large paper clip. Marilyn must have been working on them for some time, for there are tea stains and even the round outline of a cup pedestal on an inside page. The pages tell her life. Barbara knows what she needs to read. She turns quickly to the war years.

> 1942: I never believed that I could lose that wonderful life that had been entrusted to me. If I could go back, I would have killed myself before I let anything happen to him. Yet he slipped away from me in that terrible time and I have paid and paid and paid. If I hadn't had you, I couldn't have lived.
>
> In those terrible weeks before I lost him, we raced up to London to the specialists again but they said there wasn't hope. He kept getting colds and then pneumonia. I gave up my job. I left Mum with her sister Carrie for a little while. But Carrie wouldn't keep her long because Mum was unpredictable. But it was enough for me to pack up in Guildford and sell off the furniture. I found a place down in Cornwall. There weren't any nursing jobs but I got work in a hotel working as a cocktail waitress. I got a room along with my job and Carrie put Mum on the train. I watched her walk down the platform toward me. She looked like a delicate rose. My heart jumped as I watched her. She and my baby were the whole world to me. She was so glad to see us that it never worried her that we were living in one room and not the lovely three-bedroom house with pink-coloured sinks we had in Guildford.
>
> I used to walk your brother down to the seafront and he seemed to be getting better. I dared to hope. The hotel had been taken over by the RAF, and the aircrews used to hitchhike in from the airfields. It was hard to know that they might not be there the next night. They were all so young and so cheerful that you didn't mind if they got a bit drunk. One pressed me against the bar one night and demanded that I marry him right on the spot. No one knew how I was going to take it, but I laughed and repeated the vows. Then he

lumbered off with his friends. He came back the next day to apologize. His crew went missing in action the following week.

Those young men were so good to your brother. They'd bring him sweets and play with him. He'd laugh and his dimples would flash. They thought he was lovely. There was one of them in particular. He was a good-looking young man with thick black hair and eyes the shade of cornflowers. He was much younger than me, but he seemed more mature because he understood things with compassion. He'd known loss. He was someone you could trust. He was kind. His name was Jimmy Baldock and he was your father.

Then one night, your brother started coughing much worse than ever before. Nothing could stop him. I was terrified and rushed with him through the streets to the hospital. It was pitch black and there were no taxis. I left Mum at home and ran and ran. When I burst through the hospital doors, he gave one gasping cough and I knew he was dead. I started weeping hysterically and they took him from me. I collapsed on a bench in the hospital and no one came near me. The police were called and questioned me. They said there would have to be an autopsy and they wanted to know who his doctor had been because they would have to contact him in Guildford. I suppose they thought I might have done something to him. Me? Do something to that wonderful little boy? I'd have given my life before I would harm him.

I staggered home to Gran with the terrible news. She didn't say anything. She lay on her bed with her face to the wall. I looked at his toys and little clothes and I cried and cried until my face burned. Everyone in the hotel was shocked and couldn't believe he had died even though they knew he'd been ill.

There was an inquiry into his death a few days later. They had the autopsy results. They told me that his lungs had collapsed from the coughing. But then they said there would be no charges against me. Charges against me? That was the first I had heard they were thinking of it. Then they said I should send a funeral director to get his body. I never saw him again. Only the coffin I bought for him. Gran and I and some people from the hotel watched him put into a grave high up on the cliffs. It was a lovely spot. You could see the ocean from there. I knew right away that I had to have another chance to prove that I was worthy of a child. I wouldn't lose this one. I would die first. I knew Jimmy would understand the horror of my loss. I was distraught. I went to him and asked him to give me another child.

There's a gap after that until Marilyn talks about Barbara's birth. No further mention of the young man with cornflower eyes. Barbara shuffles the papers to replace the clip, but as she does so another paper falls onto the floor. It is yellowed and creased into three parts as if it had once fitted into an envelope. It is typed in uneven letters, some appearing blotchy. But what it says is readable.

> "Dear Madam. Your letter to F/Sgt James Baldock has been directed to me. I deeply regret to inform you that F/Sgt Baldock is missing in action, presumed dead, as of September 1943. F/Sgt Baldock was well respected by the squadron and he will be missed. Sincerely yours, William F. O. Stanley, DFC, DSC, Commanding Officer, 958 Squadron."

Next day she stops at the library to learn about 958 Squadron.

> 958 Squadron, "Long Shank," formed January 1943 of B Flight from 122 Squadron. Based at Leaton, Yorkshire. Long Shank is the motto of the nearby village of the same name. Flew Halifax III, IV. Disbanded 1945. Squadron secretary, F/Sgt Billy Coppin, 45 Durrendon Lane, York.

When she comes home from the theatre, she writes to Billy Coppin.

> Dear Mr. Coppin:
>
> I am hoping that you can tell me something about my father, F/Sgt James Baldock, who served with the 958 Squadron and was killed in action in September 1943. I'd like to learn all I can about him. Do you have things such as operations records and pictures of him and his crew?
>
> Thank you,
>
> Barbara MacDonald

A week later comes the reply. Mr. Coppin is in total shock and tells her that Jimmy Baldock was the wireless operator on his own crew and that he has pictures. If she would like to ring him and make plans to come to tea, he will be happy to show them to her.

9
958 Squadron

Barbara takes the direct train from King's Cross Station, which gets her into York two hours later. It's a pleasant enough trip through the autumn countryside. A short taxi ride puts her down outside Billy's house. It's one of a terrace of stone houses. All have a bay window, a front door with a dimpled glass inset traced with coloured leaves, a leaded glass canopy over the front stoop, a drainpipe down the division between the houses, and a front path with a gate that ends directly on the pavement. Because the road is narrow, cars park partly on the pavement in spaces outlined by white lines. Even with two wheels up on the pavement, though, the middle of the road is only wide enough to permit one car at a time.

The lace curtain moves in Billy's front window as she pays the taxi, and the door opens as she walks up the path. Billy is wearing a shirt and cardigan with pleated trousers. He is barely as tall as Barbara and his greying hair and silver-rimmed eyeglasses seem too old for his compact body.

"Come on in," he says. "I've put the kettle on. Took the day off from work so we could have time to talk. I was completely amazed when I got your letter. I couldn't believe that you're looking for the wireless operator on my own crew. What are the chances of that happening, I wonder?"

Barbara enters into the small hallway. On her right, a narrow staircase climbs up to a landing lit by a small, round window. To her left, double doors open into the front room. A dimly lit passage leads past the stairs into the back of the house. She imagines that all the houses in the terrace must be identical inside.

"Did you have trouble finding the house?"

Barbara hands her coat to Billy who carefully hangs it on a mirrored hall stand that holds a jumble of umbrellas, walking sticks, dog leads, and rubber boots.

"The taxi driver knew exactly where to come. He picked me up at the station, and I've asked him to come back for me."

Billy ushers her into the front room and waves her to a chintz armchair. The room obviously does double duty for living and dining. The front part is filled by a settee, a low table with piled newspapers and the open TV Times, and a television set on a stand by a fireplace that has been adapted for a hissing gas fire. The back part has a dark oak table and chairs, a sideboard, and an open door that gives onto the kitchen at the back. Through the window over the sink, Barbara can see a long narrow garden with a greenhouse at the end. As she sits down, Barbara glances out to the street through the lace curtains in the bay window. All she can see are the gate, the low stone wall, and parked cars.

"York wasn't this crowded when I was growing up." Billy has seen her look out toward the street. The nondescript houses popping up everywhere have saddened him, as well as the signs that say more are to come. He assumes she must feel the same.

"Used to be open fields and you could always tell where you were by the tower of the Minster. Now you can hardly see it. But make yourself at home, and I'll get us tea." He disappears through the open door into the kitchen.

Barbara looks more closely at the room's contents. A painted wood shield hangs over the mantle. It shows a sword held by a gauntlet in front of two lightning bolts. Barbara recognizes it as the 958 Squadron badge. Every inch of wall on either side of the mantle is filled with framed pictures. On the mantle itself, next to a silver goblet and a pottery lighthouse that says "A present from Newquay," is a photograph showing five men in RAF uniforms clustered around a map laid open on the grass. Next to that is one of Billy by himself. Barbara can't help herself. This must be the crew. She gets up to look at them.

"That's us at Operational Training Unit in Cornwall where we crewed up." Billy has stepped back in from the kitchen, carrying a tray with teapot and cups. He puts it on the table and comes to stand by her.

"That's Jimmy," he says pointing to the man kneeling on the right with his hands on his knees and smiling directly at the camera.

But Barbara had already spotted Jimmy. She thinks she can see her own face shape and smile in his. He's a slender man, well proportioned, with even features and a broad smile. The picture is black and white so she can't see colour of his eyes. But his hair is thick and seems wavy like her own, and he is as good-looking as Marilyn said.

"That's Donny Oakes, the navigator, on the left. And next to him is Tad Smith. He was our bomb aimer. They were great friends. Both Canadians. See the Canada patch on Donny's arm? Nigel, our skipper, is the one in the middle with me behind him. I was the rear gunner. Nigel came from somewhere in Kent. Your dad came from London, as I recall. Handsome devils weren't we?"

Barbara smiles. But she can't stop looking at her father's face.

"That's me," he says gratuitously after a few moments. He lifts up the picture of him by himself and shows it to her. "They came and took pictures of us in front of the Wellington. Wimpies, we called them. See the aircraft behind us. That's the Wimpy we trained on. They snapped us all together and then individually. To send to the families and girlfriends, they said."

Barbara looks at Billy's picture and glances for comparison at the man beside her.

"How old were you? You look as if you should be in school."

"I'd turned eighteen shortly before." He smiles at his younger self. The teenage Billy stares suspiciously at the camera. He looks as if he's on a playing field and expects someone to tackle him.

"What did your parents think about your being in the air force so young?"

"Not happy at all. They wanted me to wait until conscription age, but I wanted to join the RAF. They told me that Granny was in a terrible state when we were shot down. It was several months before they heard I was a prisoner. Granny died a short while after I got back. They thought she'd waited for me to come home."

He puts his picture back down and points to a small, framed picture on the wall. It is no larger than the average seaside postcard. To Barbara, it looks like a typical English market town with a square in the middle, a green, and shops all around it.

"That's Leaton. The village outside the airfield. We used to go down there to the Three Martyrs for a drink."

"The Three Martyrs?"

"People sometimes forget that we ever had a civil war. The area round York was mostly loyal to the king. They were the Royalists. But there were pockets of parliamentary sympathizers. Leaton was a known trouble spot. One day, the Royalists chased three local protesters into the church and killed them in the main aisle. The local clergyman was furious, especially when the king's troops hung the bodies from the churchyard trees. But overnight someone unknown took them down and hid them under a flagstone in the church. A leg bone was eventually taken from one of the men and put in a box. Don't ask me why. He was a tall man for the day, hence the name "Long Shank" for the village and, later, the name of the squadron. At one point, the box was hidden in the pub's cellar. Hence the name, The Three Martyrs."

"It's funny how places get their names isn't it?" she says.

Billy rubs some imaginary dust from the picture frame and takes it off the wall to hand to Barbara. She has to be interested in it, he thinks. He can remember how they walked round the shops and crossed the market square to go into the pub.

Barbara peers into the picture. One shop's awning says Griffith's Grocery. A shop front with bulbous bottles announces a chemist's next to it. And next to that are the newsagent and post office. The church is down the other end behind a lynch gate.

"When 958 Squadron was there, the green at the end was all vegetable plots. You've seen the old poster, haven't you? 'Plant a garden or a child might go hungry.' The village took that seriously. The grocery was a café then, and we used to eat there when we were stood down. Now here's one you'll want to see."

He takes the Leaton picture from Barbara, replaces it, and takes down a black and white wedding picture. Six men in RAF uniform hold up swords to form an arch over the couple. The bride's head is slightly forward and she's chuckling. The groom's head is thrown back, his mouth open in a full roar of laughter.

"The skipper's wedding. He was marrying Letitia, except everybody called her Lettuce. Look at the men holding the swords." Billy is obviously the one on the right front. He's smiling but gives the air that he's taking his job seriously.

"Is that Jimmy on the left?"

"Yes, it is. Tad is behind me on the right, and you can make out Tommy behind him. George is behind Jimmy and Donny's behind him. George was the engineer. He'd joined us at the HCU, the Heavy Conversion Unit, where we learned to fly the Halifax bomber. We needed a second gunner as well, so that's when Tommy came on. We'd finished the HCU course and been posted to Leaton when that picture was taken. We were feeling good about ourselves. The wedding was a do by wartime standards. Letitia's father was the local squire and had an old manor house. You know, the type with leaded windows from floor to ceiling and ivy up the walls. They hadn't been bombed, so things seemed normal except for the usual shortages."

"You seem to be having fun in the picture."

"That was George. He could be a proper devil if he'd a mind to. His family went to Australia when he was a lad. I can remember him telling us how the RAAF turned him down at first because he was too young. But that happened to most of us. We were all in a hurry. We didn't know what we were getting into."

Billy shakes his head as he puts the picture back and points to another one. "That's Leaton Airfield as it was—three runways making a triangle, a perimeter track, frying-pan dispersal sites, Nissen huts, the NAAFI, and the mud. Some called it Leaton-in-the-Swamp because it used to get huge puddles when it rained. It had been an old World War I grass field and wasn't meant to be permanent. All you can see now is the control tower made into somebody's house. I've often wondered if it still leaks over the stairs. I remember seeing buckets put there to catch the drips."

He leads Barbara further along the wall, commenting on everything as he moves along. "That's the charter for the formation of the 958 Squadron association, and these are commendation letters. One's from Sir Arthur "Bomber" Harris himself. I've got a nice print of Halifaxes flying over the Minster signed by him as well. The silver goblet with the squadron crest is the official gift for dignitaries at the 958 Squadron dedication service in Leaton churchyard. There were thirty 958 Squadron veterans there, and the RAF sent a letter of congratulation." He takes down the framed RAF letter for her to read and reverently replaces them when she is done. Then he shows her the framed front page from the York newspaper that has pictures of the dedication ceremony. Billy is standing prominently between a clergyman and an RAF Air Marshall. They are looking at a stone pillar incised with the squadron badge. The story is captioned, "Leaton's Own 958 Squadron Remembers Lost Airmen." There is no sign of the twenty-nine other airmen and families that Billy had mentioned were also there.

"Let's have our tea," he says after he thinks she has had sufficient time to read the articles and letters. "The missus went out to do some shopping. Thought we'd like to have some time alone to talk. She's heard all this before."

They sit down and Billy fills their cups and offers her a shortbread biscuit. She notices that he is wearing a large signet ring with the squadron badge. As she drinks her tea, he puts his head a little to the side and lifts his glasses to study her.

"You look like Jimmy. It's mostly in the face shape, I'd say, and in your eyes. He was a quiet bloke. Of course that's what they said about me, but I let off steam when I went home. All that stopped when I got back from the prison camp and got married. We've been together thirty-five years next January."

Barbara appreciates their achievement. Thirty-five years is good in anyone's book. Particularly in the theatre where the temporary tends to be permanent and supposedly permanent things, like marriage, tend to be temporary.

"How do you like the tea?" he asks as she takes another sip.

"Very nice. Smoky and rich."

"Betty's Café," he says. "Wouldn't bother brewing anything else. Of course, when I was with the squadron, we'd by-pass the tearoom and go down to the bar. Have you seen the mirror yet?"

She shakes her head. She hasn't heard anything about a mirror.

"Aircrews carved their names on it. It was damaged in the war but it's still there. It was filled with names and squadrons. So many didn't come back. It was a terrible waste of young life."

"Are your names there?"

"In the lower left of the big panel. Nigel put them there the night before his wedding. But you have to look hard to find them."

He rubs his hands together and watches her for a few moments. This is the first time he's been so personally involved with someone looking for the past. His own crew. Who would have thought it?

"So what would you like to know?" he asks finally. "Keep in mind that I was eighteen when we were shot down. They treated me like a kid brother."

"Whatever you can tell me is more than I have. Why don't you tell me about you?"

He feels relieved. That much he can do.

"Me? Well, let's see. I joined the RAF volunteer reserve when I was seventeen. Got through gunnery school and was sent to the Operational Training Unit, OTU, in Cornwall to get crewed up. Those days—at least with us—they brought pilots, navigators, bomb aimers, and rear gunners together and said form yourselves into crews. It was all about who you got to know. When the pilots were in the air, they needed a rear gunner in case the Germans came calling. That's how I got to know Nigel. The navigators and bomb aimers took navigation courses together. That brought in Tad and Donny. Then they needed a wireless operator and Nigel already had chosen Jimmy.

"Once there were the five of us, we started going cross-country as a crew on the Wimpies. Got lost once during a raid and had to circle until it was over and the runway lights could be lit. Nigel said we were so low on petrol that another few minutes and we'd have bought it. Then we went to the HCU to learn how to fly the four-engine Halifax. George and Tommy came on there. Nigel nearly took us into the control tower on his first take-off in a Halifax. They made Nigel do bumps and circuits with an instructor for a time after that. But next time he did all right. Then we were posted to 958 Squadron."

"How many Operations had you flown before you were shot down."

"Two to France. Milk runs they called them. Just to get our feet wet. Then they gave us a fortnight off. I was glad because I could take my ration coupons home. I used to cadge chocolate off the WAAFs when I could and take it home with me."

Billy takes off his glasses and wipes them with a handkerchief. He looks out of the window and blinks. He is annoyed with himself. He doesn't like seeming sentimental to this young woman.

"I remember one night we went to The Three Martyrs. That was the only place beside the NAAFI café where we could have a drink and have Tad with us. He was an officer, you see. He had to sleep and eat in the officers' quarters. The place was crowded, so we had to sit on the stairs. I was nursing a beer. George was getting up to his larks. Donny'd also had a few—he used to say he was better in the air when he'd had a drink. So had Tad. Nigel and your dad were in good shape. Tommy was being his usual mysterious self. What I remember most is how we got back to the base. We were crammed into Nigel's little car so tightly we couldn't move. Jimmy's in the back with Donny, George, and Tad. I'm in the front with Tommy. I'm almost sitting in Tommy's lap. I am sitting in his lap when Nigel changed the gears and turned a corner. Suddenly, Nigel starts with 'Bomb aimer, directions.' Tad yells out, 'Right, right, steady,' and Nigel veers all over the road. We all start shouting directions then and get thrown from side to side. That's how we get back to the airfield, directing Nigel as if we were going for a bomb run. With the little slit of light we were allowed to display on the headlamp, it's a wonder we didn't land in the ditch or hit a cow."

"You made it though."

"Nigel was a good pilot and a good driver. Jimmy used to be forever working on that car. One look at it and it broke down. But he kept it running even if we had to go scavenging to find the parts. Tad worked a swap somehow. He had his family in Canada send him sweets, and he traded those for a few gallons of petrol. Enough to keep us going. There was lots of laughter. Don't ever think that we thought we were tragic heroes. But that's enough reminiscing. I know we've got a short time together and I don't want to bore you. It's that last flight you've come to hear about, isn't it? The one where Nigel and Jimmy were lost. I'm going to assume I'm right and tell you what I can remember."

Billy frowns slightly. He's gone over that last flight many, many times in his mind. He's talked about it endlessly. He's even written about it in the squadron newsletter. But lately he's noticed that some details have lost their immediacy. The smell of burning fuel and the thud of the bullets tearing into the fuselage no longer haunt his dreams. He can't be sorry about that though.

"We were told at noon that we were on the battle order, so we hung around until it was time for the briefing. They'd padlock the telephone booth once Ops were on, so I couldn't call home. But my Mum knew that if I hadn't called by afternoon, then something was up. The Wingco told us at the briefing that we'd be going to Hannover, but I don't remember much else about it except they warned us there'd be night fighters about. We get off on time and get over the enemy coast and somewhere over Germany I spot an enemy fighter. I yell for us to corkscrew. The skipper takes her down and round. I'm blasting away with the guns and I think maybe I've hit the fighter. Then he's back, or maybe it's another one. I yell for us to corkscrew again. I fire again. But he comes up at us from below. I can feel the aircraft's in trouble. It starts vibrating heavily and pitches my turret from side to side. I can see flames. The skipper puts her into a sharp dive but next thing I know he's brought her mostly level and is telling us to bale out. I have to reach around into the aircraft to grab my parachute. I clip it on and cross my fingers that the turret won't jam, rotate it until it's open, and then drop out backwards. I fall for a while and then remember that I'm supposed to do something with the ripcord. I pull on it and then not too much later I hit the ground. I hide for about a day but then I get captured and the war's over."

"Do you see what happened to the others?"

"You have to remember that the rear wheel well and a door separate me from the others. I only know what I've been told. Donny, Tad, and George said they went out the front escape hatch. Donny said that Jimmy was in the wireless compartment last thing he saw. Nothing unusual about that because, as the navigator, Donny was supposed to open the hatch and go first. Tommy couldn't get out of the entrance hatch, so he had to get through the rest area to go out at the front. He was the last one out because of that."

"What happened to everyone?"

"We were in different POW camps and didn't hear much until some time after the war. Tad and Donny went back to Canada but came over for the 958 reunion and the dedication. George went back to Australia. Tommy didn't keep in touch much, but you hear about him. He's built up half of London. I've always thought it interesting that he spends his life afterwards building up a city that was bombed. Not by us, of course."

Billy looks at her moodily for a moment. The pause gives Barbara the opportunity to ask the question that has perplexed her.

"Do you have any idea why Nigel and Jimmy didn't get out?"

"Knowing the skipper, I'd say that he stayed to fly the aircraft so that the rest of us could get out. All these years, I've toasted him on the day we were shot down. I feel I owe my life to him. Don't know about Jimmy. Maybe he was injured. Maybe there was another explosion. But Tommy may know something. As I said, he was the last one out, but he hasn't talked about it."

"You were all so young to have such responsibility," she blurts out.

"Nigel was the oldest. We used to kid him about it. But he couldn't have been more than 24. You had to be young to get into that cramped aircraft and become a bomb ferrying service. That's what we were. A taxi for a set of guns and a load of bombs. It's insanity if you think about it now. But we didn't think much about it then. We were doing our duty. Everybody cheered us in the pubs. 'Good lads,' they said. 'Give them some what for. Bit of their own'."

Billy's lips tremble.

"Did Jimmy," she cannot bring herself to call him her father, "talk about himself or a family?"

Billy swallows and gives her an unconvincing half smile. Barbara thinks she detects a slight catch to his voice. Has the question made him uncomfortable?

"If he did, it would have been to Nigel. Jimmy was a good man. He was quiet and private. He'd sit there smiling and you knew he was taking everything in because he'd come out with something unexpected now and then. He'd impersonate the skipper—had him down perfectly—and made us all laugh. Even Nigel. The Three Martyrs had little, dark corners. The tables were the right size for a crew to sit around, and it had kept the gaslights. It was a lovely place when there was a fire going in the hearth, and there was always beer for the aircrews. Nigel and Jimmy liked to sit in front of the fire and talk about motor cars and what was happening in the world. Nigel was brainy, you know. He'd been at university."

Billy signals the end of this part of the conversation by picking up a flat, brown envelope from the chair beside him. "Here are some things for you. From your letter, I gathered that you didn't have any so I thought you should. And I've put a few other things in there."

The envelope distracts Barbara from asking further questions even if she had wanted to. She takes out the contents. He's included copies of the crew picture, the wedding photograph, the newspaper clipping on the dedication, the RAF letter, a small pin with the 958 Squadron badge, and addresses. Tommy lives in Somerset. Donny and Tad have addresses in Ontario, Canada. She looks at Billy and tries to intuit what has made him want to change the subject so abruptly. Is too painful for him to remember? Does he doubt she is who she says she is? The latter, at least, she can confront directly.

"Did you wonder about me when I contacted you?"

Billy looks at her in surprise. He had assumed she was being truthful. Why ever wouldn't she be after all these years?

"Never gave it a thought. There'd be no reason to wonder, would there? It was a long time ago. It was wartime and things happened. I'm glad that Jimmy has someone looking for him. It keeps us all alive. The worst thing would be for people to forget." Billy's eyes mist as he looks around his walls. "People have short memories these days. In another few years, there won't be anyone alive who can remember this. What good was all the loss of life if no one's going to remember?"

He takes out his handkerchief and this time dabs his eyes. He gives her an embarrassed smile. "Donny and Tad said they'd be happy to talk with you. Tommy's been more reserved about things, but he says he'll see you. He was a bright lad, that one. He got bombed out and it made him dark. I think it'll be good for him to talk if he's willing. Tommy and his wife spend their winters in Spain. He says he'll let you know when he's back if you drop him a line. Nobody's heard from George for forty years. Last we heard he was in Australia farming somewhere. I'm glad that you're asking about us. It's good to look at things again through new eyes."

Barbara feels the selfish desire to get on the train back to London and sit and stare at the pictures. She puts them and the other things back into the envelope and strokes her hand across the brown surface. The front door bangs open then and a little terrier comes racing to the table. It stops when it sees Barbara, wags its tail, and starts barking. Billy's wife bustles into the room with a shopping bag with vegetable tops sprouting from it.

"Here are Martha and Corky. Corky's the dog."

"Oh Billy don't be so daft."

Martha is a comfortable woman about the same height as Billy. Barbara senses that she is the kind of person who determines early what's important in life and doesn't worry about the rest. She unties her headscarf and ruffles her greying wavy hair. Her voice has a Yorkshire draw on the vowels.

"Now Billy's been telling you all about it, has he? They all looked so good in their uniforms. Many a girl had her head turned by the sight of them. But so many didn't come back. You took a big risk to go out with them. They'd come to the dances, just boys they were, and you knew that next time they might not be there. I used to work in the NAAFI so I'd see them all. Did Billy tell you that I remember your dad?"

She settles onto the chair across from Barbara and looks speculatively into the teapot.

"How about some fresh tea, Pet?"

"Do you want me to unpack your grocery bags?"

"That would be nice."

She smiles at Barbara and says quietly that it will give them a few moments to talk. Billy ambles off to the kitchen and they can hear water rushing into the tin kettle and the rattle as he puts it on the stove.

"Billy's and my families knew each other and lived not far from Leaton. They wanted all the women to work. I applied for the NAAFI job at Leaton because it was close and was lucky enough to get it. I remember your dad and the others coming in for a cuppa in the NAAFI in the evening. They had their regular meals in the mess, so they'd come in for the odd bite outside hours. Billy would come in on his own but most often with the others. Your dad was the quiet one. The two Canadians were always laughing and talking about Canada. The Aussie, I can't remember his name ..."

"George Williams," says Billy as he brings in the pot and stumbles over the dog, which runs under the table, yelping.

"There, Corky. That's what you get for being underfoot as usual," he says.

Martha reaches out and takes the pot to safety. "Thanks, Love. That's right—George. He was a character. But it was my Billy who was the wild one." She glances at him fondly.

"Days long past," Billy smiles back. "I had to prove I was a good boy before you'd take up with me."

"I'd have taken you regardless. I was that glad to see you come back with you all thin and pale and your hands trembling. Walking ghost is what I thought. Wasn't about to let you know that though. Had to give you some trouble. Did you unpack the bags yet?"

Billy acknowledges his inattention and disappears into the kitchen.

Martha stirs the tea leaves speculatively and makes a practice pour into a cup. It seems dark enough. For a sudden moment, her gesture reminds Barbara of Marilyn. It makes her wonder what her mother would think about dredging up the past like this when she went to so much trouble to hide it.

"Can I offer you some more tea?"

Barbara accepts and pushes her cup across the table.

"Now about your dad. Did Billy tell you that you look like him? Saw it right away when I came in. It's been a long time, but the thing I remember most about him are those bright blue eyes. The other thing I remember is that he never complained about anything. That's a nice quality, isn't it? Oh the others would go on about the powdered eggs. He wouldn't. He'd eat them and say they were quite good. He thought everything was all right and thanked you for doing anything for him. He was ever so polite—a nice man. Not like some others I could point to."

"I heard that," Billy calls from the kitchen. "We were sergeants and proud of those stripes. You'd better salute us and no half larks about it. We had to swagger and show them off."

"Right," Martha says dryly. "But Jimmy had another quality that I also remember. He had a strength. I have no idea what his life had been like before he came to Leaton, but I got the impression—you know, woman's intuition—that there was sadness that he never talked about."

"Now how could you have known that?" Billy asks as he comes back. "He never said anything about that."

"Well, that's my point, Love. He never discussed it with you. I'd call that strength."

"I didn't discuss myself much either."

"You little idiot," Martha says fondly, "you didn't have anything to discuss. Perhaps it was you and your mother that he wasn't talking about, Barbara. What did your mother tell you about him?"

"Nothing much until just before she died."

"So you grew up knowing absolutely nothing about him?"

Martha looks at her sadly. She cannot imagine how it feels to be looking for something that you can never know. She wonders for an instant why the secrecy was needed. But then she dismisses the thought. It's not her custom to question other people's reasons. Reasons always exist. That much she knows.

"Mum said he was a decent man and that he loved flying but was a bit afraid of it."

"A bit?" snorts Billy as he sits down at the table. Martha's groceries are forgotten for the moment. "We were young enough to believe we were immortal, but when you saw a bomber coned in the search lights ahead or heard flak exploding like a hammer on the fuselage you knew what you were in for. We were all afraid but once you got on an Op, there wasn't time to be. It was after you got back or before you left. You lived in a constant state of nerves. But we did what we had to."

"How did it affect you, all those crews not coming back?"

Only the luxury of time and survival has allowed Billy to find an answer for that question. He's never known why one crew survived and another didn't. Luck had to be what it was all about. But you couldn't think about it then. When you climbed into the aircraft, you had to believe you'd be the one that made it.

"We did everything together as a crew," he tells her. "Besides the crew it was your girlfriend on your mind. There wasn't much reason to get to know the others. It's sad as I look back on it, but that's the way it was. You couldn't allow yourself to think about anything other than doing your job. There were a lot of 958 squadron that I didn't know until the reunions after the war. I felt closer to my fellow kriegies because we'd spent so much more time together as POWs. There's an active POW organization. Did you know that?"

Barbara shakes her head. She's intrigued because she's sure she would have heard these stories from her father if he had made it out of the aircraft.

"Only good thing to be said about it is that we survived. We were often hungry between Red Cross parcels and used to exchange recipes. Nothing anyone in his right mind would eat, like a quart of cream, a pound of butter, and a jar of strawberry jam on a large sponge cake. But it sounded wonderful to us. We built a small radio and hid the parts all over the camp to keep them from the ferrets, the plants the Germans put in the camp to learn what we were up to. So we knew when the war was nearly over. Toward the end, the Germans kept moving us to keep us away from the Russians. We had to slog through deep snow and sleep in barns. Finally, the guards gave up and left us to fend for ourselves. When the Americans wanted to send lorries to get us, the Russians wouldn't give us up. It had to be Russian lorries. Damned fool nonsense. But the Americans fed us well when they got us, what we could keep down. We were in a roguish mood when we were flown home. We laughed at the poor American chap who had to demonstrate how to use a parachute. He went beet red. Back in the UK we had to take the train. When a civilian couple got into our railway carriage and looked disgusted at our appearance, we pretended to scratch and itch until they got up and left. We thought that was funny. But it wasn't funny at all when we had to find jobs and get on with our lives. Most of us had a hard go of it. I'm glad that I had family to give a hand."

Martha looks over at Barbara's cup and sees that it's empty. She reaches for the pot, but Barbara looks at her watch and gives a start. More time has passed than she had thought.

"I'm sorry," she says as she stands up, "but the taxi's coming back for me in a few minutes. I have to get back to London. There's a performance tonight."

"I know this is a lot to think about," Billy says, "but if you can think of anything else you want to know, give us a call."

"And stay in touch," Martha adds. "We'd like to know how your search turns out."

"You've both been absolutely wonderful and I've learned a great deal. I hope that you'll come to the theatre one night so I can repay your kindness. If you'll let me know you're coming, I'll have some tickets waiting for you."

"That's sweet," Martha replies. "We'll be sure to do that, but we don't get down there often."

Barbara looks back when the taxi comes for her. They are both standing in the doorway waving. Martha is holding Corky and looks open and happy. Billy looks slightly apprehensive. Is there something he has not told her? If there is, Barbara wonders whether time is going to reveal it, or whether she even wants to know.

10

Sir, You Can't Pass Here, London 1941

Jimmy caught the London train back from the RAF induction centre at Oxford. It took well over three hours to get to Paddington. They were stopped for some time somewhere between Reading and London, too far between stations apparently to be able to pull into one and take cover. In the distance, they could hear the ack-ack guns and the sounds of fighters mingled with the drones of the German aircraft. Something large exploded nearby and shook the carriage, sending shrapnel clattering onto the roof.

Inside the carriage, despite every seat taken and the corridors packed, all was silent. The train was almost completely dark with only a faint glow from a single bulb. Reading was impossible. Cigarette smoke curled up to merge into the dingy brown left by years of other evenings and other smokers. Jimmy squinted to read the large headline on a folded newspaper on another passenger's lap. The *Daily Mirror* screamed the headline "We Could Lose." Jimmy wondered how that got past the censors, except perhaps it was meant to be a call to arms. A further call to arms, it would seem. The country was already mobilized and in full production with women working in the factories and those without dependent children urged into the war effort. It was the first time in England's history, except perhaps for the time of Boadicea, that women had been so much a part of war. The sounds overhead receded after a time and the train began to move again but very slowly.

"Glad that's over," said one man in a raincoat. There were murmurs of assent in the carriage.

"Did we get hit?" another asked. He voiced the general concern that the falling debris might have been incendiaries that set everything on fire.

"Should doubt it," said the raincoat. "It was probably some debris from a plane."

"Let's hope it was Jerry's," said a young man across from Jimmy.

"Hope it didn't land on the line," said a woman soothing a child.

If the line was damaged, passengers had to jump from the train and walk to the nearest station. It could be difficult over railway ties and gravel in the dark, particularly carrying a child.

"They'll walk ahead and make sure it's clear."

The raincoat seemed to know what he was talking about. When the All Clear sounded, there was a feeling of relaxation. The passengers had held to the reassurance that life would continue if they were collectively self-controlled enough. Now they could let down their guard.

Jimmy didn't know what to with himself or where to look once they were moving. The carriage blackout had removed the windows as the only place to stare. He studied his hands. He looked at the floor. He closed his eyes and let his mind wander. He thought about the past three days and how disappointed he had been when he wasn't selected for pilot training. He thought about his family. His wife Rose and his dad were waiting for him at home. He'd missed them. He thought about Nigel and felt bad that he hadn't told him about his family. Nigel was a nice chap. Someone Jimmy could like. But there'd be time later on to tell him about Rose and why he wouldn't be looking for girls with him. If he ever saw him again. Jimmy didn't share his family with everyone. There was something warm about knowing they were there in his life. He wanted to keep them to himself.

Finally, he just looked around the carriage. The woman across from him wore a dark overcoat and small black hat and veil. Her child looked around two. Jimmy smiled at the child, but it sucked its thumb and stared back with large, dark eyes. He wondered what his own child would look like. Would it have the family black hair and blue eyes? Or would it look like Rose with her glistening brown hair and rosy complexion? The man in the raincoat next to the woman looked about sixty. Jimmy guessed him to be retired military, maybe army. The young man by the carriage window was someone Jimmy remembered seeing at the RAF Centre. He was watching the young woman on Jimmy's right. She was wearing a WAAF uniform. On leave, Jimmy guessed, coming up to London to see her family. She was leaned back against the seat with her eyes closed and her arms folded. The man on Jimmy's left was about forty, dressed in army uniform. Had some time off, Jimmy fantasized, probably been at Dunkirk. The man also had his eyes closed but from time to time he opened them to look at his watch. Maybe ordered to Aldershot or some place like it. Jimmy tried to look unobtrusively for a regiment badge but couldn't see one. In the end, Jimmy leaned back against the seat and resigned himself to listening to the train's on-going groans and clicks.

Paddington Station was filled with people whose trains had been delayed or cancelled because of the alert. The station office windows around the upper walls were all open and people were leaning out to watch the crowd below. There was a camaraderie, a sense of life being lived right on the edge. Who knew if their houses would be there when they got home or whether everyone would even be alive tomorrow? Whenever the loudspeaker came on to announce a platform, a sea of people moved in that direction. At the same time, the departure board came alive with the top to bottom flicker of destinations and stops. Some destinations said they were cancelled and made suggestions for alternative routes. Even though it was unlikely that everyone would get home that night, there was palpable relief. Life had been interrupted and now it was resumed. At least as long as the electricity stayed on.

Jimmy stopped briefly to talk with a constable outside the darkened station before finding his way into the underground. The constable was watching the crowd as best he could. Thieves and pickpockets were active in crowds like this. During an air raid, people were distracted and didn't mind their things as well. There had been cases where bodies were robbed after a bombing. It took only seconds and the thieves would be gone by the time the police and wardens could get there.

"Were there many hits?" Jimmy asked the constable.

"Some fires about in this area, sir. Can't tell about the rest of the city. Most seemed to be going up north somewhere. Our chaps got some. Good for them."

"Well, good night, then."

Jimmy looked up at the grey helium barrage balloons moored in the sky to protect the City of London. The burning fires below made them look bronze. One was shaped like a boxing glove. Some people thought they were magnetized and could bring down German bombers. More luck to them if believing that made them feel more secure. All the balloons did was discourage dive-bombers. Then he headed down into the underground. The platform smelled of humanity, pushed along by the hot gust that preceded a train coming through the tunnel and into the platform. His train was the third to come and it took nearly forty minutes to get to his stop. By then he was left alone to climb the grimy stairs up to the street. Halfway up, he could smell charred wood and stirred-up dust and hear the sirens. He began to run. Not here. Not again. It was a long time before the station reopened last time and even then it was all temporary and the terrible smell of bombing and death had never left.

He ran across the empty road in front of the station. He was still running when he reached his corner and was stopped by an elderly ARP warden. The flickering light of flames turned the lines in the old man's face into deep gashes. Grey-black ground smoke swirled along the street and plumes of steam from doused flames created a grey gash against the black sky.

"Sorry, sir, you can't pass here."

The man put out a protective arm and put his hand on Jimmy's shoulder. It was his job to prevent anguished civilians from becoming hindering the fire brigade and the rescue squad. He hadn't ever had this much authority in his life before and wanted to be a good public servant. Jimmy looked desperately into the man's face, pleading his need to be allowed to pass.

"But this is my road. My house is down the end."

The ARP warden was not an unkind man. He wanted to help if he could. They'd told him that was his mission: to protect and to serve. He took an even firmer hold on to Jimmy's arm. The news he was about to give wasn't good. He'd seen dazed survivors before.

"Sorry, Sir, there was a direct hit. It's too dangerous for you to go down there. There are houses down and the road is blocked."

"Do you know which houses?"

Jimmy's heart pounded and he had trouble swallowing.

"Well, Sir, since you live there, you can go over and ask the constable at the next barrier. But don't go further. They're pulling people out, and the Heavy Duty boys and the fire brigade have ladders and hoses all over the street."

Jimmy pushed his way to the barrier on the other side of the street. The dust had become a stench of ground up mortar, brick, burned wood, household gas, and explosives. His breath came in short thuds and he felt dizzy. The constable recognized him and gestured for him to stand next to him by the barrier. Several other people were pressed there already, watching the fire brigade pump water in a large arc onto smoking rubble. It had been hours since the bomb exploded, but the flames were stubborn.

"Sorry, Jimmy, there was direct hit. You can't go down there."

Jimmy looked down the road. Flames licked up between cracks in the rubble piles, and bricks were funnelled like landslides across the pavement and the street. The flashes from the fire illuminated the stark walls of what had been a row of terraced houses. Here and there he could see scraps of flowered wallpaper. He could see a picture hanging over a toilet supported by its plumbing. A kitchen stove clung to the one wall left standing, the oven door hanging by one hinge.

The road was filled with piles of shattered doors, window frames, and personal belongings—a child's toy, a shoe, an umbrella with no fabric cover.

"Was anyone taken out?" Jimmy's voice was anguished.

"We've got some killed, and a number taken off in the ambulances. They'll be sending runners over the ARP hut with the names once they have more information."

Jimmy didn't reply. He stood in unbelieving silence looking at the flickering reality of what had happened to his street. His house was too far down for him to see beyond the rubble and debris of the first collapsed houses. He knew he couldn't walk away without knowing. He waited some time for his moment. When the constable was busy with someone else, Jimmy pressed back against the walls of the Green Goblin, the public house on the corner, and slipped behind the barricade.

Slowly, he edged down the road, staying in the shadows. The fires had made everything hot, and he could feel the bricks burning through his coat. He picked his way around splintered wood beams and shattered glass, slipping behind the firemen and rescue workers who were too occupied with the fire to notice him. He passed a gaping hole in the ground filling with water from ruptured pipes. Numbers 40 through 46 Cumbers Way had lost their fronts. He could see inside into the framing that had held the houses together. Then he stopped in front of 38. His house.

Still pressing himself against the damaged brick wall across the street, he stared in mute incomprehension. The number was readable on the stone parapet at the steps up to the front door. But where there had been a building, there was now a deep, smoking hole and a towering mound of broken wood, plaster, and stone.

"Is this your home, Sir?" Another ARP warden had spotted him the flickering firelight.

Jimmy nodded but couldn't speak or move. The warden saw his dazed look and took him by the arm. "Let's go back behind the barrier, shall we? We don't want another casualty now do we?" Jimmy did not look back as they walked slowly down the road toward the barricade, broken glass crunching beneath their feet.

"Do you have somewhere to go for the night?" the warden asked after he deposited Jimmy safely behind the barrier. Jimmy shook his head. "Well, Sir, you can't stay here. This isn't safe. Why don't you go down to the shelter for the night? You look like you could use a cuppa. There's nothing you can do here."

Jimmy nodded numbly.

"You didn't want to be doing that, Jimmy, going down there like that," the constable scolded as he drew Jimmy further behind the barricade. "There's nothing to see there. You could look in at the warden post across from the station. The list will be up there once we know anything. Go on down to the centre. Perhaps your people went there before the alert."

"Did your house get it too?" Jimmy asked him. The constable lived several houses away from him.

"Damaged, it looks like. But the wife was down at the shelter. Maybe yours is too."

Jimmy nodded and stumbled his way down the road past the station. He recognized the man at the sandbagged warden post when he got there. Barney, the local butcher, had his shop bombed out. He'd been glad to get a job for three quid a week as a warden. He was the only one full-time. Everyone else was a volunteer. But it was good that Barney was there. He knew everyone in the neighbourhood. There he was with his helmet with a big W, his armband, his silver badge, and his conical, green air-raid box. His familiarity was a comfort. You never know a man until there's danger. Barney looked as stunned as anyone. But his face was set and he seemed to be holding himself together by doing his job. Jimmy stood patiently among the others waiting his turn to ask.

"Have you seen my family, Barney?"

"Can't say that I have, Jimmy. We've got one report come by runner but nothing on your family. But check the shelter. That's where we're sending everyone."

"Did you get hit, Barney?" Jimmy asked.

"Don't know yet. Thanks for asking, Jimmy. There's no word on my street. Can't leave here to check. So, like you, I have to wait."

Jimmy walked along the road to the shelter. Ambulance and fire bells seemed to come from all across the city. There'd be many people looking a place to stay the night.

The shelter was packed when Jimmy got there. The Women's Reserve ladies were out in green coats handing out tea to the several hundred people who had spread coats and newspapers on the floor. Jimmy divided the room into quadrants and began walking up and down. At first, he saw no one he knew. Then he saw an elderly couple from up his road. The man's face was white and strained, he had a bandage on his head, and his arms were scraped in the way of elderly people with paper-thin, transparent skin. He sat on the floor with a mug of tea and stared at nothing. His wife looked pale and vacant.

"Harry," said Jimmy eagerly as he crouched down next to the man.

Harry looked up at him and took a moment to recognize his neighbour.

"Are you all right?"

The man's lip trembled as he nodded. Then he caught himself and nodded again with more determination.

"Bloody Huns," he finally managed.

Jimmy kneeled down beside him, apologizing to a woman for bumping her as he did so.

"What happened?"

"Direct hit on the street. Don't know which house got it. Blew out the windows and the wall. We're under the staircase. When we try to come out, the front's all gone. Nothing left. They have to get ladders and pull us out. They said we were lucky. Wanted to know why we weren't down at the shelter. But you can't be always running to the shelter. You'd be there all night. We're all right, but the house's done for."

"It was my house that they got," Jimmy said. "Nothing's left. Have you seen my dad or Rose?"

The man shook his head.

"They picked some people out. Laid them out on the ground, but they were covered by the time they pulled us out. They fixed us up and told us to come to the shelter. It's the dust that's the worst. It's everywhere. And there's no place even to wash it off."

"Have you got a place to go to?" Jimmy asked.

The old man shrugged. "Maybe our daughter's. Don't know. She's got the kids and already has boarders from the Blitz. Made her double up the kids so she could take in a bombed-out family. Don't know. They told us they'd get to us when they could. Damned dust."

The old man wrung his hands and tried to wipe them on his shirt.

Jimmy patted him on the shoulder and then stood up and resumed his search. With each circuit of the room, he felt more desperate. In the end he admitted his defeat. His wife and father were not at the shelter. He asked at the desk about them. No one had heard anything. There was nowhere even to sit by then. He slumped down on the steps from the street outside and took a cup of tea when it was offered. Like Harry, he had nowhere to go.

Slowly the reality sank in. His wife and dad were gone. They had to be. They had stopped going to the shelter some time ago.

"I'll take my chances under the table," Rose had said. "If I'm going to die, I'll be at home, if you please." His dad didn't disagree. They got a free steel shelter they could put up in the house and get under when the siren sounded. It was supposed to protect you unless there was a direct hit. Nothing could protect against that. Not even the shelter.

Now everything was gone. He'd go by and look tomorrow but he already knew there wasn't enough left to look for some reminder of his life. No torn pictures, no dented saucepan, no chipped teacup with its thick white sides, the little things that people collected the next day to hold onto the past—all was utterly gone. There was a deep, deep hole, shattered bricks, and a fire consuming whatever the bomb might have spared.

His family was gone. All he had left was memories. He remembered the terrible night when his mother died two years ago—a tear drying on her cheek when he whispered goodbye. How strange he thought it was that his dad never talked about losing his wife until Jimmy understood that some things can only be borne in silence. He'd met Rose at the bank where they both worked and he'd not waited to ask her to marry him because, with the war, there might be no time later. They'd moved into Dad's tiny flat because there was a housing shortage. They laughed together as they screened off the dining room to make a bedroom for them. They'd taped up the windows and made blackout curtains with cheap fabric and soot. They'd talked about their future together and laughed again when Rose tried to cook BBC recipes using carrots, turnips, and potatoes.

"Never replace the Sunday joint," she'd said.

"I could really fancy a sausage," his dad said wistfully. "A nice one, all dark brown outside."

"I could get you one, Dad," Rose said. "I've got some dripping saved to fry it in."

He shook his head. "Not something that tastes like sawdust and dried cauliflower."

"Sorry, Dad," she laughed. "That's the best I can do."

"I didn't think they were too bad," Jimmy offered. "Could be worse."

"How?" his dad had asked archly.

Dad's irony would come out unexpectedly. Never underestimate the Baldock men was his favourite comment.

"You'd eat anything, Jimmy," Rose laughed. "I suppose you like that awful American stuff. What's it called? The pink stuff."

"Spam?" Jimmy offered helpfully.

"That's it. Nasty stuff. Salty. Doesn't taste anything like a nice piece of gammon."

"I don't mind it," Jimmy replied. "Better than nothing."

"That's not saying much," his dad had said. "Might be all right if you could put something on it to cover the taste."

Rose let out a merry laugh.

"Come on, Dad. Don't you know there's a war on?"

"Not you too," Dad had howled. "Hear enough about that on the BBC. At least it's ITMA tonight. Wouldn't miss that, so Auntie does some good."

They'd huddle round the wireless, listening to the broadcasters' plummy tones and then Tommy Handley's rapid puns and word play. Everyone on the street listened to him. It was a national pastime. On summer evenings, you could walk down the street and not miss a word because everyone had it on and the windows were all open.

Jimmy stumbled along with his memories, which were forcing themselves into his mind in place of tears and shock.

He remembered how they'd pop round to the Green Goblin for a half pint. You didn't go for the beer, which was watered down. It was always lively there with regulars from the streets surrounding it. Rose had a sweet singing voice and there'd be cheers when she showed up. Someone would bang away on the piano and she'd sing the Vera Lynn songs. She'd make Jimmy join in. "Come on," she'd say. "You've got a good voice so let's hear it." Jimmy would join in then, but he was never one to push himself forward. Barney the butcher had a good voice too but he sang so loud that he drowned out everyone else. Jimmy thought that was bad manners.

He'd been restless after he volunteered. Being in the bank wasn't a reserved occupation. He knew the call would come soon and he was ready. Many fellows he knew wanted the Navy but most would go in the army because that's where they were needed. Jimmy knew he wanted the air force. But the RAF didn't take everyone and you had to qualify. The recruiting posters showed a pilot waving jauntily: Are you the cream of the crop? the poster asked. They were all volunteers because the RAF never conscripted, and there was always the possibility too of staying in England. That was important to men with families.

Then a few days ago the letter finally arrived. He was to report to Oxford. Rose had been quiet when it came.

"Did it have to be now?" she had asked him.

"Sooner or later," he had replied laconically.

"But I thought we'd have more time."

She'd known it had to come. The men were all going. The young ones were joining the cadets. The old were volunteering as wardens and guards. The war seemed to need everyone who could get up in the morning. Both she and Jimmy were on night fire patrol at the bank watching for fires and prepared to put sand on incendiaries.

On the day, three mornings ago, when he'd left for the recruiting centre, his dad was stolidly eating some bread and Rose's homemade apple jam with his tea when Jimmy came down.

"So it's today, is it?" his father said, more statement than question.

"Yes, it's today."

Jimmy sat down at the table and watched his father.

"And you're going to Oxford, are you?"

They had been over this several times and Jimmy knew that the old man didn't know what to say.

Jimmy nodded.

"And they're testing you, you said?"

Again Jimmy nodded. His father retreated into silence and looked away from him. He seemed to swallow and then opened his mouth. Jimmy waited in silence to see what his father wanted to tell him.

"Anyone want more tea? The ration coupons came yesterday so we're rich."

Rose came into the room with the teapot.

"How's the jam, Dad?"

"Nice."

"You get more from the sugar ration if you make jam with it," Rose said. "Don't think jam works if you put it in tea. That's the problem. But I've saved some sugar for you, Dad."

Jimmy knew she was trying to be bright and cheerful to hide her worries. He went over and gave her a self-conscious hug. Baldock men weren't given to open displays of their feelings. But this was different. He patted her stomach.

"Take good care of you both. I'll be gone only three days."

She smiled at him. They'd known for a week that she was pregnant. She handed him his cup of tea. He could see the concern in her eyes.

At the door when he left, Rose smoothed the lapels of his jacket and told him to get to be a pilot since he wanted it so badly. They kissed and Jimmy stroked her stomach.

"It's just three days," he repeated as she clung tightly to him.

His dad shook his hand and wished him luck. They both waved him off down the street—the same street now clogged with rubble and flames. Jimmy remembered how he'd looked back that one last time. The front garden railings were long gone for scrap, so the street looked as if it was missing teeth. Outside each house was a dustbin and separate bundles of paper wrapped with string, a box for bottles, and a bucket for food scraps to be fed to animals somewhere. The bundles were neatly stacked. Jerry was not going to be allowed to disrupt order and good manners. He'd waved one last time and turned at the pub to go to the underground station.

Jimmy left the shelter and walked back along to his road. His body sagged with the reality of what had happened. A clawing emptiness took hold. Why did it have to be when he wasn't there? Why had they gone and left him behind to be alone? He looked down the road, hoping for the miracle of familiar shapes walking toward him. But there were only the ARP wardens and a few people coming back from the shelters to see what was left. At the corner, the elderly ARP warden had taken up watchful position at the barricade. The area was quieting down and smoke and steam curled around the fire hoses as the fire brigade started recoiling them.

"Still can't let anyone down there, Sir."

Jimmy could see that the constable was there too and was watching to see that Jimmy obeyed orders this time. But Jimmy didn't want to cross the barricade. He needed to confirm in his uncomprehending brain the reality of what he'd seen.

If there had been anyone in there, he knew they hadn't had much chance. He knew he'd check at the police station and warden's post for the injured lists and he'd leave his name in case they came looking for him. But he already knew.

He hunched his shoulders, put his head down, and started walking through the black streets, his way lit by lingering flames from houses hit on other streets and pale starlight. He had nowhere to go. There was nowhere to walk to. He didn't care if anyone stopped him and wondered what he was doing. Walking was the only possibility left to him in a world gone mad.

11

The Road to Port Hope

Barbara's flight leaves Heathrow nearly an hour late. It doesn't make any difference to her but some passengers are complaining about missing connections in Toronto. There are several small children in the waiting area, some screaming. Modern transport, she thinks. She wonders what her dad and the others would have thought if they could have looked into the future of aviation. But despite all the omens, the flight isn't bad.

She goes to the rental car agency at Toronto airport. She's more apprehensive about driving on the other side of the road than about meeting Donny Oakes and Tad Smith and staying at Donny's house. Donny and his wife wouldn't hear of her staying anywhere else. Three days is all she has. She promised Sheridan it would be three performances. They sat down together and talked for some time about her search for her father. He seemed to understand very deeply.

The rental-car agent asks if she has ever driven on the right-hand side of the road before. When she says no, he looks doubtful and insists on driving with her around the airport. The biggest problem for her turns out to be not knowing how far away the on-coming cars are on the passenger side. In the end, he advises her to get into a traffic stream and follow the others. It works out well because there aren't traffic roundabouts. The roads are clearly marked, and the agent has given her directions that include exactly which lane she needs to be in at what time.

The traffic through Toronto is congested but that helps because everyone is creeping along. Once outside the city, the crowds are gone and all she has to do is stay on the highway except to pull off into the ubiquitous café shops called Tim Hortons along the way.

Ontario appears to be flat and she catches only occasional glimpses of Lake Ontario as she drives along its shore. She cannot see the far side when the trees clear. The roadsides have thick thatched grass with gauzy heads and evergreen trees that serve as a windbreak. Even so, the car is buffeted by windy gusts from across the water.

Donny and his wife live on the outskirts of a small town called Port Hope, about an hour east of Toronto. When Barbara turns off the highway, she finds herself on a long, country road that threads its way through farmland. Go past the village they had told her, and then look for the barn. You can't miss it. But the village turns out to be six miles from the highway and the barn is four miles on beyond that.

Finally, she finds the barn. It is a large lumbering red wood building with animal pens outside and piled-up farm equipment leaned against the walls. She mentally crosses her fingers that she is correct, turns right and continues on a gravel and dirt road until she finds a driveway on the left leading up to an enormous two-storey house with cement walls on the first floor and wood panels on the second. A double garage occupies half the lower level with a veranda on top. On one side the land runs down to a stream marked by trees along its bank. On the other there is a large shed with two doors. One is open and there appears to be a tractor inside. The countryside around is misty rolling hills that remind her of Yorkshire. It is all green and damp and obviously fertile. She parks behind a large caravan that has a red maple leaf pasted on the back.

Donny and his wife are sitting on the balcony in the autumn sunshine at the point where the balcony's wood railings come to a point like a ship's prow. They wave her to come up the stairs at the side.

Donny shakes her hand vigorously. He is completely recognizable from the crew picture. Then he had a square face with prominent ears and his hair was dark and slicked into a wave at the front. Now grey hair wisps around his ears, he has thickened, and he wears glasses with little lines across the bottom. But his jaw still juts out and his greyish hair stands up in front as it did when he flew the Halifaxes.

"Welcome, welcome. You've made it all right. We were getting worried and thought we might have to send out the dogs to find you."

He turns to the woman smiling beside him.

"This is Noreen, my better half. Put up with me now for nearly forty years."

Noreen has short waved hair and metal-framed glasses. She's wearing black check slacks and a yellow shirt. She laughs freely and offers Barbara tea or coffee. Then she goes into the house to get the teapot.

"I'll be out in the kitchen for a sec," she says as she goes. She pronounces out as if was oot.

"Come and sit down here. It's nice weather, not raining and the snow's not here yet, so we thought we'd sit outside."

Donny pulls out a chair for her and turns it so that she can look out over the hills around them.

"Can't believe that you'd come all this way for a couple of days. Tad and Margie are coming over for dinner and staying over so you'll have as much time as possible with us. He was as amazed as I was when Billy told us about you."

He takes out a cigarette.

"Mind?" he asks. "Nasty habit I picked up during the war. I've cut it down but not out. I suppose you have to die of something."

Barbara studies him curiously as he flicks the match and cradles the flame. She warmed to him on sight. He's someone that women would like, she thinks. Someone who might take a sick stray cat to the vet to be put down and then end up paying hundreds to save it.

"We're what, five hours behind you? You must be tired as all get out."

"Not too bad," she replies. "I went straight to the airport after the matinee and nodded off on the plane. Coming west is a bonus. I gain time. I'll lose it going back and it's overnight, so that'll be harder."

Noreen returns with the teapot and cups. Little tags with a flower on them hang over the side of the teapot indicating that Noreen is brewing teabags. Barbara is surprised that she notices that. But then it occurs to her that her search for her father has been punctuated by cups of tea.

"Tad and Margie will be here for dinner and then they're staying over to have some time with you," she says.

"I told her that already, Hon."

"Oh all right then. Now have you started to tell her about her father?"

"Give me time," he chides back. "Let's set the programme first. Barbara's here for such a short time. Tad and I will do what we can to remember. Then tomorrow, Tad's planning to drive you around to Port Hope in the morning. When she heard about that, Norrie said she'd like to come too. There's a shop down there she likes. I don't imagine that Margie will be shy either, so there's a crowd going with you. Hope you don't mind."

"It sounds wonderful."

"Whatever am I thinking about? Here's the milk and sugar." Noreen pushes the creamer and sugar bowl across the table. "Don't stand on ceremony here. If you want something, you speak up."

"There's much to say," Donny begins and then hesitates. "Where do you want me to begin?"

"Well," Barbara says, "I had a good talk with Billy Coppin."

To her surprise, Donny bursts out laughing.

"Sorry, Barbara," he says as he sees her confused expression. "So you met with Mr. Squadron? What did you think of him?"

"He struck me as a man with a lot on his mind."

"Well that's giving him credit. Don't get me wrong. He's great in his own way and he's done wonderful things for the squadron. But I remember him as a little pipsqueak who didn't have a pot to piss in. That is, until he adopted 958 Squadron."

"Donny!"

"All right, Hon, don't look so scandalized. I'm sure Barbara's heard worse. Billy found his calling in life after he got back from the stalag. 958 became his. Which was fine with the rest of us. We had lives to live and didn't have the time to get a squadron badge, or have it put in the floor of Saint Clement Danes, or to set up a memorial in Leaton. He did, and God bless him for it."

"Barbara may not know about Saint Clement Danes," Noreen says.

"Right. That's the RAF chapel. Right in the middle of the Strand. Traffic has to go around it on both sides. It got bombed out during the Blitz, but they rebuilt it. It has a book in it with all the names of lost aircrew, and it has the squadron badges in the floor. Trouble was that 958 Squadron had been started late in the war. No one had time to come up with a badge. Then Billy decided that the squadron's honour demanded it. He got the sketch done, got it through the College of Heralds, and then got the RAF to put it in the floor next to the pulpit. God bless him for it, as I said. But after that, 958 Squadron was his. The rest of us were bookends."

"Billy told me you were over there for the dedication of the memorial."

"Oh yes," Noreen answers for them both, "and was it ever nice. The RAF was there with the flags and an honour guard. We all lit candles and held them up. And there was a flight of jets went overhead. They were honoured right, eh?"

Donny looks a little embarrassed.

"A big fuss, if you ask me. But Billy doesn't do things by half when it comes to the squadron."

"So tell me," Barbara asks, "where this all started for you? How did you get into the RAF and 958 Squadron?"

"RCAF," he corrects her. "Canadians assigned to the RAF. It started right here in Ontario. I grew up down the road in Port Hope. Noreen was one year behind me in school. That's how we met. I volunteered after high school along with a couple of friends. We all wanted to be pilots. Thought we'd save the world. I'll never forget what our corporal bellowed at us when he first saw us: 'Cream of the crop? You've all curdled'."

Donny takes a drag on his cigarette and stubs it out.

"I trained as an observer, which meant I got a cram course in navigation, gunnery, and bomb-aiming. It wasn't far from here and I could get back from time to time. Noreen and I started seeing each other. Hadn't before, eh?"

"I thought he was stuck up," Noreen laughs.

"And I thought she was a kid. Little did I know what lay in wait. I didn't want to go further than that with me going overseas. But I didn't get much say."

Donny reaches out to squeeze Noreen's hand. She smiles back and then winks at Barbara.

"Anyway," he continues, "After an awful cruise, if you can call it that, over to the UK, I was sent down to a reception centre at Bournemouth. That's where they sorted out the Canadians and figured out what to do with us. Nice place except for the German fighters. You'd look out and one would whiz by, then gunfire would rattle as they fired in the windows. Big thing there was to keep your head down. It was a busy time with extra training because none of us had experience flying in tight airspace. Tad was a bomb aimer and by then I'd been settled as a navigator. We'd met up on the ship coming over, shared a cabin four decks down with four other fellows right over the propeller. You could hear that thing rattling all night. Anchor hotel we called it. When we got there, we spent what little time we had off at Bournemouth walking up in the hills and going to dances."

"Get to her dad."

"I'm getting there. Don't rush me. She needs to know some things before I get started on that." Donny pushes his glasses further up on his nose and picks up the story. "I got sent up to a navigation school for a while and kept track of Tad. You can imagine how good it was to learn we were being posted to the same OTU, Operational Training Unit that is. When we were told to find our own crews, we went right for each other. Then we went looking for another crew that needed a navigator and bomb aimer. Luckily Nigel our skipper came looking for that. He already had his wireless operator. That was Jimmy, your dad. So all we needed was a tail gunner. Billy looked as if he wasn't old enough to shave, not that the rest of us were that much older, but the skipper liked him So then we were crewed up, all five of us ready to start flying a two-engine Wellington, or a Wimpy as we called it."

Donny lifts up a sheet from the table and hands it to Barbara. It's the same crew picture that Billy had given her, the crew in front of the Wimpy.

"That's us at the OTU," he says. "We were about ready to pass out to a Heavy Conversion Unit to learn to fly the four-engine jobs. Some man came by and shot pictures of us alone, a couple as a crew. There was one of us standing in front of the aircraft, but we all looked droopy. This one's the best. The one where Nigel is reading the map and the rest of us are trying to look pretty."

"Well you were pretty. Those uniforms did a lot," Noreen says. "You looked dashing when you came back on leave before you sailed over to England. I was taken with you. Couldn't tell if it was you or your uniform."

"Pre-embarkation leave," Donny says. "That's what that was. They gave you two weeks off before you went overseas. I came home an innocent lad and when I left here I was engaged to be married. The Germans had nothing on Noreen when she wanted something."

"All right," Noreen says, shaking her head, "since you obviously are not going to talk about Jimmy until Tad and Margie get here, why don't you make yourself useful and take Barbara's bags to her room? Then you can show Barbara around so I can get dinner going. She might be interested in how we built this house."

Donny lumbers to his feet, but Barbara is already up. They go down and get her luggage from the car. He disappears with her things for a moment and then they walk slowly behind the house.

"This land's ours down to the trees. We've got about three acres, and I know all about it when I have to cut the grass. We've got deer and other wildlife. Norrie used to feed the cat out on the veranda but that attracted raccoons. Couldn't get too upset about that, even though they're real pests. One time there was an entire family here. Mother and six little ones all up on the porch eating the cat's food. Don't know where the cat was. Hiding probably. I went out to politely ask them to leave and the mother bared her teeth at me. After that we left them be."

"Do you still have them?"

"Don't know if they're from the same family, but after the cat died we see them only occasionally. No food for them, eh?"

Barbara looks at the farmlands all around them. The trees lining the stream are all shades of gold and red. They remind her of the leaf piles she used to throw herself into when she was a child. She thinks how much Marilyn would have enjoyed being here. Her mother was always up for adventures.

"I saw your tractor in the barn when I came in," Barbara says.

"That's not a tractor. That's the sit-on lawn mower. Noreen wants grass and that means mowing. I treated myself to that a few years back."

They walk over to the shed and peer in at the mower. The smells of dried grass and oil mingle in the air. A blade attachment for the mower leans against the wall. Donny points at it.

"That's for the snow. From time to time, we have to clear right down our driveway and out to the road you came up on. It's mostly rain in these parts but we have been known to have a couple of feet of snow. Gets dangerous if you're out in it and there's a good wind blowing. That's when you see cars in the ditch all along the highway. But I'm to tell you about the house."

They walk round to the front and stand by the steps leading up to the front door. Next to the door there's a wooden board with a notepad and pencil with the words: "If at home you do not find us, leave a note that will remind us." At the bottom of the board it says "Souvenir of Winnipeg, Manitoba." Donny sees her reading it.

"Picked that up on a trip across to BC—British Columbia. Once the kids left, we bought the motor home and take it out whenever the spirit moves us. We've been across Canada several times, drove up to the Yukon in it, and took it down to Florida last year."

Barbara's head swims at all the new geography. She's glad he doesn't expect her to remember it. But he has walked up to the foundation and tapped the stucco.

"When I came back from the UK, we got married right away. There wasn't housing so we had to move in with Noreen's parents. That worked fine for a while, but it was hard on them and Noreen got pregnant right away. I was working in my dad's grocery business in Port Hope. I had some money coming to me from the Canadian government for my service so we bought this land. Wasn't worth much then because it was a long ways out of town, so we could afford it. Then we had to figure out how to build a house. I borrowed some money from my dad. It was enough to dig out the foundation and have the cement slab poured and the basement walls put up. It was like an air-raid shelter inside, but we had a bathroom and kitchen and one big room. We could make do. We threw a tarp over the cement roof and hooked in the electricity. Then we lived in the basement over the winter.

The following year, we put up the wood framing for the second floor. I'd come home from work each day and do as much as I could. By the next winter I'd got the roof on and the walls in. We nailed plastic over the window openings, enough to keep the weather out upstairs but not enough to live in. So it was another year in the basement. We used to come up the stairs and sit in the empty front room, imagining how things would be when it was done. We'd planned for a large front room with a picture window, a big kitchen that we could all eat in, a dining room, and two bedrooms up here. The other bedrooms and laundry room were to be down in the basement. We dreamed about the day we could move in and never have to worry about being cramped again. When we did finally move in, our oldest, Carole Ann, was nearly two and she thought that everyone lived under ground. Noreen calls it our years of igloo living because when it snowed all you could see were the upstairs door we were using as a front door and the ventilation pipes from the kitchen and bathroom. The garage and the deck came later. We've lived here all our married life and each year we've added on. Noreen says we'll never be finished."

"Was it unusual for you to build the house yourself?"

"No. It was common then. There were shortages everywhere after the war. Took a while for Canada to change over from war production. Meanwhile the men were coming home all at once and wanting to start families. Some were bringing back war brides, like Tad did with Margie. That was hard because where we had two sets of parents to help, Tad was much more on his own. He got whatever jobs he could before he went in with another veteran on a contracting business. They did all right because there was a housing boom. But he stayed over in that Big City you came through—Toronto—and they got back into production faster than some of us out here in the country."

The crunch of gravel announces a car's arrival.

"That's Tad and Margie," Donny says.

A brown car with an enormous luggage compartment in the back has drawn up behind Barbara's small rental car. From it emerges a man in a blue plaid flannel shirt carrying a wine bottle. Barbara can see some of his light sandy hair straggling out from beneath a billed cap that has a bird's profile and the words *Blue Jays*. It takes her a moment to realize that this must represent a sports team. Beside him is a cheerful woman in a flower-print dress and a cardigan who is carrying a dish covered with silver foil.

"You must be Barbara," Margie says as she hands her dish to her husband and gives her a big hug. "I'm Margie. I'm pleased to meet a fellow Brit."

Tad deposits the dish and bottle on the car bonnet and shakes her hand. Barbara can see that he is looking closely at her. She is getting used to this now. She knows he's looking for resemblance to Jimmy. It's so long ago, though, that she wonders if he can remember things that distinctly. Again she is wrong.

"You've got his eyes," he says. "I've never seen anyone else with that blue."

"You remember that?"

"I've not forgotten much about those days," he replies. "You don't forget."

"Well, let's get on inside," Margie says. Her voice is a mixture of her Yorkshire origins and her long residence in Canada.

They crowd into the ample kitchen. The whole house seems to be panelled in light wood, and the appliances and looped carpet are various shades of green.

Donny opens the bottle and pours them each a glass.

"Aren't you supposed to let that stuff breathe?" Tad asks.

Tad doesn't know much about wine. He usually drinks beer. But he thought that Barbara would expect something special and he relied on the sales clerk to make the choice. Now he's anxious about it.

"Nah," replies Donny, "that's the red. What do you think, Norrie?" Donny hopes he's right. He's not a wine drinker either.

"Well, you can't tell by me. Is it cold? That's what matters. Give us all a glass and stop the nonsense." Noreen knows the men don't know anything. She thinks it's funny that they're trying so hard to impress their visitor.

"Yes, Dear," says Donny as he hands Barbara a glass.

"That's local, made around here," Tad tells her "Thought you'd like to try something different."

"Thank you," Barbara replies. "I didn't know that Canada had a wine industry."

"Primarily in British Columbia, but it's picking up here." Tad beams with pleasure that he at least knows where the winery is. The clerk told him the rest.

"Very nice." Barbara doesn't know much about wine either. But it tastes faintly sweet and light. There's nothing not to like. She smiles and Tad is pleased.

"I'm making wild salmon tonight," Noreen says behind a cloud of steam as she opens the oven door. "Thought that Barbara'd like to have something Canadian."

"And I've made pumpkin pie for dessert," Margie adds. "Bet you don't get much of that in the UK."

Barbara shakes her head. She's not sure what the Canadians mean by pumpkin. But she's prepared to like everything because her hosts are trying so hard to make her welcome.

Noreen seats them all at the dining room table. It's made of a pale golden wood. She tells Barbara later that it's maple.

"Don't stand on ceremony here," Noreen says. "Just dig in."

"This salmon is wonderful," Margie tells Noreen after they have helped themselves. Barbara agrees. She likes the sweet nuttiness of Margie's pie too when that is served. She could also get used to the iced water Noreen gives everyone, but she feels self-conscious when she uses her knife and fork in the English way when everyone else uses only a fork.

The dinner over and offers to help clear the dishes soundly refused, the men take Barbara into the living room with more cups of tea. The serious talking begins.

"You'll have to forgive us, Barbara," Donny says. We don't get too many opportunities to talk about the war with someone who wants to listen. If it gets too much for you, you let us know. As I mentioned earlier, there were eighty of us at the OTU and after three weeks or so of ground instruction mostly with our own trades, we were told to crew up. Mostly, it was size the chap up as you looked at him."

"It was more casual than I thought it would be," Tad agrees. "One day we were all in the room and we were told it was time and good luck to us all. Donny and I had gone around together as Canadians from Toronto, and we wanted a crew where we could be together. Nigel knew Donny and he came and asked us both if we'd like to join his crew. But before we could answer he said that there was this other chap that he wanted to crew with, a wireless operator. Would that be all right? We said we'd look him at him, and he called your dad over. He seemed a quiet, conscientious type and I liked his look, so I said yes right away."

"Only thing was," Donny adds, "whether he'd enjoy a pint or two. So I asked him outright. He said he most certainly did enjoy a pint but couldn't drink too much as it made him ill. That was good enough for me, and we shook hands all round."

"Anyone want coffee or another piece of pie?" Noreen calls from the doorway to the kitchen. "Margie and I are having a cup out here and you're welcome to have some. There's plenty."

Donny looks inquiringly at Barbara and Tad, then calls back that there are no takers but thanks anyway.

"Would you really have said no if he hadn't been up for a pint?" Tad reacts as if this is the first time he's heard of it.

"I wanted to know who he was. You know, Barbara, even after all these years, your dad's still a mystery. He was a good chap, and I've got good memories about things we did as a crew. But I wasn't surprised to hear about you because I don't think he ever spoke about family. Do you remember him talking about himself, Tad?"

"No. I don't. We heard a lot about Nigel. His mind went a mile a minute and he was mad on Canada. Had done his training out on the prairies. And then there was his wedding. We'll have to tell you about that. But even Billy, our rear gunner, used to talk about his parents and the girl he was sweet on in York. We learned lots about Australia from George. But I don't think Jimmy ever did talk about himself."

"Not that I can recall at least," agrees Donny. "But it may have been that there was so much going on. People from all around the world were coming and going through the squadrons. Look at us. Seventeen thousand Canadians flew with the RAF. There were fifteen Canadian bomber squadrons. Our neighbours to the south get all the glory, but they didn't come in until much later. So there we were, crewed up. We five started doing cross-country runs, stooges as we called them, and practice bomb runs using unarmed bombs. Your dad would be in the wireless operator's office under the pilot's seat. We didn't see much of him when we were on an Op. But we'd hear him now and then coming in with an update. I remember thinking once what a nice voice he had—steady and low. He sounded good. Not like Billy whose voice sounded like a squeak."

"Well, he was one, wasn't he?"

Tad bursts into laughter and Donny joins in. Barbara remembers what Billy said about them treating him like a kid brother.

"I'll never forget the first time I saw a Halifax when we got to the HCU," Tad says. It was huge. I couldn't believe that we'd be able to get it into the air and we nearly didn't the first time."

Donny nods in agreement. He's never forgotten how he gritted his teeth and hung on while the Halifax scraped along the ground. They'd escaped out of the entrance hatch. The aircraft was completely done for, good only for parts after that.

"We were flying tired planes that were clapped out, meaning that they had already done their time with operational squadrons," he explains. "That's all that could be spared for instruction. Something or other happened when Nigel was taking off the first time and we nearly hit the control tower. The Halifax, halibags we called them, were known for being kind to their crews. They had much better survival rates than the other bombers. It worked that way for us. We skidded along the ground and stopped just in time. Luckily no one was hurt. But you'd better know we got out fast."

"When we picked up Tommy Lewis as the mid-upper gunner and George Williams as the engineer at the HCU," Tad says, "we had the crew we needed for the Halifax."

Donny nods. "George was an Aussie. Came from the Brisbane hills and all he wanted to do was get back and farm up there. The green behind the gold, he called it, the hills behind the beaches. We were lucky to have him. There were times we needed him to make us laugh and often it was at his own expense. We got sent up for survival training and had to get into a swimming pool, right an overturned dinghy, and get in. In case we went down in water, you understand. Well, we had to get on these heavy flight suits before we could try it. So there we are struggling to get into them. Other crews had used them and they were wet and miserably cold. Then we're supposed to jump in and swim for it. George told us he was a good swimmer and proceeded to dive in first. The dive was impressive and we clapped for him. It took some time for him to come up though. When he did emerge, it seems he'd hit his head on the bottom. He was all right, but we didn't let him live that down for a while."

"When we got our posting to 958 Squadron," Tad says, "we had become like brothers. Then one day Nigel tells us that he's getting married and invites us to the wedding. That started things. It meant a bash. We went up to York and went pub crawling and then ended up in Betty's Bar, or the Dive, as it was called."

Barbara stifles a yawn but cannot completely hide it.

"I think that's enough for tonight," Noreen says briskly as she comes in from the kitchen. "This poor girl has had a long day and needs to be getting some sleep. She can hear about the bash tomorrow. Tad, we've made up the bed in the basement for you and Margie, and we'll all get together for the trip into town after breakfast."

"Sounds like a great idea," Donny says as they go their separate ways. "We'll be off to Port Hope in the morning and tell you some more. But you sleep well tonight and we're delighted that you're here."

"Would you like anything special for breakfast?" Noreen asks Barbara after she's taken her to her room.

Barbara doesn't think it's a good time to admit to her poisonous diet. She says she will have what everyone else is having. It gets settled on what Noreen calls hotcakes and coffee.

12

The Readiness is All, Summer 1943

The HCU was situated ten miles south of York in flat farmland. It was ideal flying terrain because there were few obstacles for low-flying aircraft. It was also ideal for laying the concrete and tarmac needed for runways. A broad swath of airbases was laid out around York, and for all of them the tower of the medieval York Minster was the beacon that told them they were leaving home and welcomed them back when they returned.

The HCU's briefing room had the usual curved corrugated tin walls converging in an arch overhead. It's hard to imagine what the air force would have done without these pre-fab Nissen huts. One long half-cylinder, two ends, and a pot-bellied stove that glowed red right up the stack. Cold in winter, hot in summer. This one was big enough to hold the crews assembled here to learn to fly the four-engine Halifaxes. It was a tough course, seven days on, one weekend off.

Jimmy was sitting in a row of chairs with Nigel and the others. All around them men lounged in their seats, talking to one another, obviously wondering what came next. Jimmy didn't have any idea himself except that they were to be briefed about becoming operational.

Some months before, Jimmy had been sitting in the first briefing at the OTU in Cornwall when he felt a thump on his back. He couldn't believe his eyes. There was Nigel grinning broadly. He hadn't seen him since their basic training together in Blackpool.

"Where have you been," Jimmy blurted out.

"I've been in Canada, Old Chap. And I can't wait to go back. One day, after the war, if I'm lucky."

Jimmy looked at the insignia on Nigel's uniform. The double wings. So Nigel had made it.

"What was it like over there?"

Jimmy had spent his training time at Bristol and then a year on the south coast with Coastal Command. Canada sounded exotic. Nigel nudged over the man sitting next to Jimmy and sat down. He was his usual chatty self.

"The trip over was hell. Nearly everyone was sick. Great huge grey waves and alarms about subs. I didn't worry much about the subs. They'd be too wise to be out in those gales. I was more worried about how to stay in the hammock. They strung them close to one another, and when one started swaying, there went the lot. Landed in New Brunswick in fog. Couldn't see a thing, but we got onto the train and off we went for days. We stopped in Montreal first and then went along the frozen lakes. Amazing, Old Chap. Landed at Regina, out on what they call the Prairies—miles and miles of flat farmland. Lorries took us out to the airfield. Never been so cold in my life."

"So you're glad to be home?"

"Not on your life. Did everything I could to delay coming back for a time. I was an instructor for a while. Other chaps hated it. But I loved the black earth, the green corn—except they call it wheat—the sloughs with the migrating birds, and even the beaver. The girls were pretty and the town put on dances. Loved the land and the people. I'm all for going back there after the war."

"Well, from the sound if it, it's made you a poet."

Jimmy's head had spun from all the description.

"Suppose it has, Old Chap. But in the end, I wanted to do what I'd trained for. I wanted to fly and wanted to get into the action."

Nigel looked at the flashes on Jimmy's uniform. "I hear we're supposed to crew up here later. What about getting a jump on it? You don't make a hash of wireless messages do you?"

"Shouldn't. I spent a year practicing them. Then I passed the tests."

"Well, then, are you up for my crew when the time comes? I want to find good men who can get us there and back. I already know how solid you are."

"I'll be glad to if we get a choice."

"Then consider yourself in my crew."

Nigel looked doubtful. "That's all right with you, isn't it?"

"Of course it is." Jimmy tried to conceal his smile. He was pleased to be asked and had been secretly worried about what he'd do if no one wanted him. "Hard to believe you've been over in Canada, though, and we've met up."

"Luck of the draw, Old Chap. Always was. Let's take that as settled then."

So there it was. On the first day after getting to the OTU, Jimmy was crewed up with a pilot. Nigel had taken him on trust that he was good at his job. There was no way Jimmy would let him down.

Over the next few weeks, Nigel kept an eye out carefully for the rest. He flew with several different tail gunners when he went up with a screen, a pilot on rest from a squadron after completing thirty Ops, and then later on his own when he practiced circuits and bumps. He liked the little kid from York. Nigel took navigation classes with Donny and liked his looks as well. It was a plus that he came from Canada, even if it was from the eastern part. Nigel asked Jimmy about it, but Jimmy was agreeable with whatever Nigel wanted because he knew only the wireless operators.

When the CO came in and gave them a short message, which essentially boiled down to "You're on your own, Lads," Nigel was ready. He approached Donny to be their navigator. Donny was willing but said that he'd like to fly with a fellow Canadian—excellent bomb-aimer, also good at navigation, an officer, reliable, knew his stuff. Would Nigel be willing to consider him? That's how they got Tad. Then there was Billy, and the others liked him well enough. So Nigel had the crew he wanted.

They stooged cross-country on Wimpies learning to be a crew. They got lost once, and once they got completely turned around over the North Sea and had to radio Query Direct Magnetic so a ground station could give them a course But through it all, their luck held. They survived, and with every flight they became more confident in one another's abilities.

And so they had come to the HCU to learn to fly the four-engine Halifax bomber. That's where Tommy Lewis and George Williams were added to the crew. Those were grueling weeks, but again they survived. Now they were in the HCU briefing room to be congratulated and given their posting as well as a couple of weeks' leave.

"I've got some news, chaps," Nigel said as they waited. "I'm getting married. It's madness of course, what with the war, but Lettuce wants it. I'd like you all to be there. It's going to be at her family's place in the country."

If the crew had other plans for their leave at that point, they were glad to change them for their skipper. It was a celebration they wouldn't miss. They were also happy to celebrate when they learned a few minutes later that they were posted to Leaton. Billy was especially happy because it was close to his home.

Nigel's marriage and their completion of the HCU training meant there had to be a bash. There wasn't a friendly mess at the HCU, so the decision was made to get rooms in York the night before the wedding. Nigel would leave first thing in the morning, and the others would follow.

Later, Nigel took Jimmy aside. 'I've got a favour to ask, Old Man. My brother's going to be my best man. That is, if he can get leave. I was wondering if you'd be willing to be in the wings, so to speak. If my brother can't be there, would you stand up with me?"

"I'd like that," Jimmy said simply. He liked to see life pushing on. He hadn't told Nigel about Rose and his dad yet. But he knew one day he would. Nigel had become the closest thing he had to family.

"I'm not sure if my father's coming or not. I told him about it. We'll have to see. Probably will since my brother's up for it."

York was jammed with aircrew when they got there, but they managed to find rooms right in town. The party then flowed through the ancient, cobbled streets from pub to pub, with laughter and toasts and jokes. Spirits were high. They were through. They were going to their squadron. They were alive. They wound up down in Betty's Bar. George was worse for wear. Tommy was sardonically tight and even cracked an unusual smile now and then. Billy's cheeks were pink. Nigel was bemused by it all. Tad and Donny were given to bursts of laughter. Even Jimmy looked amused and happy. There was something to celebrate.

"We've got to commemorate this evening," Donny said a little unsteadily. "What can we do? We can't let the Skipper go out without something to show for it."

"Have you looked at the mirror behind the bar?" Tommy had done some scouting around. He had seen another crew writing on the mirror and had gone to ask.

"What's there? Tad was always open to suggestion.

"Go look. There are names and squadrons scratched in the glass."

Donny went sent to look. The mirror was full of scratched names and squadrons and dates. Some were so faint, he had to look at them sideways. There were dozens of them.

"That's perfect," Donny said when he came back. "Let's go put up the crew so people will know we were here. What do we do it with?"

"They use diamonds to scratch glass," Tad said, "Anyone got a diamond?"

No one had so Donny went back to the bar to inquire.

"No need to worry," Donny said when he came back. "They've got a pen over there that you use."

"All right," said George. "Nigel, you have to write our names."

Nigel allowed himself to be dragged over to the mirror.

"Down there," Tommy said and pointed to a spot where Nigel would be able to scratch on their names as long as he kept his writing small.

"It's bloody hard work," Nigel said as he did it. He had to scratch carefully to get anything that looked like readable names.

"You've spelled one wrong," observed Tad as he turned his head sideways to squint at the writing.

"Too late now," said Nigel as he stood up amidst cheers.

Then they stumbled off into darkened York, past the Minster, and over to their rooms. In the morning, Nigel left early as planned. Jimmy and Tommy were up before anyone else to have their breakfast. Billy came down soon after them. Donny and Tad came down a few minutes before breakfast closed and asked if anyone had aspirins. George had to be rousted to catch the train down to Letitia's village.

When they got off the train, everyone seemed to know who they were. When Jimmy and the crew asked directions at the railway station, the stationmaster told them their business.

"You're here for the wedding, then, are you?"

There was no denying it, and the station master, whose grey hair slid untidily from under his cap, was pleased with his deduction. No one had the heart to point out that there would not be six other men in RAF uniform arriving at the station all at once.

"Well," he said in a West Country drawl, "you go up the High Street, past the shops, and turn at the bank. When you're done," and with this he winked, "the pub's down this end around the corner here. Wouldn't do to have the pub too near the Church, now would it? The reverend might get depressed if he compared the trade." He chuckled at his own joke. "I'll be at the pub myself after the wedding's done."

"You'll be there at the church?" Donny wondered how well packed the church would be if the entire town was coming.

"Oh, not me. But I'll be there to cheer Miss Letitia on when they come out. But she'll be a missus then. The entire village will be there outside. We were told to look out for you and send you on up as soon as you got here."

Donny nudged Tad as they walked away. "Bit like Port Hope. You can't fart without everyone testing the wind."

They followed the old man's directions, but it wasn't hard to see the church steeple overseeing village life. The old Norman church was behind a lynch gate. It had a shell-like facade of knapped flint and Tudor panelling over the porch door. In front of it, a large yew tree spread its darkness over gravestones worn blank by time and weather. The grass grew in pale clumps wherever light was able to filter through, creating a mosaic of green and mud beneath the tree. People walked about on the gravel pathway, filling the churchyard with the crunch of their footsteps.

The reverend was watching for them. He came bustling through the porch door, his robes swaying round him like curtains. He was portly with an almost angelic face framed by grey curls.

"Welcome. Welcome. Nigel is waiting for you."

He ushered them into the church and deposited them into the vestry at the back. They could see the aisle and altar through the vestry's carved wooden screen. In the sunlight, the church's stained windows cast the colours of faith and hope onto the congregation.

"Glad you made it," Nigel said.

He was standing with an older, unsmiling man in a grey silk suit. Nigel made the introductions. This was his crew, and that was his father. There did not seem to be other relatives from Nigel's side. The hum out in the pews suggested that the bride's family and friends had turned out in force.

"Jimmy, I'm going to ask you to stand up with me, if that's all right with you. My brother isn't able to make it."

Jimmy nodded. He managed to contain his small, pleased smile. It was good to be wanted. To feel part of a family again, even if it wasn't his own. His crew had stepped into a massive void in his life, although he had never told them that.

"Gentlemen," the reverend said to the crew. "I have a special request for you."

He pointed to some swords that looked as if they had been used in a school pageant: William the Conqueror versus Harold of England. The hilts had worn tassels that appeared to have been chewed by the moths that always seem to inhabit rectory storage rooms.

"I'm going to leave these inside the porch door. The bride and groom will pause inside and we'd like you to hold them so."

He demonstrated by lifting one in an arc over his head.

"You will form an archway for the couple outside the porch door. The photographer will set his camera up down the pathway and we'll get a nice picture."

"If Jimmy's standing at the altar, how does he get back here?" George asked.

George's Australian voice seemed to take the reverend by surprise even though the patch on George's shoulder said Australia. The man blinked for a moment and stared at the crew before he continued.

"He's standing up with Nigel," George explained. The reverend had been startled by the question.

"The reason I ask, Mate," George continued genially, "is that without Jimmy there are five here and I think an archway needs an even number."

"Oh dear, yes," the reverend replied. "Let me see what we can do about this."

"Whatever you decide," George said equally genially, "it has to be another uniform or we won't match."

"Yes indeed," the reverend said and disappeared with another swish of robes. He was back in a moment. The crew could hear a piano inside. The ceremony was about to start.

"As soon as the ceremony is over," the reverend informed them, "you crew-members slip off to the side of the chapel and walk up to the front. The best man will wait for the bridal couple to start down the aisle and then should walk down the side of the pews, come straight out here, and take up a sword. Nigel, when you bring Letitia back down the aisle, give your best man a few moments to come to the front door. We'll ask the guests to remain seated."

That business done, the reverend turned to Nigel's father. "It's time now," he said, "for you to walk down to the front pew on the right. The rest of you gentlemen, please walk down and sit in the rows behind him."

The reverend took Nigel's arm and ushered him and Jimmy out of the room.

"I think we can go in now," George said. "Anyone else reminded of the White Rabbit? Or maybe a wallaby?"

Whether the atmosphere within the church had overcome them was unclear, but no one answered George's question. They followed Nigel's father down through the rainbow of colours thrown from the stained glass windows and sat behind him. Letitia's side was packed. Nigel's occupied three rows only because the crew took two.

At the altar were a beaming Nigel and a stolid Jimmy. Their eyes were trained on the back of the church where an increasing murmur indicated that the bride had arrived. Everyone stood when the piano managed to bang out the wedding march in somewhat louder tones. When Lettuce turned down the aisle, she was radiant in something that looked like parachute silk. Her golden hair fell in ringlets down her back and her simple dress emphasized her graceful arms and the sweep of her neck. They all thought the same thing. Nigel had found himself a looker.

After the service, the crew more or less piled out on time and lofted their swords. Nigel and Letitia paused under them for a picture to be taken.

"I hope you're ready for a Long Shank," George said softly to the bride as she and Nigel walked under the canopy of swords. The photographer captured the moment when Letitia and Nigel burst into laughter. In the picture, Billy looked slightly puzzled. He hadn't heard George's comment. Jimmy had but contained his amusement with his usual smile. Tommy is too far back for his expression to be clear, but Donny and Tad are chuckling. And the swords looked better than they had any right to.

With the picture taken, Nigel and Letitia were driven amidst the cheers of the villagers to her family home. Her parents and Nigel's father followed in another car, and the rest walked. It wasn't far along a country lane that seemed to be in another universe from squadrons and Operations. The Tudor styled house loomed up on a hill ahead, brickwork glowing, leaded casements shining in the sun, and the roof bristling with chimneys from multiple fireplaces.

"Must be a horror to heat," Tad said sagely as they walked up the driveway.

"I don't think they bother," Donny replied. "They seem to like it cold over here."

"Not really," said Jimmy. "Can't afford much. You light a fire and when that's gone it's off to bed."

"It's a wonder your population isn't larger if that's what you do." George knew Tasmania's winters could make people huddle in bed and listen to the spit of rain on the windows. Melbourne could be cold when it was rainy as well. But the English chill went right through you. If you said anything about it, though, people looked at you strangely and said you should wear more clothes.

"We do all right. You might be surprised," Jimmy answered

"Do you suppose there'll be anything to drink?" Tommy was expressing the general concern.

"Well, I'm all for the pub if they don't." George meant to see what the village had to offer if the house was dry. "Jimmy, you're our resident expert here. What happens at do's like this?"

"Don't ask me. I've never been to anything like this. I should imagine watercress sandwiches, you know, cut in squares. Strawberries. That sort of thing."

"Lovely," said Tommy.

"Now, Chaps," said Donny sternly, "this is the skipper's do. We go in and behave properly. Once they've gone off on the honeymoon, we'll repair to the pub."

The five walked in a properly respectful manner up the driveway and entered into the line of people waiting to congratulate the newlyweds. The house smelled of beeswax polish and a vase of flowers obviously picked freshly from the garden. Nigel and Letitia and her parents stood at the foot of the curved, wooden staircase welcoming their guests. Nigel looked happy but a little bewildered at all the family that he was expected to remember. Letitia kissed each of her husband's aircrew as they came through the line.

"I'm so glad you could all come," she told them. "It means a lot to Nigel."

"Wouldn't have missed it," Donny told her for them all.

Letitia's mother had the same gold hair as her daughter and shook their hands. Letitia's father was older than his wife. He was wearing tweed and it was easy to imagine him as part of Dad's Army, pulling down signposts, demanding identification, and making everyone's life miserable. No one would say anything though because he was the squire and that wasn't done.

"She's part of the squadron now," Donny told her mother. "We'll make sure that Nigel takes good care of her."

"She's going to look for a place to live somewhere near where you're going," her mother said. "I forget where that is."

"Leaton," Tad replied. "Outside York."

She nodded absently. She hadn't thought her daughter would go so far away. But she had accommodated to the idea of wartime. She worked with the ladies relief fund and had teas in her house to help out with the war effort. The war had turned around all life's certainties. No bombs had fallen here, but there were children being evacuated from London that needed to be housed with local families and there were shortages everywhere. Everyone had pulled together to make the wedding possible because everyone loved Letitia.

"York's a lovely city," Jimmy contributed awkwardly.

"She'll be coming back home," the Squire boomed, "if she needs anything."

"Don't you worry. I'll take wonderful care of her." Nigel had overheard the conversation and offered his reassurances.

After that the crew went to the refreshment table. Tommy needn't have worried. The party at the house had the predicted little sandwiches but also wine and a dry country cider. George would have preferred beer but managed to be gracious while sweeping his eyes around the room. A dark-haired girl with doe eyes caught his fancy. She was pretty and even her clothes looked unusually stylish for wartime Britain. He disappeared in her direction and was soon busy talking with her. Judging by snatches of their conversation, he seemed to be telling her about Australia.

The rest of the crew scattered round the room.

Like George, Tommy picked out a suitable companion for a pleasant conversation. He edged over to a bridesmaid, a fair-haired girl who turned out to be Letitia's cousin. When Jimmy glanced at him, he noticed that Tommy was being uncharacteristically talkative. Perhaps it was because he had a glass of cider in his hand. Jimmy watched him curiously and even saw him smile. It was indeed a gala.

Billy eyed the wine and cider suspiciously. He'd wait for the beer at the pub. Jimmy could hear the occasional laughter from Tad and Donny's direction. A local MP had come over and asked them what they thought the possibilities were that the war could be over by next year. It's good that no one ever reported what Donny told him. It seemed that the world would be saved once this crew joined 958 Squadron.

Jimmy preferred to look around the room at the guests for a while and then took his drink out onto the terrace with its hourglass-shaped cement balustrade overlooking the grounds. He dreaded giving the toast, but he knew he had to since he had stood up with Nigel.

Everyone gathered round when Jimmy was cued to his duty. He raised his glass and spoke with sincerity: "To our skipper and his bride. Here's wishing you a good take-off, fair weather for your flight, and only happy landings."

It was the best that Jimmy could do. The rest of the crew joined in with hear and hear and the wedding guests applauded. For Jimmy, it was pure eloquence and he smiled shyly as his cheeks turned pink.

As the afternoon neared its end, Nigel and Letitia came around to say a final goodbye before heading off on their honeymoon in the Lake District. They were due at the railway station. Letitia had changed into a coral suit. She looked smashing.

"Do you happen to have a sister?" George crooned, temporarily abandoning his dark-haired companion.

"Sorry, only me," she laughed. "Take care of Nigel at Leaton, won't you? And take care of yourselves."

"Goodbye everyone," Nigel called as they headed out of the door.

The guests followed them out and spilled over the grass and the pavement. Someone threw a handful of paper streamers. Then they piled laughing into the car and were off to the station.

Jimmy watched them leave through the window. Nigel's father came and stood morosely next to him. The man had been like a statue through the ceremony and the aftermath. Jimmy had completely forgotten he was present.

"A nice ceremony, wasn't it?" Jimmy said politely.

"Yes," the man said slowly.

He turned to look at Jimmy as if he had just noticed him. "You're the wireless operator."

It was Jimmy's turn to give a single-word reply.

"My older son's a fighter pilot. He's won the DFC."

Jimmy said nothing.

"That's flying. Up there alone. You don't have other people with you making it easy."

"There's nothing easy about four engines and flying hundred of miles over enemy territory in the dark," Jimmy said quietly. "We all have a job to do and Nigel is the skipper."

The man seemed not even to have heard.

"In a single-engine aeroplane, you do everything yourself. He's got markers under his cockpit. He's shot down enemy fighters."

"We also shoot down enemy aircraft in Bomber Command," Jimmy observed.

The man said nothing.

"We're grateful for the fighters," Jimmy added. "But Nigel is responsible for all our lives."

The man frowned and did not meet Jimmy's eyes. He seemed to thinking about something else. Then he turned on his heel and left the room and went out of the house. Jimmy watched his back disappear down the garden and then onto the road toward the station.

It was then that Jimmy noticed that his hand was shaking. He looked around for the others. George had gone back to flirting. He had his hand draped over a chair back and seemed to be hanging on the dark-haired girl's words. Tommy was talking to Letitia's cousin. Billy was nowhere to be seen, probably outside somewhere. Donny and Tad had their backs to Jimmy. They had taken up position at the refreshment table and were talking with the reverend. Jimmy had no reinforcements and with a feeling of mounting anger, he knew he had to do something. He turned away from the window and forced himself to rejoin the wedding guests.

When the crew walked back down to the village, they went straight into the pub. Settled in a dark corner, a half-pint each, Jimmy found it possible to tell them what Nigel's father had said.

"Easy?" snorted Tad. "When I'm on my stomach hung out over the bombsight, it's easy?"

"I don't think he meant that," said Jimmy. "I think he meant it more personally that he thought Nigel wasn't as good as his other son."

"I've nothing against the fighter chaps," said Tommy, "but you can't go around comparing us like that."

"Good thing I didn't hear him," boomed George "or I'd have bounced him one."

"Here's to 958, when we get there, but most important here's to the skipper." Donny raised his pint amidst the hear-hears and the slam of the glasses back down on the table. Some of the other patrons turned to watch them and gave them a cheer.

Jimmy felt his pride surge in Bomber Command, in his squadron to be, and in what he did on board the aircraft. Most of all, he felt a wonderful feeling of pride in his aircrew and a sense of truly belonging.

"So where is everyone headed?" Donny asked.

"I'm going up north to see Margie and her family," Tad said.

"Going to York," Billy said. "Told my parents to expect me."

"Don't know yet," George offered.

Donny looked up. "I'm going to London, George. Why don't you come along with me? What's a little bombing? What about you, Tommy?"

Tommy gave a little smile. "I thought I'd stay here for a while. I've got an invitation to play tennis."

"Tennis?" said Tad incredulously. "Have you ever played before?"

"No. But how hard can it be? It's just a ball and a bat."

"Racquet," corrected Donny. "Some people take the game seriously. Does she know you don't know how to play?"

"How do you know it's a she?"

"Because," added Donny sagely, "you wouldn't be doing it for anyone else. Was it that little blonde girl at the wedding? Lettuce's cousin?"

"Maybe."

"One day and he's done for," laughed George. "Next thing, we'll be holding up the swords for you."

"Well, we wish you luck," said Jimmy.

"And where are you going, Jimmy?" asked Donny.

"Thought I'd go down to the coast. See where I trained."

"What's there?"

"Oh you never know," Jimmy replied and said no more.

13
Canada's Always Been There

Port Hope turns out to be a grown-up village of several intersecting streets laid out along the shore of Lake Ontario. This is where Donny grew up and he drives the five of them around. When they stop at the war memorial he gives Barbara a brief history.

"Men from Port Hope have been in every war from the ones with the US to the present. Canada has always been a part of the fighting, but not always of the peace. The UK bowed to US pressure and gave away large parts of Canadian soil to the US. Upper New York State and parts of Washington State should have been ours. If you talk with Canadians about it, they're still bitter."

Then they drive down and get out at the beach along the waterfront. They walk along a harbour wall beside the river out to where they can look back at the town.

"The river channel is much deeper and wider than it was," he explains. "They had to dredge it out after the flood last year. There was a heavy snowmelt and the river overflowed into town. It washed away some fine old buildings and the eastern part of town went under a couple of feet of water."

"It flooded out most of the shops on the lower end of town," Noreen agrees. "The sidewalk was broken up in great big chunks. Our grocery store was all right, but we're far up the hill."

"That's right," Donny laughs. "It took out your dress shop for a while. Well that may be the only good thing that could be said about it. It clipped Norrie's wings for a while."

"Oh go on with you." Noreen laughs but she also sounds annoyed. "I go over to Cobourg or into Oshawa," she explains to Barbara. "They're bigger towns and have nice shopping areas. But there's a dress shop here that I like and there's an appliance shop that has everything."

They stand for some time looking out at the lake. It still looks like an ocean to Barbara. Grey waves lap hypnotically on the shore and it reminds her of some place she once visited out on the Thames estuary.

"It's a lovely little town," she finally says.

"It's deliberately kept the small-town feel," Donny admits. "There's history here and we'll take a drive around. But I wanted you to see it because, in many ways, this is typical of where the Canadian aircrews came from. Now Tad, here, came from Toronto, so I can't speak for him."

"Hey, I lived in a place like this outside Toronto. I hadn't been downtown more than a few times before I volunteered. Whatever you're going to say applies to me too."

"What I was saying, before I was so rudely interrupted," Donny says, "is that most of us came from places like this. We were small-town boys who had never been away from home, let alone outside Canada. There were teachers from Alberta. Farm boys from the prairies. Bank clerks who wanted some adventure. Youngsters from right here who knew everyone in town. I got talking once with a gunner from a place called Weyburn. That's out on the prairies in Saskatchewan. His family ran the local newspaper and lived on a farm outside town. He used to ride a horse to move the cows down the road from one range to another. So there he is one day running cattle. Next thing he's in the cramped skies over York. He used to say that he felt like the sky had folded in on him. He was failed to return on an Op. Never heard. But I hope he made it."

"We had no idea what we were getting into," Tad says. "And then all at once we're in the real world and they're shooting at us. Picture us as young and first time away from home. Pitifully young, some of us. I heard of a rear gunner who had done a full 30 Ops by the time he was eighteen. We called Nigel the old man and he was about 23. I know he was at university when he signed up because he said so, so he must have been around 20 when he volunteered."

"They all looked young," Margie chimes in, "Billy especially. I thought he was younger than he said he was. I said so once, and he fishes out his identification card. But Billy, I say to him, did you tell the truth to them when you went in to sign up? He's indignant. Says he had to show he was through school before they'd take him. That's the way it was in England."

"And that was true here in Canada as well," Tad says. "I tried to join up but they wouldn't take me until I'd finished school. They told me to go away and not to come back until I had."

"I was impatient too and wanted to get on with it," Donny says. "There wasn't conscription in Canada. Not officially anyway. We volunteered and then after we were trained they said 'Oh by the way there's a war on in Europe, you'd like to go there, wouldn't you?' That was to be sensitive to French Canada. You may have noticed that we have two languages here. But there were many French Canadians in the aircrews. They had one squadron that was French-speaking. Most of them, though, elected to stay in the English-speaking squadrons. I once asked a chap from Quebec why he didn't go to the Alouette squadron when he had the chance. He said he wanted to practice his English. You know, now and then someone says that we didn't all get along. That's not true, is it, Tad?"

"We were all Canadian aircrew and that was it. You can't believe everything you hear from people who weren't there."

"Why don't we drive to the café up the street, Don?" Noreen says. "Margie and I can pop off and do a spot of shopping and you can talk some more without us."

Donny turns the car up toward the main street and drives slowly up looking for a parking spot.

"There's one," Noreen says loudly. "We're in luck. About halfway up. Well done, Dad."

"Women!" Donny mumbles under his breath as we get out and Noreen and Margie go off chattering happily.

"Can't live with 'em, can't live without 'em," Tad commiserates.

"'Scuse us, Barbara. Shopping trips to Port Hope and Cobourg seem to have come with the marriage contract."

Donny picks up the story as the women walk off down the street and they go into the café and seat themselves. They settle into a booth with high backs and get served coffee from a round glass pot.

"Once the Commonwealth Training Plan started up," Donny continues, "Canada started getting men from all around the world. There were training posts here in the east, but a lot in the Prairie Provinces. Manitoba, part of Alberta, and Saskatchewan are flat, so they were ideal. Now your dad never got out here. Wireless operators were trained in the UK and had to do a year's practice at an active duty station before they were assigned to a squadron. That was one of his regrets. He always said he'd have liked to come abroad. He'd never been out of the UK, you see."

"I remember him saying that," Tad agrees. "Nigel used to go on about the prairies and Jimmy would sit there and listen. I know Nigel wanted to come back to Canada and Jimmy might have come as well. I think it's this country's size. Everything is nearby in England. Here it's going to take five or six days, more if you stop, to get across to Vancouver. Some people thrive on that."

"Margie had some trouble with it though, didn't she?" asks Donny.

"She did at first. She was homesick when she first arrived. My parents helped. I expected to be in for it when I told my family that I was bringing home a war bride, but they took it well. I think they were just glad to have me come home in one piece."

"So many others didn't" Donnie observes solemnly.

"I think the main thing was that there were things here to remind Margie of home. It wasn't that unfamiliar, not like she was going to a completely foreign country. Her parents came out from time to time and she went back when we could afford it. She took the children when they were old enough. So she never really lost contact. But Canada became her home and when she took citizenship she thought of herself as Canadian."

"Can I get you something else," the waitress asks as she refills the coffee cups. "We've got some nice homemade pies."

"What kind?" Donny asks.

"Apple, blueberry, lemon meringue, mud, and coconut custard."

"Anything appeal, Barbara? I'm going to try the lemon meringue."

"What's a mud pie?"

"You've got to try it. Let's have a piece of mud pie for the lady. And I know you, Tad, a piece of the apple as well."

"Do you want the apple heated? How about ice cream on the side anyone?"

"Not for me," Barbara says hastily.

"I'll take some on the apple," Tad says as the waitress swishes off.

"Well, I think we left off last night when Tad was talking about the night before Nigel's wedding when we wound up at Betty's Bar," Donny begins.

"It was a favourite aircrew bar for Canadians," Tad explains. "It was mostly aircrew because the area around York was packed with airfields. They kept a diamond-tip pen there so you could write your name on the mirror. We told Nigel that he had to write all our names. He'd had a few, although he was presentable."

"Not like George."

"Or like you. Barbara, if Donny had tried to write his name, I think he'd have broken the mirror and then we'd all have had back luck."

"Can't think how much worse that could have been."

Tad ignores him. "Nigel scratches our names on the mirror except that he misspells Jimmy's name. Instead of Baldock, he writes Baldack and for the rest of the evening, we call Jimmy Mr. Baldass."

Barbara frowns slightly and Tad feels the need to explain. "A little aircrew humour."

"Let's get on with it," says Donny reprovingly. He doesn't want Barbara to get the wrong idea about the crew. They weren't saints but there's no need to go into that.

"When we were over there for the 958 reunion, we went to look at the mirror. It had been damaged and they'd moved it from behind the bar, but it was still there. And there down in the corner were our names. Next morning Nigel's off to his wedding. It's about an hour's train ride from there."

"So we had time to drag Donny and George out of bed and pile them on the train." Tad chuckles. He knows exactly how to get Donny's goat.

"You did not," says Donny indignantly. "I came down under my own steam. And what about you, you old scoundrel? You weren't feeling so hot yourself."

"Whatever our condition," Tad says, "we show up at the wedding and it goes well."

"Then we have to decide what to do for our leaves," says Donny. Your dad disappears off somewhere. God knows where. Tommy's after a girl. So's Billy and so is Tad for that matter. And that leaves George and me to go up to London. I won't bore you with the misadventures, but by some miracle no one gets killed or arrested and we meet up again at Leaton."

The waitress returns with the pies. Mud pie turns out to be a thick chocolate mousse in a crust with a large dollop of whipped cream on top. Donny's lemon meringue has to be five inches high and Tad's apple is buried under the ice cream.

Donny takes a forkful of his pie and Tad continues the story as if there has been no interruption. "That was the leave when Margie and I got engaged. She knew I wasn't a great prospect, that I could get killed any time, but she said yes. Since she lived outside York, she'd come down to Leaton whenever I had some time off or I'd hitch a ride up there to see her. Nigel's wife Letitia—we all called her Lettuce—moved into rooms over The Three Martyrs. Billy's girl, I forget her name, worked in the NAAFI. Donny was always on about Noreen who'd send him packages from home that we'd all get into. He had to hide the maple fudge. Tommy was plain mysterious about May, but then I think he figured we would put her off if she had much to do with us. George was a great bloke, as he called himself. Terrific fun. He made friends wherever he went. Your dad was the one who didn't seem to have anyone. But he was happy enough to be with crew and have a drink in the pub. And there'd be plenty of laughs."

"Did Jimmy ever say anything about a child?" It's the question Barbara has wanted to ask but been afraid to.

"Not that I can remember," Donny says.

Barbara feels the awkwardness of her position and glances self-consciously at the table. Donny notices her gesture and understands it.

"Barbara, this is as good a time as any to talk about some things," he says firmly. "As a your father's crewmate, I want to tell you that no one should judge what happened then. I learned that when a Port Hope friend came back to the squadron one night bragging about an encounter. Well, I knew he had a wife back in Canada, yet I understood. We were young men in need of affection and kindness. Many hadn't even been with a woman before, and we'd go to dances and be satisfied with kissing and dancing. But we were curious about life. Large numbers of aircrew didn't come back and you didn't want to miss out. We wanted to know what things were all about while there was time."

"Of the lot," Tad adds, "George was the most experienced. He was a good-looking chap. Tall, broad-shouldered. We'd go to a dance at Leaton, and he'd have the pick of the girls and would disappear. I used to watch him with real admiration. Now there's a man who knows how to live, I said to myself. But we were all looking for warmth. Not to tell tales out of school, but Letitia told Margie that she and Nigel got married not because she was pregnant but because she could have been. So things happen in wartime and have to be accepted for what they are. The rules don't apply."

"And the rules don't apply to the aftermath either," Donny says. "They told us all to get on with our lives and forget about it. As if we could. Oh by the way, they also said, be prepared to recognize that your women are going to be more independent. They've been working in factories and running the household. Norrie quickly set me straight on that when I got back. She wasn't about to let me have the checkbook, not without both our names on it."

"It was a time of change, all right," Tad adds. "Some men never talked about the war. They wanted to get on with life. Others stayed quiet because they didn't want to have to justify what happened. As if one could justify what happens in war. Donny and I stayed friends. We'd get together with some of the others—and there were returning aircrew vets everywhere, particularly over at Trenton—and we talked about things when we needed to."

Donny shakes his head. He gets depressed when he pictures all those young lives lost. A whole generation of Canada's future. He gets even more depressed when he thinks about the people he has come to call the revisionist bastards. They are the ones who want to rewrite history and turn the bomber crews into callous murderers.

"It was the courage of those young flight crews that sticks with me," Donny explains. "That's what makes it so hard when you see people who weren't over there making accusations. No one's right in war. War brings out the best and the worst in people. The big thing is to keep one's humanity."

Tad gives a compassionate glance at his friend. He's heard him struggle with these issues before. "I had nightmares," he tells Barbara. "Margie would wake me and tell me I was screaming "Bale out, bale out," in my sleep. My hands would be shaking and my back would be wet. I think I was trying to understand why I got out and the others didn't. Sometimes, I couldn't shut my mind down. Even now, all I takes is for me to look at the squadron pictures to remember the shock of surviving. I didn't see the others again until after the war. Margie and I married as soon as I got back to England, but then I was sent back to Canada and had to wait until she could join me."

"I think surviving was pure luck," Donny says. "I felt that the time we came back from the first Op. Was over to France as I recall."

"Archeres," Tad agrees. "No night fighters, not much flak. We dropped the bombs on target."

"We had a great navigator."

"Praising yourself is no recommendation," snorts Tad. "The bomb aimer had something to do with it."

"All right," Donny continues as he brightens up, "we're back and we're cocky about it. First Op and there we are safe and sound. All the training has paid off. And it was fine training. I have to give the RAF and RCAF their due. They scrubbed one Op so our official second Op was also over to France. We got over and back without any problem. Then we had some leave. I don't think anyone went anywhere much that time. We hung around Leaton and York as I recall except maybe for Tommy. But next time we were on battle order we had a fair idea that it was going to be different."

Tad remembers the mixture of excitement and fear as he realized they were going to drop their bombs on Germany. He'd tried to be casual about it, but even Donny had a wide-eyed look when he heard the target. It was the big one, their first test as a crew over well-defended enemy territory. He tries to help Barbara imagine what it was like.

"We'd go out and check the aircraft in the morning and then wait around to see if we were up for the night. This particular day we could see that our ground crew was busy, so chances were we'd be on the battle order. Sure enough, when the list was posted we were on."

"Crews generally tried to guess where they were going," Donny continues. "It depended on the ratio between the bomb load and the petrol. More petrol meant fewer bombs, which in turn meant a longer stooge. Another clue was the type of bomb being loaded. We'd put two and two together and come up with five. But we still did it."

"Nigel bet on Germany," Tad says. "I remember that because I bet on Holland. They'd been bombing Rotterdam and I thought they'd go back. Nigel turned out to be right."

"We got briefed and then went over to the flight shed to get the parachutes and escape gear," Donny says. "Then it was onto the lorry to go out to dispersal. Everything seemed ordinary enough except this was the first time to Germany. I don't know about the others, but I was nervous until I got into the Hali and the familiar routine took over. After we'd checked everything, I went to the take-off position. That was the safest place to be because it was behind the main spar. We got off on time and everything seemed normal until Billy yelled for Nigel to corkscrew. He's spotted a night fighter. I hung on for the corkscrew. There's nothing I could do in those situations. It's all up to Nigel and the gunners to get us out of there. There's an almighty bang and an engine's on fire. Billy yells again and we corkscrew again. This time I bang my head on something and get bounced around. There's a splatter of something against the aircraft, and we start pitching madly. I suppose cannon shells must have hit us. Next thing I know, Nigel is saying to bale out. I unstrap myself, clip on my parachute, and get over to open the hatch. A fierce blast of icy air rips off my boots as I go through it. Nothing I can do about that. I fall for some time, pull the cord, and pray that the parachute opens. The girls back at Leaton could probably hear my scream when I felt the jerk as it opened."

"I followed Donny out," Tad says.

"Did you see Jimmy as you went out?"

"I didn't," says Donny. "I was focused on getting that hatch open. It was my job to see that it was and to get out of the way so the others could follow me."

"I did," says Tad. "Just a glimpse because the wireless position is tucked away next to the steps. He was clipping on his parachute. I was in a hurry to bale out, and I assumed he'd follow me."

"But why didn't he?" Barbara asks. "I could see that Nigel needed to keep the plane level for you, but why would Jimmy not be able to get out when the hatch was almost at his feet?"

Donny spreads his hands in a gesture of incomprehension. "I've wondered why myself. He should have been able to."

"You might ask Tommy when you talk with him," Tad says. "He was the last one out."

"Where did you land after you jumped?"

"I landed next to a canal," says Donny. "Another few feet and I'd have been in the water. So I was lucky. There was a road running alongside. I dragged my parachute across it and hid it and me in some bushes. My escape didn't last long, though. A German patrol came along in the morning and I walked right into it. They didn't speak much English but one managed to get out the famous line 'For you, the war is over.'"

"My parachute got caught in some trees and I was left hanging," Tad says. "I was going to cut myself free but in the dark I couldn't tell how high I was. In the morning, I could see that I was a foot or two above the ground. But by then I was easily spotted. So much for being an evader and getting back to England."

"Donny, you were in the same camp with George, weren't you?"

"And Billy. Tad got taken off to the officers' stalag where they spent their time digging escape holes. But when they first caught us, they piled Tad and me into a truck and drove off to some place where we picked up part of another downed Halifax crew. Then they drove us to an interrogation centre to see what they could get out of us."

"Yes, and what an amazing experience that was," Tad says. "They knew more about the squadron than I did. This one German officer even read off to me an article from the Toronto newspaper saying that I was going overseas. He could see the shock on my face and laughed. The Canadian papers got sent to neutral countries and then apparently made their way to Germany. Made you feel vulnerable, which is what it was meant to. Then they took me off by myself to the stalag. It was bleak but we did things to pass the time. Main thing is that we're here. We survived."

"Did you try to escape?"

"I helped with the digging and the escape packs, but my name didn't come up in the drawings. That last attempt was a tragic mistake and good men were gunned down afterwards. Fifty men died and I knew them nearly all."

Noreen and Margie come bustling into the café at that moment laden with bags. They pull over chairs from the next table and crowd around. No one seems to mind and the waitress comes over for the orders of coffee and hot tea.

"Did you leave anything for anyone else to buy?" Donny says as he surveys Noreen's purchases.

"Oh don't be such a smart aleck," she replies. "Margie and I picked up a few necessaries."

She looks at the half eaten lemon meringue pie on her husband's plate.

"Can I have a bite? I love their pies here."

Without waiting for Donny's reply, she takes his fork and spears a mouthful.

"What do you have?" Margie asks Tad.

"Apple. But don't let me stop you from trying it."

"I won't."

"Would anyone like to try the mud pie?" Barbara offers. "I've eaten half but it's so rich I can't finish it."

A couple of forks appear like magic.

When the waitress brings the bill, Barbara reaches into her purse to struggle with the unfamiliar coloured bills, but Donny will have none of it.

"Put your pocketbook away," he insists. "Your money's no good here. You're family now."

Back at the house, Barbara throws the few things she brought with her into her bag ready for the morning. She plans to order flowers for Noreen in thanks for her hospitality.

"Has it ever been nice to have you here," Noreen says as they eat what she calls good Alberta steak for dinner. "Next time, though, you've got to stay longer. Two days is simply not enough."

"What time are you leaving tomorrow?" Margie asks.

"My plane leaves at 4:00 p.m. I'll be London in the morning with time to rest and get ready for the evening performance."

"It's been such a rushed trip. I do hope you've found something useful. And that these two behaved themselves."

Noreen glances sternly at Tad and Donny.

"Everyone's been wonderful," Barbara says sincerely.

"Well I'm glad you've enjoyed your stay, eh? Because we'd get after them if you hadn't."

"Now what did we do?" Tad throws up his hands in defence.

"I don't trust either of you further than I can throw you."

"See what I have to put up with?" Donny laughs.

Noreen ignores him with an expression of regal disdain.

"Seriously, Barbara," she says later that evening as she puts her arms around her and kisses her warmly on the cheek, "you feel like part of the family. We're all going to miss you. Next time, you simply have to stay much longer."

"I'd like to."

"When you get back to the UK," Donny says as he pats her awkwardly on the shoulder, "I want you to remember that you've now got family here in Canada. We're your air force family. We were brothers on that crew, and that means the families too. You're part of us now."

"Yes," chimes in Margie. "You've got family here in Canada."

14

Our Own Good Opinion, January, 1981

One evening, Sheridan calls a cast meeting after the evening show. "Champagne in the Green Room, boys and girls" he says cheerily to them. "Don't miss it, anyone. It's celebration time."

No one has any idea what he's talking about. Barbara daydreams that Chandler has changed her mind about taking the lead when Maggie leaves or has married some inappropriate rock star and is going off somewhere to have a baby. But that seems silly since if that was the case Sheridan would hardly be standing the cast to champagne.

The show goes well but everyone becomes almost unbearably curious as the evening wends on. There is much speculation during the intervals but no definite information about what Sheridan wants to celebrate. After the show, they find that a table with filled champagne glasses has been set up in the hallway outside the Green Room. Cast and crew are invited to take one and cram inside. The well-used armchairs and sofa are quickly taken and people have to stand or sit on the tables. Sheridan does not appear to notice the crush and seems to be in fine form, standing on a chair to be heard and seen.

"Does everyone have a glass?" he booms from his perch. "If you don't, go and get one. It's going to be good tonight."

Barbara is pushed up against a bulletin board at the back and nearly splashes her champagne when she is jostled. She hopes that he gets on with it, whatever it is.

"Ladies and gentlemen," he finally says with grave formality, waving his glass in the air to prolong the moment. "We all know how wonderful Maggie is, but tonight I am glad to announce that our good opinion has been properly acknowledged. It is my privilege to announce that our leading lady, Maggie Carpenter, has been nominated for the Lawrence Olivier Award, or "Larry" as we enviously know them, for best performance by a female actor in a leading role."

Spontaneous applause breaks out and voices cheer their leading lady. The good cheer is mixed with relief. Such nominations are worth an extended run. Maggie, who has managed not to be crushed against the wall and in fact is standing next to Sheridan at the front, smiles and acknowledges the congratulations. She manages to look neither surprised nor smug. She's not a star for nothing, Barbara thinks.

"The nominees will be formally announced tomorrow but we have the advantage of a little early reconnaissance. The winners will not be announced until February," he continues. "But I should note that if the judges are even reasonably intelligent they will select her as the winner. A toast: To Maggie, congratulations and the best of luck, although you don't need the latter."

"Hear, hear" goes round the room.

Barbara sips her champagne and begins to consider how to make her escape. She starts inching her way toward the door, when Sheridan makes it clear that he is not done.

"But wonderful as that is, there is more. Barbara, stop trying to slide away."

Barbara stops and turns around. She looks guiltily at Sheridan and around the room.

"Come on up here and stop trying to get away."

Sheridan waits until Barbara makes her way through to the front. She stands beside him and Maggie feeling like the class dunce.

"Ladies and gentlemen, there is more. As gracious and wonderful as our star Maggie Carpenter, she would be the first to admit that she cannot do it alone—unless of course it is a one-woman show."

Barbara gazes in wonder up at Sheridan, wondering if he has drunk a champagne bottle by himself some time earlier in the evening.

"So, I am delighted to inform you—and her—that our own Barbara MacDonald has also been nominated for a Larry. She has been nominated for best performance by an actor in a supporting role. Barbara: please accept our heartiest congratulations on a well-deserved nomination."

Now Barbara receives the applause. Maggie smiles at her and Barbara wonders fleetingly what is going to happen if only one of them wins. She hopes it's Maggie if that's the case.

"Both nominations, I might add, are being duly recorded on the outside playbills as we speak."

He lifts his glass and all the glasses round the room rise up in unison.

"Ladies, to you both. Thank you for your talent and your professionalism. And now," he says raising his glass again, "if any have been so immoderate to have drunk your champagne, hasten now to refill your glass. There is more."

A few people push their way out to the hallway and return with full glasses. Sheridan waits for them with an air of amusement and mischief.

"As I said, there is yet more. I have the most immodest pleasure of indicating that your own director has also been nominated for, what else, his direction of this play."

A general and loud cheer goes up. There is some justice in the world, Barbara thinks. It would have been terrible if he hadn't been nominated.

"And our ensemble as a whole can justly take pride as well. Our play has been nominated for this season's best revival."

Cheers erupt in the green room. "A clean sweep," someone yells.

It is indeed a stunning success. Barbara feels a little sad that Martin Quinn, who plays Lily's former lover, hasn't been nominated as well for best actor. But he doesn't look unhappy. The nominations mean extended work. He must not have expected it. It's a woman's play after all.

Sheridan gets down from the chair, collects Maggie and Barbara, and puts his arms around them. The camera's flash startles Barbara.

"Take another one," Sheridan directs, "Barbara's eyes were closed. Make sure they're open this time!"

And so a picture is taken that will always be on Barbara's wall. It shows Sheridan beaming, his moustache hiked at an angle, wearing a cashmere turtleneck sweater under his jacket. He looks polished, suave, and happy. Maggie is smiling, her hair beautifully set and her suit impeccable. Did she know in advance to wear Dior? And then there's Barbara. She's wearing a cardigan over a lumpy tweed skirt. Maggie looks healthy and wealthy. Barbara looks self-conscious, awkward, and like a shop girl.

"This stops right now," she thinks to herself when she sees the picture the next day. "I'm going to do something about this."

The this she is talking about is herself.

She clips the Olivier announcement from the newspaper for her scrapbook. Marilyn was the one who started that and kept it up to date. She'll have to do that herself now. Maggie's competition is stiff. The other two nominees are seasoned stage actresses and one has also won an American Tony award. Barbara is up against a newcomer to the theatre who plays a drug addict and an older actress who plays a murderous housewife. Both women are good. Being nominated with them makes Barbara feel proud and even more determined.

That afternoon, she knocks on Maggie's dressing room door. It takes courage to go inside once she hears the invitation to enter. Maggie is sitting in her velvet dressing gown looking—marvelous. The flowers arranged on her make-up table scent the room. She looks at Barbara's reflection in her mirror. For the moment Barbara is tongue-tied at the impertinence of what she is about to ask. Then she realizes that there is no turning back.

"Maggie," she manages to blurt out to the leading lady's back "Can I ask you where you get your hair done?"

Barbara stands there like a panicking school girl in front of the head mistress, or at least in front of the head mistress's back. She watches awkwardly as Maggie looks up at her short-cropped, messy hair. She fully expects to be thrown out. Then Maggie's eyes drop to her clumsy uncoordinated clothes. Barbara stands frozen in embarrassment. Then an unexpected smile appears on Maggie's face that quickly broadens into a throaty chuckle. She twists her chair around to face Barbara and spreads her arms wide on the armrests.

"So are you finally ready to go after Sheridan?"

Barbara's mouth falls open and she plops down uninvited into Maggie's plush side chair.

"Don't look so flabbergasted," Maggie says. "Everyone knows how you feel about him."

"How I feel about him?" Barbara stammers.

"Now don't you tell me that you're not smitten with him. One look at you when you're with him and it's plain as day."

Maggie swings her chair back to face the mirror and dabs on her make-up. Barbara sees the challenge represented in that movement. Don't waste her time unless Barbara is serious. Maggie stares into her mirror and watches. She hadn't expected Barbara to ask her for help. But in the past she has had to suppress the urge to take Barbara aside and tell her to get on with it.

"Who's everybody?"

"Oh, don't worry. No one's holding it against you. They're all on your side. They think he likes you too, but they haven't gone so far as to place bets on you getting together."

"My God. They place bets?"

"Not yet," Maggie says casually. "But maybe soon."

"Do you think he knows? Has somebody told him?"

"I shouldn't be surprised. But more important is what you want to do about it."

Maggie stretches prettily, then swivels her chair around and looks at Barbara appraisingly. There is potential here, she thinks, if Barbara is put into the right hands.

"Hair is a part of the picture," she instructs Barbara. "But there's everything else that goes with it. Everything that builds image and presentation. If you want to get the works, are you prepared to pay for it? It's going to be expensive to do it right."

Barbara hadn't thought much about the cost. For her, getting her hair done was sufficient. Maggie's in another category, and she seems to be enjoying herself.

"Can you picture Sheridan and me together?"

"Doesn't matter what I think. Can *you* picture yourself together? If you can't then there's no point investing the time and money. You've made the head wife a pivotal part of the play, and she's become Lily's equal. You created that. You took a role and made it your own. You need to do that again in real life."

"Whatever it takes," Barbara says, a little more gamely than she feels. She has a twinge of conscience about what this transformation is going to cost but she's afraid to ask.

For her part, Maggie likes being part of a nascent transformation. How delicious, she thinks, and all for a good cause. She likes Barbara and wants her to succeed with Sheridan. He's a good friend, but both she and Roger agree that he's been unstable in his choice of women. A settled Sheridan is good for business. Barbara has a quiet strength if it can be freed from her uncertainties. She'll be good for Sheridan. She'll bring him calm and will be an antidote to his impulsiveness. If they can bring Barbara out of her shell, Sheridan will keep her there. Good for both of them. Maggie has already made the match in her mind. But every princess must be made ready for her prince.

"Then go to Joubert at the Savoy. Tell him I sent you because he only accepts referrals and won't take you otherwise. And don't try to cut corners. Take his entire morning session. He'll do your hair, nails, and make-up and give you lots of advice whether you think you need it or not. Trust him because he knows what he's doing. Then go to Yvonne, my personal shopper at Harrods. Let her help you select two outfits. You need to develop your own dress sense, but she will be able to tell you what looks good on you in styles and colours. After that you can start doing the rounds of the dress shops yourself. Those two outfits will be the basis for your wardrobe and you will be expanding after that."

She laughs outright at the bewildered expression on Barbara's face.

"That's how I started. I bought one couture suit and then bought nothing else unless it went with that. If you're clever with colour, you can buy things on sale or at Marks and Spencer and change the buttons and do wonderful things with them. The trick is getting the colours right."

"Marks and Spencer's?"

"Don't you dare tell anyone. But there was a time when I was grateful to shop there. They had good quality things if a bit dowdy until you played with them. Calloram Computers existed only on my kitchen table. I had a baby and we'd sunk everything we had into starting the business. So you can believe that things were tight. My leading lady at the time was Veronica Lindman and she took me aside one day to tell me how she'd started out. She said she still shopped there for her underwear. It's become a tradition to pass it on."

Well, Barbara thinks to herself, if the most famous actresses in London can do it, so can she. She doesn't say so, but her jumbled mixture of fear and hope reminds her of the tremulous day when she took her mother to the hospital. You never know how things are going to turn out. Nevertheless, she hides her feelings and stands up resolutely enough. She doesn't want to be thought a coward.

"Joubert it shall be," she says.

She tries to project confidence and sound convinced. She knows she is being asked to surrender to the feminine principle that to change one's life requires changing one's appearance. The idea scares her. But she knows that she has committed herself to more than a cosmetic morning. And she also knows that she can't stop now. If she doesn't follow through then Maggie will think her a weakling. And she does not wish to lose Maggie's respect. As she leaves Maggie's dressing room, she wonders how many acts of courage have been done by people too afraid not to do them.

Joubert turns out to be shrewd man with watchful eyes and a self-conscious talent for self-promotion. He uses the stereotype of Gallic indifference to express scorn for opinions other than his own. He does not invite argument or input. He charges enough to limit his clientele and is selective even among those who can afford him. His clients interpret his unavailability as exclusivity, an idea he reinforces by turning away anyone who strikes him as being vulgar. He has a waiting list of those who want to say they are his clients. These are the ones he doesn't want. His sees his Gallic rationality as the needed antidote to British barbarism.

He eyes Barbara suspiciously as she walks in and sits down in his chair. He sniffs at her appearance. She can't blame him. Once he is convinced that the darling Miss Carpenter has indeed referred her and she is therefore worth his attention, he commences a running monologue with his assistant as he studies her. Barbara starts noticing little things. Like his almond-shaped, manicured nails.

Like the curious way he doesn't finish his sentences, leaving it to his assistant to sort it all out and make the notes. Like his curious self-indulgence in offence.

"You call this a haircut? Non, non, non. Who ever? No don't tell me. Jamais, never, never wear hair cropped close like this on a face like yours. It looks careless and indifferent. Cropped hair is for teenagers and women who have given up. It will take three months to have enough growth. No more cutting. Yes, it needs a fringe to hide the forehead lines and lines around the eyes. Must be angled so … Hair needs to under. . curled forward like so. With length we lift it up like so. Today we will start the shape … and talk about care. Absolutely no more cutting."

He directs the last comment at the cringing Barbara who knows that he has seen through her attempts to cut her own hair. As she sits there under the lamps and listens to the man and his assistant, she starts to feel as if she no longer owns herself. She has become a clinical case, a research challenge to be analyzed and treated. That's how he's treating her. The litany continues.

"Thick hair, bien, fuller the right side. Left part. Waves. They are a problem and will need to be part of the fringe. They may stick up when it's brushed. Colour needs to be lightened. Use thinning scissors. May need to be straightened. Unbroken dark brown is too harsh for a woman her age. She has made herself look much older. We can take years off."

"Can you make me look twenty-four again?" she asks hopefully.

Joubert ignores her. He is completely focused on what he hopes to accomplish and is determined to shape her into his idea of what she ought to look like. His tone implies that he has little hope, but maybe he can work a miracle. If so, it will not be her face but his talent that accomplishes it.

"Hair needs highlights. Cheeks need gold under base. Light coral colour for cheekbones. Eye colour is good blue. Unusual. Smoke-grey for liner, mix azure and midnight for shadow … sienna in eyelid crease … white under brow, number 3, no use number 2. Number two on the makeup. Some sun damage, use number 1 concealer."

He looks at her hands. She has a strong desire to curl her fingertips under.

"Nails bad. Clean and shape the nails. You use colour polish?"

She shakes her head. From his expression, she realizes that it is not a good thing.

He turns her hands over and looks at them from different angles.

"Put poison on them," he says to his assistant.

He stops and frowns.

"Poison?"

"Pepper," his assistant offers.

"Bitter pepper, yes" he says. "One taste and you will never bite them again. Sleep with your hands in cotton gloves. Vaseline at night."

Now Barbara feels guilty and childish. He has made her feel that biting one's nails is an affront to civilization. Her hands no longer belong to her. She wonders whether the outcome will be worth all the fuss. She also thinks about all the hungry children that could be fed with what she's spending on herself. But maybe Joubert sends donations to feed them, she thinks giddily. Right about now her eyes are glazing. She stops listening until she realizes that he is prioritizing what he is about to do to her.

He starts with her hair, and another well-coiffed and made-up assistant washes it with something that smells of musk and lily of the valley. It smells expensive. He keeps up a steady stream of instruction that is duly recorded by the first assistant for Barbara to follow in the weeks ahead. The assistant's long nails fascinate Barbara. Artificial, she decides. No one could have intact nails with little sparkling things on them and keep them all the same length while trying to live a normal life. But how does she pull up the zippers in her clothing? The reveries end when Joubert finds out what she has been using on her hair.

"Baby shampoo? Non, non, that is too drying," he shouts. "Use honey and lanolin shampoo for dark hair. Pas else."

Then he supervises as her hair is lightened. He personally trims what little there is, muttering all along. She has enough schoolgirl French to understand some of what he's saying. She wants to laugh. But then he would know that she was eavesdropping on him. With each clip her hair falls into place. Then her face is steamed and oiled and her eyebrows waxed. She gets a cup of tea as her reward about mid way through.

He blow-dries her hair himself, pulling and tugging at it. He's impatient with it and Barbara winces. He doesn't seem to notice or to care. When he doesn't like it, he sprays it with something wet and starts all over. From time to time, he stops to pull out a hair. It stings. He ignores her grimaces. The make-up bottles are lined up across the table. He uses one at a time and chatters away with instructions and reprimands as he makes the applications, starting with the outer part of her face and working toward the centre. Barbara is amazed at the almost scientific precision of his work. She wonders if he ever gets bored.

Finally, he stands back and seems satisfied. He hands her a mirror and slowly swings the chair around so she can look at herself. At first she doesn't recognize this woman with the large blue eyes and the soft apricot complexion. But when she smiles, the woman smiles back at her.

Joubert nods. "Better," is all he will say.

When she leaves, she leaves behind three months' salary.

Joubert's parting shout is to hold her head up. She suspects that this is to display what he has accomplished. She giggles in the relief of having her face back in her own control. But her eyebrows are arched, her hair is showing some slight sign of what it will become after the next three appointments, she has had a crash course in how to use all the cosmetic bottles and brushes in her carrying bag, her nails are clean and painted with something that smarts badly if she touches her tongue to it (Joubert made her try it), and she feels tremendous. She walks on air over to Harrods where she loses an equivalent sum on a basic blue suit that, the shopper says, matches her eyes, a cream silk blouse, and a slim black skirt with a top that can take her from day to evening with the addition of Gran's pearls. She now has a smile on her face that seems contagious. People notice her and smile back.

She can't wait to show herself to Maggie. She goes straight from Harrods to the theatre. She wants Maggie to be the first to see her, so she slides into the theatre quietly hiding behind her bags and trying not to let anyone see her.

Maggie studies her carefully. She asks to see her new clothes and has her hold them up.

"Not bad at all," she says. "Good colours, nice looking cut. They'll do nicely."

She walks up and examines the make-up.

"What did Joubert say about your hair?"

"He said it needs three inches before he can do anything with it."

"Turn around," she says. "Let me see the back. He's given you the start of a Parisian cut. It will be straight across the back and then curl forward in front of your ears. It will look good on you."

She glances in her mirror and pats her own hair. "It's about time for another session with him myself."

It's then that Barbara knows how good she looks.

"Be sure that Sheridan sees you before you have to wipe all that off," Maggie says sagely. "Joubert is impossible, of course, but he's the best at what he does. Consider this an investment."

Sheridan is busy talking with Joe when Barbara catches up with him. They don't seem to recognize her at first. It takes a few moments of conversation before Sheridan stops in mid-sentence.

"Barbara, what have you done to yourself?"

Not the reaction she was looking for. But it recognizes the difference between her selves, before and after.

"Crikey," says Joe.

She tries to be casual and not give the usual response of "Do you like it?" which implies that she's looking for admiring comments.

"I thought it was time to make a change."

"You've done that all right," Joe splutters.

"You look splendid, Barbara," Sheridan manages to say. "But I thought you looked fine before. What made you decide to do this?"

"Let's say I realized it was time to get on with my life."

Barbara realizes that she is being owlish. She is deliberately recalling their conversation at the pub when he asked when she would be ready. Will he remember? She has sent him a signal but has no idea what to do next. She will have to wait and see.

In the week that follows her renaissance, though, she has some distraction from wondering about her chances for the Olivier or with Sheridan. She has achieved a break through in what has become an obsession to learn about her father. She now has his service record.

She felt guilty when she filled out the application for it. She had to certify that she was Jimmy Baldock's daughter. But they asked no questions and didn't want proof. She submitted the payment and they politely sent the two pages that are the entire record of the last three years of his life.

But he does not to leap to life from the pages as she had hoped. The service record reminds her of how little she knows about him. Most of it is a list of letters and abbreviations. She knows this has to make sense to someone. She has a fleeting moment of distraction when she imagines clerk-typists sitting at rows of desks with overflowing baskets, stolidly pressing on the round iron keys of heavy black typewriters to enter the details of individual troop movements and reassignments. She wonders what these—undoubtedly—women thought as they put in the details of families who should be notified in case of death, recommendations for training, and personal details such as gunnery scores. Did they do their jobs and not think about all the death or potential death they were recording? Were they in some country house's basement or in a bunker surrounded by sandbags, hoping there would not be a direct hit during a bombing raid? They were the ones who typed in the maze of abbreviations. They would know what this all meant.

But Barbara is not about to give up and she pieces together what she can. She knows now that he was called up to Oxford, and the record shows that he was placed in reserve. Undoubtedly he was registered for conscription, but he must have volunteered before he was called. The Aircrew Selection Board tested him for three days and said he was healthy and intelligent enough to be part of an aircrew. Then they sent him home to wait. Was he apprehensive? Was he looking forward to his new status as a flyer? Did he have a youthful swagger and the certainty that nothing was going to happen to him? How did he feel when he found out they were going to recommend him for training as a wireless operator? Marilyn said he wanted to be a pilot. There was something about the jaunty wave from the cockpit that attracted the young men and their girls. She has the feeling these are things that she will never know.

Then one day she has even more to think about. Tommy has written to tell her that he will be coming home from Spain at the end of April.

15

Of Theatres and Computers

Maggie and Roger are throwing a party and everyone is invited. Roger wants to celebrate a new computer contract with the EU. Maggie wants to celebrate the cast and crew and welcome Chandler Taylor to the play. Maggie won the Larry for her role. She is delighted. But so have Sheridan and Barbara. True to the oddities that work around these awards, the play did not win in the other category. But no matter, as Sheridan likes to say, the company is larger than its parts. Everyone won. This party should be eclectic, computers and theatre.

This is also farewell to Maggie for a while. She doesn't want to commit to another show every night for now. Her children are young, she says, and she needs more time with her husband who is still building his business—as if it's not doing nicely. Calloram Computers has been named among the top ten businesses in the UK and Roger Calloram has been identified as a major player in Europe. She's going to concentrate on making films so she can take long breaks when she needs to. But she'll come back to the stage, she promises. It's her home.

She and Roger live in Dorman's Land on a country estate. They have horses that they keep in a six-stall barn with gleaming tack and polished saddles, detached cottages for their liveryman and housekeeper, a gun room for Roger Calloram's antique rifles, a garage with four cars, one of which is a Landrover, and their own pond. The Callorams can leave their doors unlocked because they have a pair of loose Nutria rats. One look at their long orange teeth discourages anyone who might even think of breaking in. Roger likes to feed them dried apples from his own orchard. It's the type of country estate that the wealthy English can do so well.

The distance from London is not a problem for Maggie because she's driven in each day. But it is for Barbara who doesn't have a car. The train from London stops at the country station nearby, but Maggie's house is across some fields. It's March so the path will be wet, certainly cold, and there are cows in the field and stiles to climb at both ends.

These challenges don't bother Joe and the rest of the crew without cars. They're looking forward to what they call a spot of fresh air. Barbara, on the other hand, can't see pushing cows aside, dodging cow piles in the dark, and climbing over slimey stiles in high-heeled shoes. She needs a plan. She reasons that if she can get herself out to Canada, drive on the other side of the road, and get home safely, then she should definitely be up to getting to Maggie's house.

She starts to inquire discreetly about how people are getting to the party. Most are driving but coming from the wrong direction. Or like Joe they are going on the train and walking from the station. That doesn't solve her problem with the cows and stiles.

In the end, she asks Maggie. They've become friends after what Maggie calls her coming out. They've gone shopping together, deposited outside Harrods by Maggie's chauffeur and then carried off to the Savoy afterwards for tea. Maggie has continued Barbara's lessons and told her that they need to go further a-field. There are wonderful specialty shops she hasn't shared yet, she says. Places where you can get woollen coats and embroidered cardigans that never make it to the London shops. Barbara's head spins when Maggie talks about her world.

Maggie sits thoughtfully when she hears what the problem is. She understands the situation but from her own point of view. Barbara may think it a question of dignity, but to Maggie it is entrance and image.

"I should have anticipated this," she says. "I can send the car over to the station if you let me know which train you're coming down on. But better yet, Roger's invited his managers from work. Let me see who's coming and perhaps you won't have to take the train at all."

Two days before the party, she has a solution. She takes Barbara aside and announces that the problem is solved.

"Roger's people don't live anywhere close to you, so it didn't work out. But Sheridan says he would be happy to give you a lift. I told him to pick you up at 5:30 since it will take time to get there." She puts her head on one side and asks coyly if that's all right.

Barbara feels her cheeks start to burn. In a split second Barbara has seen her impending danger. How is she going to handle this if he shows up with a young, beautiful model? What if Miss Gorgeous looks at her with pity because she has a date and Barbara doesn't? And what if he looks at her with smug affection because she is nuzzling him and looks good on his arm? Barbara feels both jealousy and fear. Her first impulse is to say she won't go, but her pride won't let her. Maggie seems to be aware of the maelstrom she's caused. She is smiling and her eyes are daring. She's living up to her reputation for mischief.

"That's one solution."

"It's the solution," Maggie corrects her. "It's perfect," she adds before she can be contradicted.

Barbara knows she is trapped. She asked Maggie for her help. If she turns it down she will appear ungrateful and rude. No other alternative. Barbara knows that she will have to go.

"I'll be ready," she says weakly.

Maggie smiles like the Cheshire Cat. She's in command of things and prepared to fade away if Barbara foolishly contests such a splendid arrangement.

On the night of the party, Barbara augments her black Harrods skirt with a new black gauzy blouse with cream collar and cuffs. She puts on Gran's pearls and does her makeup with particular attention. She'll be damned is she's going to appear dowdy in front of some young model who makes her living by looking good.

At the appointed time, she takes a deep breath and walks down to the foyer. She is neither early nor late. Sheridan drives into the courtyard just as she reaches the front door. He is alone.

Now Barbara is not sure how she feels since she has practiced the elegant nonchalance with which she intended to greet him and his date. Instead she says hello and gets into his car looking straight ahead in her self-consciousness. It is a dashing, sporty car. Black outside with plush red interior. It reminds her for a mischievous moment of a coffin. Black dark wood outside with taffeta lining, perfect for taking the deceased from one world to the next. She can't help herself and she giggles as he drives onto the Ring Road.

"What's so amusing?" he asks.

"Interesting colours, the red and the black. Sounds like a Russian novel."

"German. I'll have you know this is very in. The car salesman assured me of that

"I don't think I've ever seen one like it before

She knows she is being absolutely horrible. It's his car, and she should shut up and be grateful for his being willing to give her a lift.

He doesn't respond, but she can see his moustache twitch. Is he annoyed? How surprised she would have been to know that he was nervous.

"I imagined you'd say something like that. I'm surprised at how fast you managed it."

She bursts out laughing. "What made you think I'd say something?"

"Because you are about the most contrary person I have ever run across. You are quiet as the tomb when I expect you to say something. You come out and say what you think at times when I think you'll be silent. You are also the most hard-headed woman I know."

Off hand she can't remember behaviour like that. But she is intrigued.

"And that's a real problem?"

"Actually not," he replies. "It's sometime fun trying to predict what you'll do."

"All right," she says, "give me some examples."

"The night I announced the nominations. Remember that? Here was the highest honour possible for the play and you are buried in the back and trying to slide away."

She glances at his profile as they stop for a light and quells the urge to sweep back his fallen lock of hair.

"How was I to know I was included?"

"That's just it. You were included. You're playing a major character in the play. If the play's good, then it's due in large part to you. Yet you hung back. Maggie didn't have trouble understanding that. She'd have been at the front whether she was nominated or not."

"I'll concede that point," she admits. "So give me an example of when I spoke out."

"When we went out to dinner and you asked me about the women I dated."

"Yes, I'm sorry about that. I was quite tight."

"I liked it," Sheridan says and looks at her sideways. "I thought, well she's at least taking note of me."

Taking note of him? For Barbara, the conversation has taken a sharp turn into the bizarre. She can't say anything for a moment.

"I don't think anyone doesn't take note of you."

She hears herself stammer at the absurd idea that she hadn't noticed him. He's been on her mind for so long, she can't remember a time when he wasn't.

"No, Barbara, you don't escape like that. I got the feeling you were interested in me that night."

Barbara remembers with horror what Maggie said about people knowing her feelings about Sheridan. She considers jumping out of the car for pure embarrassment. But then the moment passes. She remembers the challenge in Maggie's eyes and the situation takes on a new set of possibilities. She feels wicked and daring. If they are taking bets on her, why not simply follow this where it is going?

"My god," she says, trying to sound both weakly flirtatious and slightly outraged. "Exactly what is your role tonight. Are you my transport or my date?"

"I'm your escort."

She realizes that he has matched her tone perfectly. The air vibrates around them.

"And what does an escort do?"

Her heart is pounding and her eyes are wide. She fights to keep her voice under control.

"Whatever is asked of him."

He glances at her sideways again and then looks back at the road ahead.

Her head spins. At that moment all she can think of is whether she's picked up her underwear in the bedroom. She knows exactly what she wants to ask and has the wonderful, frightening feeling that she is going to ask it.

She sits in stunned silence for several minutes and then feels his hand reach out for hers. His hand is warm and masculine and inquiring. She turns her hand slightly under his and curls her fingers around his. He gives her a quick smile. She takes her hand from his and reaches across to finally brush back his hair. Then they ride the rest of the way without saying much. Whenever they stop for a light, they glance at each other and smile shyly.

Maggie's house is a square stone building with stairs leading up both sides to a double front door with columns and a carved pediment with a griffin in relief. Cars are parked all along the carriageway, lit by the soft glow of light from the windows. The house is already filling even though it's early in the evening. Everyone says that these parties last into the small hours of the morning. They are infrequent but esteemed. No one wants to miss them.

Maggie and Roger are standing by the foot of the central staircase when Sheridan and Barbara go in. All the doors of the lower floor have been thrown open to create a flowing space through and around the house. Each room has mantles adorned with flower arrangements. One is an oval formed of tropical flowers that towers a good six feet. The furniture has been pushed back against the walls to provide sitting space and leave the centres open. Maggie points them to a bar set up on the indoor tennis court, an obvious addition at the back of the house. She is radiant in a filmy gold gown and looks absolutely stunning. When Sheridan and Barbara go to the tennis court, they can see that there's a clear demarcation in appearance between the computer guests and the theatre people. The people from Roger's business are extremely well groomed and almost invariably young, much younger on average than the group from the theatre. But there's no professional divide between the arts and sciences when it comes to the bar. They're equally well represented there and the bartender is being kept busy. Barbara gets a wine and ginger so she won't consume too much alcohol. She wants to enjoy the evening—all of it.

They take their drinks and walk through the house looking at the exquisite carved woodwork and English antique furniture in every room. Sheridan stays by her side until he is drawn away to meet arriving people, including Chandler Taylor who arrives with an entourage and sets herself up in a corner. Barbara has found Chandler pleasant enough in the rehearsals, but she's not Maggie, and Barbara hasn't warmed to her. Chandler is self-protective and doesn't encourage intimacy, perhaps because she is not yet comfortable in the theatre. Perhaps their relationship will grow. But for now, Barbara feels no need to visit Chandler's corner.

Instead, she goes back out to the tennis court saying hello and stopping to talk. Then she heads over to the buffet. She hadn't intended to eat anything because juggling a plate and a glass are impossible, but the food is tempting and she ends up with some. Now she needs to sit down. Martin and his wife and Joe are sitting at a small table in a corner and she heads over toward them. Martin has signed a contract to continue with the London cast and is pleased.

"Glad to be settled and not feel like gypsy," he's saying.

He has to speak up because the band is playing loudly. More and more people are arriving. There's a good deal of drinking, and the activity level is heating up.

"I've enjoyed working with you," Martin tells Barbara. "I wish you were staying with the London cast."

Joe agrees with him. "Have you considered staying in London?" he asks. "We'll miss you."

"I'll miss you too. But I don't know what's happening yet."

"I heard you were going to the travelling company," Martin says. "It would be a good opportunity for you and we wish you the best whatever you do."

Sheridan finds her there. Martin and Joe eye him with interest. Barbara wonders if they've placed their bets. Sheridan is with an older man whom she recognizes.

"Barbara, this is Wilson Holland, the esteemed theatre critic for the Globe. Wilson, may I introduce Barbara MacDonald?"

She stands up to shake his hand.

"Barbara MacDonald? Olivier this year. Saw you once in some horror set in Windsor Forest. What was it? Something Shakespearean. See, I *have* deliberately forgotten it to save my sanity. As I recall, you were not bad in it."

"Coming from Wilson, that faint praise is the best one ever gets," Sheridan laughs.

"Not true, not true." Wilson shakes his lumbering head and looks like a large dog shaking its jowls. He peers at her down his nose as if he is mildly surprised to discover that she is an attractive woman. He squints slightly as he leans in to look at her. Then he shakes his jowls again and straightens up. He makes a slight sucking noise as he purses his lips.

Barbara looks closely at the demon of London critics and thinks that he needs to get better dentures. They whistle while he talks and make his lower jaw jut out. An absurd thought fills her mind: perhaps he could sing 'Whistle While You Work" with the band. She resolves not to have a second drink.

"I have been known to commend people from time to time," Wilson offers with an attempt at sophisticated nonchalance and a glance at Sheridan. "Don't believe all you hear, Miss MacDonald. I play a most important role. I poke holes into things to see if they explode."

"Why would you want them to explode?" She's never heard anyone discuss theatrical criticism that way.

He draws out his chest and sucks in his breath. "Because I despise mediocrity and there seems to be an epidemic. Incompetence has overtaken the theatre. Don't ask me to come to a theatre and show me something substandard. I get cross when that happens. I've been to some horrors lately where I walked out after the first act."

"Perhaps those plays might have improved in the second act," Sheridan comments.

Wilson snorts loudly. "You have one act to convince me or I'm leaving. Get me while you have me."

"Well," says Sheridan, "whatever are you doing here among this lesser breed?"

"That's where you're wrong. Maggie Carpenter has never offered anything less than first rate. Her performances are magnificent. She has been fearless in her choice of roles and she has brought the element of humanity to every one. This party is nothing less than I would expect of her. Miss Taylor has large shoes to fill. We shall have to see how well she does. Miss MacDonald, as you are an actress, I point to Maggie Carpenter as your model."

With that he bows and walks away.

"I think he's had a bit to drink," Sheridan observes.

"Sheridan, what is it that makes Maggie so magnificent? I've been trying to understand it ever since the play opened. I can see it, but I can't describe it."

"It's a complex question when you ask about presence. And that's what it is. It's about how actors present themselves on stage."

Barbara notices that Martin and Joe have stopped talking. They apparently want to hear what Sheridan has to say too.

"When I was a student, I took a job cleaning theatre lavatories so I could be around during rehearsals. One evening I heard a director ask an actor what he was trying to accomplish by a movement. That struck me. He wasn't telling, he was asking and at the same time trusting that the actor knew. Hearing that was heady stuff for someone doing repertory parts in school productions. What I realized was that you can learn all the technical and professional techniques, things like timing, pauses, and tone—things that a good director can help you with. But there also has to be an intuitive connection between the actor and the character. If the actor can't find the character, can't grasp the core at the centre of the play, no amount of direction can make the performance work."

"Does the actor choose a role then? Or is the other way around?"

"Barbara, what do you feel when you watch Maggie on stage?"

That isn't a hard question since Barbara has studied her so carefully.

"I feel her suppressed fury and her strength. When she tells Frank she intends to destroy him, I believe her."

"That's one way of putting it. When she is in the right role, she gives her most memorable performance because she understands it. She has a theme to her acting because she understands herself and what she is best at doing."

Sheridan's moustache twitches with amusement. He knows what she is going to ask, and he is ready for it.

"Do I have a theme to my acting?"

"I'm not going to answer that for you. You need to be the one to find it. It comes with experience and knowing yourself. It's also the moment when you lose self-consciousness on stage and understand that you are there not to be noticed but to be believed."

They stay together as much as they can for the evening. Barbara tries not to fade into the background but stand at peace beside him. Finally a man with short-cropped hair and thick glasses approaches them. Sheridan introduces him as Roger's vice president for finance. It becomes clear as they talk that Calloram Computers has invested in the show. Barbara realizes that he must have been one of the people who wondered whether she had the personal acting strength to follow Maggie.

From then on, the evening passes rapidly. Barbara dances several times with Sheridan, once with the vice president, once with Roger and then with several others from Calloram Computers. Apart from Roger, who has an almost Diplomatic Corps charm, the others are preoccupied and give her the impression they would prefer to be somewhere else. She asks about their work but cannot understand their answers. All she can gather is that the Calloram Computer contract is huge, and they are focused on making a go of it.

As the evening wears on, the band moves away from a mixture of theatre tunes and soft rock into something approaching heavy metal. Or at least that's how it sounds to Barbara. Couples gyrate on the floor and the festive mood steps up another notch. The computer crowd comes to life. The theatre crowd is now more content to sit and watch, and drink. The young couples from Calloram Computers dance intently. Barbara is fascinated when Maggie and Roger get out there and join them.

She glances at Sheridan now and then when he is busy talking with the flow of London theatre people. Many are not connected with the show, so she leaves him to his business. She is delighted in her new confidence and walks around to introduce herself to people, many of whom recognize her or at least her name and want to talk about the play. Sheridan seems to know when she is looking at him and more often than not he meets her gaze and smiles. A sexual tension grows between them as the night wears on and the waiting intensifies it. At 10:00 p.m. they thank their hosts and begin the long ride up to London.

"Are you leaving so early?" Maggie asks. "I hope you found the bar."

"We had a wonderful time," Barbara tells her.

"Please thank Roger for us," Sheridan adds.

Maggie glances across the room where Roger is engaged in focused conversation with a couple of his men.

"I think he's having a board meeting," she sighs. "I'll have to go and break it up."

Sheridan drapes Barbara's coat around her shoulders.

"Let me know how it goes," Maggie whispers in Barbara's ear as Sheridan turns away to retrieve his own.

The ride home is inconsequential. They talk a little about the party and how well it went. They hold hands for part of the journey, and he reaches over to kiss her once when they are stopped. Then they drive up to the doorway of her flat. She has been rehearsing what to say and when to say it. In the end, she simply says for him to come up and he does.

Once inside the doorway, she goes into his arms. They exchange a long and passionate kiss. He runs the back of his hand down her cheek and slowly down her arm. The movement is sensuous and slow. She feels a thrill of excitement and the pure exultation of having him there in her flat and in her arms. Then he kisses her neck and her breath starts to come faster. She drops her coat on the floor behind her. She cannot remember how long it has been since someone wanted her and she wanted him so badly in return.

"Where's the bedroom?" he whispers as he drops his coat.

She tells him, and he puts his arm around her to steer them there. They leave the bedroom dark. He unbuttons her blouse and removes her bra. She doesn't realize that he has done that until his lips press on her nipples. Slowly, gently, completely assured, he lays her back on the bed and slips off her shoes and then her nylons and skirt. She groans and starts to move against him. She feels a throb of expectation and loses track of time. Then finally his weight shifts over her and she is abandoned to an ecstatic moment when nothing else matters in the world.

"Great party last night, wasn't it?" Joe asks as Barbara waltzes into work next day.

"Absolutely superb," she warbles as she passes him on the way to Maggie's dressing room. She no longer cares about the betting. She feels supremely happy. Maggie is peering intently into the mirror as she comes in.

"Wonderful evening."

"We didn't get to sleep until dawn and I look like hell," Maggie says dourly.

"No you don't. You look smashing as ever."

"Several of Roger's people had to sleep in the guest quarters and come up to London this morning. We couldn't let them drive. I'm glad we don't have close neighbours or do this too often."

"We didn't get to sleep until dawn either," Barbara giggles.

Maggie looks up at her and chuckles. She forgets her displeasure with the mirror.

"I won the bet! I said you'd get together after the party. Some of the others thought it would be at the end of the run."

"But Maggie," Barbara protests, "that was cheating because you arranged for Sheridan to pick me up. You made it possible."

Maggie shakes her head and smiles impishly.

"No, Barbara, I didn't. I'd like to take the credit, but it wasn't me."

She is looking too smug for Barbara's liking.

"Then who was it?"

Maggie holds her in suspense for several moments before she answers the question.

"It was Sheridan. He came by and asked me to arrange it. He asked me to keep it a secret. I hope you aren't angry with me."

"Angry?" Barbara bursts across the room and throws her arms around her. "Maggie, you're a bloody genius."

16

On Top of Things

Tommy Lewis's house sits astride a hill and obviously has been designed to capture an unimpeded view of the gently rolling countryside. It looks expensive in the way of meticulously restored homes on the National Historic Register. There's no plaque announcing that it's on the register, but the house looks as if it deserves it. It has two storeys with perfectly balanced rows of windows in Georgian style. To the side there is a detached garage and at the back, just glimpsed from the road, a building for stables. Barbara imagines that they have an AGA stove in the kitchen and authentic period colours on all their walls. How delicious, Maggie might say. Billy was right. Tommy has done well.

When Barbara gets out of the taxi, she crowds into the arched doorway to get out of the spring rain. She gives a good rap with the highly polished brass fox knocker on the bright blue door.

"Come on in." Tommy's wife laughs as she barely restrains a large St Bernard by its collar. "Hope you're prepared. The grandchildren are here and the house is full of animal hair. They can't play outside because of the weather plus the cleaning staff have the day off so we're not on top of things right now."

The dog gives a mighty woof and its jowls shake. It calms down as soon the front door is closed. His huge head seems out of proportion to his body and he looks as if he could take someone's arm off.

"He's really a rug of a dog," the woman says, trying to sound reassuring. She is well tanned from her stay in Spain and appears to be in her late fifties. Her hair is a lovely shade of honey wheat, highlighted becomingly by a few grey streaks. She is trim and Barbara can imagine her riding the horses that she saw in the field next to the house. For now she is engaged in imposing order on the dog. She takes her fingers out of the collar and the now-released dog comes up and licks Barbara's hand, but it's a noisy slurp that leaves her hand sticky.

"I'm May," the woman says as she tries to shoo the dog away. But the dog turns in a circle and stands on Barbara's foot. She gasps with surprise and pain. When he brushes against her, he feels solid and nearly knocks her off balance.

"No, Hans. Bad dog. Go away. Now."

The dog shakes its head and sprays them both with saliva before he gives an athletic bounce and hurtles off toward the back of the house. Claws rattle loudly on the hardwood floor and at one point he seems to have slipped and thumped into a wall. A cat's angry hiss comes from that direction, followed by the dog's yelp. Children's shouts and laughter greet his arrival somewhere in the back of the house.

"I have to apologize. Hans is a puppy and we haven't completed obedience training yet. Brandy our cat is teaching him some manners, but he's got some way to go. Hans jumped up on Tommy the other night and knocked him flat. So now we're emphasizing obedience. I'm sure you'd like to wash your hands after all that."

May points to a small cloakroom off the hallway.

"Tommy's in his study," May says when Barbara comes out. "He retreats when there's chaos in the house."

She leads her through the living room with its bay windows and heavy velvet Regency curtains, over to a set of double doors. Barbara glimpses cream wallpaper striped with moss green, gold and green upholstered furniture, and deeply shining antique wood tables with carved legs.

"Barbara's here, Love," she calls and Tommy rouses himself out to greet her.

"I assume she's run the gauntlet," he asks his wife.

"Not too bad. Hans listened when I told him to go away."

"That's a good start," he says. "That dog is going to cost four times in training fees what it cost to buy him. Come on in, Barbara." He points to a side chair beside his desk.

Tommy's study is masculine. Pipe tobacco smoke hangs in the air and the walls are heavily panelled with dark wood. Tommy fits right in. He's wearing a cashmere cardigan over a white shirt and well-tailored dark brown trousers. He looks well-dressed casual. His profession surrounds him. The built-in floor-to-ceiling bookcases hold metal construction hats inscribed with the names and dates of London buildings and rolls of what seem to be plans. Aerial views of London hang on the wall along with a silverpoint etching of York Minster. There is also a large framed picture of a Halifax bomber flying over York.

Barbara tries to envision him as a young air gunner crammed into a rotating upper turret. She can't align that image with him now with his expensive haircut and expensive clothing. He looks every bit the respected and highly successful builder of the modern high-rise apartments and office buildings that mark the London skyline. He has done well indeed.

"I'll talk to the cook about supper," May says, "and I'll leave you alone."

Tommy shuts the doors after her and settles in his high-backed leather chair.

"As you may have already gathered, my wife was raised in the country and doesn't feel complete without a full menagerie. The children take after her. So we have dogs, cats, horses, sheep, rabbits, chickens, a turkey, and even a goat. All decorative, mind you. Except for the children's ponies, all useless. We get some eggs from the chickens, but if it gets hot or gets cold or it's neither, they stop laying. And the turkey is far too old and tough to eat. But there you are."

Barbara smiles sympathetically but has the idea he likes complaining about the confusion. Tommy is one of those men who choose agreeable wives to clear the pathway to social acceptance. Barbara has seen it in the theatre. The more charming the one, the less outgoing the other.

"May talked me into riding to the hunt once. It's something she'd done all her life, but I came to it late and wasn't up to it although I'd ridden for a couple of years by then. She's got a great seat and went over the first hedge like a bird. I tried and landed in the ditch, which happened to be full of water. Told her after that she was on her own and she'd have to find another way to make me into a country gentleman."

"You weren't raised in the country?"

"Heavens no," he snorts. "City boy. We lived near Croydon and got bombed out. After that my family spread out all over the country living with relatives, and I joined the RAF. I was in business school when I signed up. In the RAF's infinite wisdom that qualified me as an air gunner. I'd never fired a weapon in my life. But no matter. Off I went to learn."

He laughs at the memory but his laugh is cynical.

"I haven't talked much about the war. Billy probably told you that I haven't kept in touch with the squadron. I'm not much for looking back. But lately I've been thinking that I should. May's asked me about the war from time to time. So did the children. I always said that it was a terrible time. What war isn't? Young lives lost. Civilians dead. Cities flattened. I didn't want to remember what I saw from the turret."

"I appreciate your talking to me."

"Billy was the one who convinced me. He said it was time to let go. I first met Billy and the others at the Heavy Conversion Unit. You always wonder who you're going to crew with, and it's a wonder that it worked as well as it did.

Jimmy and Nigel and the others crewed up at the OTU in Cornwall before George Williams and I joined them. We didn't get to choose, just assigned to them. But they looked all right and we all got on well enough, I suppose."

Barbara picks up the reserve and doubt in Tommy's voice.

"Were there tensions in the crew, then?"

"Too strong a word, *tension*. I suppose there might have become some over time. But we weren't together long enough for it to happen. They were all right. But there was a limit to what I could take of George. Too much of a good thing. Nigel didn't believe in silence either but he could be engaging. Billy was a teenager. The two Canadians tended to talk about where they came from. Jimmy was quiet. Never knew what he was thinking. I was glad to escape off to see May."

"If you'd had the choice, would you have joined another crew?"

"Never know, shall we?"

He takes down a framed portrait of the crew. But this time there are seven standing in front of the Halifax. Jimmy is on the left, standing next to Tommy. In the centre, Nigel is laughing as he rests his arms around the shoulders of Donny and George. Tad and Billy are on the other side of George. Jimmy's in profile and for some reason looks different from his earlier pictures. From the way he's holding his body, Barbara thinks he looks uncomfortable. She wonders if something's on his mind. But then she wonders why no one else seems to have this picture.

"I haven't seen this photograph before. May I ask where it came from?"

"It was taken with my camera. I asked one of the ground crew to take it for me. It's the only one that shows the seven of us as a crew."

"I'd love to get a copy of this if I can."

Tommy nods. He'd been expecting her request. He knew the others didn't have this photograph, but he hadn't felt like sharing it before.

"This was taken at the HCU, obviously," he says. "Nigel was in high spirits. He was about to be married. George and I had been added because two more were needed to fly the Halifax. We'd come back from a cross-country flight when that picture was taken, and we were getting ready to be posted to a squadron. One of the other crews had crashed the day before with everyone killed, so you could see how happy we might feel to have survived. We nearly didn't on the first time without an instructor. We're going down the runway and then we're heading for the control tower. There's one hell of a crash. Nigel's put the undercarriage down. Why he had so much trouble, I don't know. He'd had enough practice with an instructor, so it had to be some malfunction. We screech down the runway and sparks explode everywhere. No one's hurt but the Halifax is only good for parts. We stopped about six yards from the building. The duty officer comes raging out and wants to know what happened, except he didn't ask in those words. A WAAF in the tower told me later that they thought they'd got the chop and ducked under the desks. But Nigel got good at getting it up afterwards."

The telephone rings and he excuses himself to answer it. He looks at Barbara significantly, and she guesses that whoever is on the other end is talking about her.

"Yes, she's here. She made it. All right. No I won't. I won't forget." He hangs up and turns to her. "That was Billy. He says to say hello to you."

May looks in on them. "Tea anyone?"

"Lovely," says Tommy and she disappears. There is a crash in the hallway.

"What the …?" Tommy says and partly gets up.

"It's all right," May yells to no one in particular. "I just tripped over Hans."

"Damned dog," Tommy says as he sits back down. "Forgive my language. I wanted something small like a terrier, but I got outvoted. The grandchildren fell in love with St Bernards after they read *Peter Pan*. There's nothing practical about a St. Bernard. It simply exists to knock things over, slobber over everything, deposit hair, and take up space."

He shakes his head. Barbara doesn't know if it is disgust or resignation.

"Nigel expected to be skipper whether we were in the air or not. That was all right by me. He had a tiny car that we'd somehow or other get ourselves into. Then we'd go off to the pub in Leaton. I don't know how we found the petrol, probably just as well I didn't know. It was noisy and hot in that little car. Nigel had opinions on everything. He'd be talking away in the front while the four in the back couldn't hear a word. We'd be half hanging out of the windows, trying to breathe. It was a good thing that the airfield was close to Leaton. The two Canadians were noisy and liked to drink. I always expected to hear that Billy, the tail gunner, was being dressed down for something. He had no sense of self-control then."

May comes in carrying a tray with the tea things. She takes a few minutes to arrange everything and then is off again, leaving them to talk. May seems to dart around like a bird, arranging things and taking care of everyone.

"I met May at Nigel's wedding." Tommy seems to have read Barbara's thoughts.

"Jimmy was the best man, and a complete bundle of nerves. I think he was more nervous than Nigel. He had to give the toast and I think he took ten seconds to do it and looked as if he'd done a hard day's work when he was done. It was surprising that he was so shy because he used to sing well enough."

"He could sing?"

Barbara's eyebrows lift involuntarily. She doesn't know why she's surprised. After all, Jimmy Baldock exists for her in other people's recollections. The more that she talks with the people who knew him, the more she realizes how little Marilyn knew. But then it appears that not many people whose lives touched his knew him any better.

"Quite well. Someone from another crew could play the piano. Jimmy'd sing the songs and whoever was there joined in the choruses if they wanted to. The songs were squadron favourites but some were off-colour. Give him his due. He had a beautiful baritone voice. He might have gone on the stage."

"Well, I didn't inherit his musical talent. I sing flat as the floor."

Barbara has to laugh. As a child in school, she'd been told to mouth the words to a song that her form was presenting.

"Funny thing with children. Our son is blonde like his mother and always loved horses. Our daughter is dark like me and prefers to read. They're almost completely different. Now our son is in the Diplomatic Corps and we mind the grandchildren from time to time. Our daughter teaches English at a university in Wales. You never know how things run in families."

He pours the tea and then gestures inquiringly toward a wood humidor on his large desktop. When Barbara nods, he fills his pipe, tamps it down, and lights the tobacco. The tobacco crackles as he draws on it.

"There we were at the wedding. Lettuce—her real name is Letitia—turns out to have a large bouncing family. The kind that is accustomed to running across muddy fields and up and down stairs. Nobody ever walks and every one shouts. I call them the Wellington boot brigade. They were all there at the house, relatives, assorted children, dogs running round, and friends dropping in and out. And through it all, Jimmy quietly carries on as usual. He has one run-in with Nigel's father who struck me as a cold fish but otherwise everyone liked him. What wasn't there to like? It's the ones who open their mouths like George who get in trouble."

He takes several more crackling draws on his pipe and lays it down.

"May is Lettitia's cousin. I remember thinking how capable she was. That's what attracted me. She could keep everyone moving in the same direction without upsetting anyone. A pure diplomat. She was helping Letitia deal with the chaos of relatives, calmly keeping everything running—well, you can see how she is here in this house—and to this day I've never seen her upset. It was so different in my family. I'll blow up but she looks at me as if I've lost my mind. After the wedding, Nigel goes off on his honeymoon and we have a couple of beers in the local pub. We're planning our leaves before joining the squadron at Leaton. Donny wants to go to London and talks George into it. Not that George needed much encouragement. He'd show off at the drop of a hat. Used to talk about getting back to Australia and having a dog's eye with dead horse. Apparently that was a meat pie with sauce. Tad had been invited to spend some time with a family up north. Billy said he'd promised to go back to his family in York. When I said I was going to stay around the village, I took flak about losing my head over a girl I'd just met. But she was the one decent thing I'd found. I remember Jimmy not saying anything about where he was off to until someone asked him directly. Then he said he was going back down to where he trained on the Coast."

"Back to Cornwall?"

"I don't think so."

"Did he say why?"

"I had a talk with him once. He'd been in the bombing in London so he knew something of what I'd been through. He knew that dreadful feeling when your home is shoveled out of the street. He told me that he'd also lost family in the bombing. That final leave before going to the squadron told you about priorities. Some were going to London for the excitement; others were going to family or girlfriends. Jimmy was plain mysterious. He said he was going to the coast but not why."

"Tommy, if I may ask, I don't get the sense that you felt close to them. Why did Jimmy choose to talk with you about losing his home when he didn't tell the others?"

"I think it may have been someone to talk to who'd been through something similar."

Barbara feels perplexed. Why would he trust Tommy when there was Nigel he could talk to? Or even Tad and Donny? She offers a bland comment in the hope that Tommy will explain more.

"Everyone says he was a private man."

"Yes and no. Nigel and Jimmy would talk when things were quiet. But it was usually noisy in the mess. I remember Billy going around the room jumping from one armchair to another. The point was not to let his feet touch the ground. Then Billy and George liked a game called Tank. There were bruises and damage bills after that one. I didn't care to get involved. I always suspected that Nigel had turned down a commission in order to be with his crew. He might have done better if he'd taken it. But it was awkward. Tad was an officer and he had to sleep in the officer's quarters. Couldn't come into the sergeants' mess. So, yes, Jimmy didn't talk all that much about himself. But, as I said, he spoke to me about the bombing in London, and I know that he'd talk with Nigel although I have no idea what they talked about."

"You didn't feel a close friendship with them, then?"

"As I said, each seemed to have something in common that I didn't share."

The office door opens and May peeps in.

"Sorry, Love, but the children would like to say hello if that's all right?"

"Oh why not?" Tommy says. "Do you think while that's happening we could get some more hot water?"

"Of course."

May opens up the door to reveal two boys and a girl. The boys are dark haired and the middle one, the girl, is blonde. The children are fiddly but curious. May introduces them.

"This is Philip. He's eleven. Letitia is nine. And then the youngest, Christopher is six."

Barbara smiles back at the children and introduces herself. They stare at her with wide eyes.

"Are you a famous actress in London?" Philip asks her.

"Well, I'm on the stage," she replies, "but maybe not so famous."

"Were you in Peter Pan?" Letitia asks. "We saw that."

"No," Barbara admits. "I don't think you'd like my show anywhere near as well."

"All right now," May says, "you've met her, so you all be off before Hans chews up the back door again." She smiles at her husband. "More hot water in half a tick."

"You were a prisoner of war, weren't you?"

Barbara wants to keep him engaged with the past.

"I was in a stalag in Czechoslovakia. The others were sent to different stalags. We were finally released by the Russians but not until after the Germans had marched us from camp to camp through the snow."

"You must have been relieved to hear the war was over."

"To be honest about it, I was numb. I remember feeling oh the war is over, now what? May had written to me over the two years I was in the stalag, and she had become the major focus of my life. I knew I would have to prove to her family that I could support her decently. No one was going to look at me as a son-in-law unless I had money. So when I heard it was all done in Europe I wanted to get home and get started building a life she'd want to share. That and get a bath and enough to eat for a change. Last thing I wanted to do was dwell on what we'd been through."

"Building a life must have seemed an overwhelming prospect with the country in ruins."

"I knew it wasn't going to be easy. All at once, you had four million people demobbed and looking for jobs. There wasn't much waiting for us. In fact, the first years after the war were worse than the war itself. Food was still rationed. There was no money to rebuild. The men returned to no jobs and a housing shortage. We'd supposedly won the war, but it was Europe getting all the help. There were unrest and strikes. Many emigrated to Australia and Canada. I might have done that too but there was May to think about. It took me many years to get financially stable enough to ask her to marry me. So we were late getting started with the family. It didn't take much to realize that there was going to be a big demand for rebuilding bomb damage once the money became available. I got a job in a bank and made connections with financiers interested in investing."

The hot water arrives, and this time May sits down with them. "It's stopped raining so the children have gone off to feed the chickens. I thought I'd have a cup of tea with you."

"I was telling her about how we met."

"Letitia's wedding!" May laughs out loud. "That was an experience. I think John Broadbent, that was Nigel's father, was taken aback with the bustle in the house. We'd never met him before, although Letitia might have. You'd have to ask her. Letitia asked me to keep an eye on him, as she wanted to make a good impression. I kept trying to introduce him to people, but he didn't seem up to it. Then in all the commotion I forgot about him until Letitia asked me where he is. Couldn't find him anywhere. Then I looked out into the garden and there he was sitting ramrod straight under a tree. 'Won't you come in for the toast?' I go out and ask him. And he does so reluctantly."

"Does Letitia still live in the country?"

"London. She married a doctor about five years after the war and he adopted the little boy."

"That was Nigel's son?"

May glances at Tommy. "Didn't you tell her what happened?"

"I was getting to it. Now that makes two of you. Billy phoned earlier to make sure I told her about the prang. That's RAF for crash."

"Good for Billy," May says.

Tommy looks at Barbara as if he is measuring how much he should tell her. Go on, she wants to tell him. She needs to know.

"Billy told me that you wanted to know why your dad and Nigel didn't get out."

"Yes, it's played on my mind ever since I heard about it."

"It all happened very quickly. That's what I remember. We were on fire and Nigel said to bale out. We'd practiced getting out quickly so we automatically knew what to do. But I ran into a problem. The aircraft was pitching and I couldn't get the entrance hatch open. That meant I had to go out the front. I was thrown around and there were two spars I had to get over. I kept banging against things and fell over. I was afraid I was going to get hung up because there were things sticking out everywhere. I practically threw myself over the front spar and pushed past the engineer's panel. George wasn't there so he'd already gone. I got to the top of the steps and looked over at Nigel. He pointed down and then gave me the thumbs up. Donny and Tad had gone. I assumed Billy went out of the rear turret. But I wasn't thinking about much except getting out. I lurched down and jumped out of the hatch."

"Did you see Jimmy at all?"

"I remember seeing something move as I went down. Jimmy must have been in his position. The way I remember that is because I wondered if he was trying to send a report back to Leaton. But I can't be sure. It all happened quickly. I really don't know."

"Did it seem that he could have got out?"

"I think I noticed that he had turned his seat around, so, yes, my impression was that he was ready to follow me. Except, of course, that he didn't."

Barbara sits in silence digesting this for a moment. It puzzles her. If he could get out, why didn't he?

"Could the aircraft could have stayed in the air?" she finally asks. She knows that crippled aircraft sometimes made it back to England even after most of the crew had baled out. There was even an occasion when everyone baled out except the rear gunner whose intercom hadn't been working. The aircraft landed itself and the rear gunner was stunned to find he was alone.

"I would have been surprised, although you could never tell with the Halifaxes. But I think the key is that Nigel wasn't able to keep it flying. He could, if anyone could. He got to be a good pilot in the end."

"The reason I asked," Barbara says as she touches the rim of her tea cup reflectively, "is that I was wondering if Jimmy might have gone up to try to help Nigel."

"If he did that he was disobeying a direct order to bale out. I wouldn't have thought he was the type. He was someone who followed rules."

"All of them were decent men," May says quickly. "I think that's what struck me most about them. They made light of things. You didn't know what they were going through, but anyone could see the casualty lists. Nobody tried to hide the losses. Every night they flew, more of them were lost. I often wondered how Bomber Command could send them out night after night, knowing that many wouldn't come back."

"It was our job," Tommy says. "We signed up for it. Nobody wanted to be LMF, taken off flying for lack of moral fibre, which essentially meant cowardice in the RAF. It was a tough go, but it had to be done."

"Granny," Letitia calls from the hallway, "Christopher is trying to ride Hans."

"I'll be right there, Darling." May gets up to leave. "If I don't see you again, Barbara, it was good to meet you."

"We debated asking you to stay to tea," Tommy explains after May leaves. "But we came to the conclusion that it wouldn't be fair to you. Hope you don't think we're being inhospitable."

"Not at all," Barbara replies sincerely. "I have to be off. I've appreciated the time you've given me." She doesn't say, but the thought of Hans resting his head in her lap while she was sitting at the table was enough to put her off.

"Is there anything else you want to ask me?"

Barbara isn't sure, but it seems to her that Tommy looks slightly bored. She wonders if he would like to be rid of her and with her the past that she's been stirring up. She studies him for a second and wonders how to play a hunch. She isn't sure where she is going with it or whether it is real. Perhaps it was the hint in Billy's voice compounded now by Tommy's studied indifference. But her mind is racing with suspicion. She takes a deep breath before launching into the chasm of her doubts.

"I hope you will forgive me if I share some misgivings with you. I got the feeling that there was something Billy that didn't want to tell me. I'm groping in the dark here, but if you know what it is, I hope you would."

"It was a long time ago," he replies noncommittally. He seems to be implying that he has forgotten a lot of things.

But Barbara is not convinced by his suggestion that he has forgotten. Not talked about the past admittedly, but that's different from forgetting. He seems to be a man who would not forget. He also seems to be someone who would not be likely to indulge in subterfuge even in friendship's name, particularly since he claims not to have felt that close to the rest of the crew. Barbara wants to proceed with delicacy. Who might he be protecting then? But as she watches him pick up his pipe and relight it, Barbara recognizes that Tommy is not a man of delicacy himself and would not appreciate anything other than directness. Since she has nothing to lose, she decides not to mince her words.

"Was Jimmy ever LMF?"

He can immediately sense the change in her approach and looks at her with some surprise. He answers her questions with the same directness.

"No."

"Did he get in trouble on the base?"

"No."

"Did he get into fights?"

"No. If that ever were to happen, it would be Billy. But it didn't."

"Did he steal?"

"No."

"Did he do something to be ashamed of?"

"No. I wouldn't say that."

"Then may I ask what it is?"

But Tommy is not to be budged so easily. He counters her persistent questions by turning the interrogation back to her.

"How much did your mother tell you about him?"

Barbara feels the gates begin to open. She realizes, if he does not, that they are negotiating how she will be told.

"Nothing more than who he was and how he died."

"Did she say anything about his having a family?"

"She said he lost them in the bombing before she met him."

Tommy takes a few moments to weigh Barbara's personality. He dislikes messy scenes, but this woman doesn't seem as if she would make one. He had thought that Billy was foolish to withhold the truth. It was bound to come out.

"He had a wife. I take it that it wasn't your mother."

"My mother said she'd died."

"Perhaps he wasn't completely forthcoming to your mother?"

Barbara blinks. Tommy taps out the ashes from his pipe and the smell of tobacco envelops the room. She sits in silence for several moments, feeling as she did when her mother first told her about Jimmy Baldock. Married? She has thought of him as being single. He couldn't have been married. He shouldn't have been married. Then her confusion turns into embarrassment. She cannot bring herself to look at Tommy. God, what must he be thinking? Is he enjoying this? Could he be lying? But then why would he?

Tommy is not enjoying her confusion, but he feels a satisfaction in removing her illusions. Billy should have told her. Then she could have made informed decisions about how far she wanted to go with this. She needs to face the truth even though it may be harsh.

"I suppose," he continues in an analytical tone, "you have to ask whether your mother was telling you the truth about his being your father. Or maybe you already have asked yourself that. On the other hand, lots of men had affairs. I suppose you could say it was everyone trying to live for the day."

Barbara's cheeks burn red. "Did you ever meet her?" she finally blurts out.

"None of us met her then. I don't know why."

"Then how do you know?"

He is not at all offended by her bluntness. He would have done the same in her position.

"Jimmy told me about her before the final Op. He asked me to keep an eye on her in case he didn't come back."

"Forgive me, but why you? You said you weren't close to him."

Barbara's lips tremble. She feels Tommy's judgement. And she can feel herself starting to resent him for it.

"Why not me? I was staying in England. The rest of them were headed back halfway around the world—if they survived. As it was, he'd told Nigel who then was killed. There was Billy and who'd tell him?"

"Is she alive, this wife?"

"I don't know. She remarried and lives in Wiltshire or used to. I haven't talked to her for a long time."

"You've spoken to her then?"

"Not for many years. I wrote her when I got back from the stalag. She's had a problem accepting that the rest of us got out and Jimmy didn't. She as much as accused me of shoving out past Jimmy and causing his death since I was the last one out. It didn't make me want to keep up with her. I didn't think it was worth the effort."

Barbara cannot bring herself to look at Tommy. She doubts that he has anything much more to offer that will not be unpleasant . She knows she needs time. She has to work things out.

"This is a lot to think about," she finally says quietly. "Perhaps I should leave now."

He does not seem surprised when she stands up.

"I'll send you a copy of the crew picture at the HCU if you still want it," he says.

He phones for the taxi and walks her to the door in silence. She has no interest in starting up another conversation with him. He seems satisfied now that he has given his version of the truth. There is nothing more to say.

"Thank you for your time" she says simply at the door. "And please say goodbye for me to May and the children."

As Barbara gets in the taxi, she does not look back.

At the railway station, she sits down heavily on a hard wooden bench to wait for the train. Through the dirty windows, the countryside looks sodden and slate grey. It reflects her mood, although she doesn't know how to feel. She can't be angry with Tommy. He told her at her own insistence. She was the one who wanted to open the door to the past, so it's her own fault in that respect. She gave no thought to what her search might involve. She painted a pretty picture in her mind of a doomed romance between her parents and then went about to prove it. She now feels hollow and deceived. She has been misled. She knows that now. Perhaps by everyone. How foolish and gullible has she looked? Is she now talked about with pity? But then she thinks about Billy. If he'd told her the truth in the first place, she would have stopped her search right there in his front room. He was on top of things. He knew. And he withheld the full accounting. She hears the train approaching and stands up. She knows it's Billy now who will have to deal with her.

17

Close Your Eyes and Imagine

Barbara goes to her flat after the meeting with Tommy and sits in Marilyn's chair where she burst into tears. On the train coming home, she wrestled with irrational surges of emotion. She is angry now with her mother. It was bad enough believing she had been abandoned by the man she thought her father. Now she has to face something worse: that the people around her don't even believe she is who her mother says. She can talk to herself all she wants about it being wartime, but her illusions have been dashed and she imagines a tawdry, adulterous affair. It keeps ringing in her mind: he was married. How could he? How could her mother?

The phone rings. Sheridan has been looking for her. He wants to know how it went with Tommy and whether she's coming over to his flat before they go to the theatre. She cherishes the warmth of his voice, and he can sense that something's wrong.

"I'll tell you all about it when I get there." She tries to sound bright and in control. "I'm all right. Really. I have to make a phone call."

He sounds worried and tells her not to be long.

She revels for a moment in the fact there is someone concerned about her. They've been virtually living together since Maggie's party although she's kept her own flat for the time being.

"Welcome to my world," Sheridan said the first time that the London gossip columns mentioned them in the same paragraph: "Seen around town: a much-married director and an award-winning actress. Any bets how long this one will last?"

"They'll move on to other things when we bore them to death," she said. "Besides, how do you get to be much-married?"

"I think they expect that we'll get married with the usual outcome," he said sardonically.

"Well, that remains to be seen," she replied without committing him to ask or her to accept. But they both know where their relationship is headed, even as they knew they would sleep together the night of Maggie's party. She knows what he's thinking without him having to say it. She's comfortable with him, and above all she trusts him.

She washes her face and puts on lipstick. Then she sits down and rings Billy's number. The repetitive bring-bring of the receiver makes her think for a moment that he's not home, but then he answers, sounding slightly out of breath. For a split second she debates the wisdom of what she's about to do, but she's committed herself to finding the truth and can't stop now.

"Billy, this is Barbara MacDonald. Do you have a moment?"

"Of course," he says, but his tone suggests that he knows that something's up.

"I think you know that I spoke with Tommy today."

"Was he able to help with your questions about escaping from the Halifax?" It's clear that he's hoping that's what she's calling about.

"Well, yes. But it's raised some other issues for me."

There is silence on the other end. He waits for her to continue. Barbara wonders if he dreads what might come next. She can't draw conclusions from his silence.

"Tommy says that Jimmy was seeing someone when he was at Leaton. Can you tell me anything about that?"

There is silence, but she intends to wait Billy out. He doesn't know exactly what she knows. A part of her feels awful about being so indirect. But another part relishes it. He didn't tell her himself, so now he can squirm.

"I didn't know anything about it."

There is both affirmation and evasion in his response. Barbara feels wickedly in control. It might be fun except for the deep hurt inside her. Billy may not have met this other woman at the time, but that doesn't diminish her significance. His short reply convinces her that there is more going on.

She plays her unpleasant trump card. "Tommy said that he was married to her."

A heavy sigh on the other end. He knows that he is beaten. He had hoped not to be in this position. He knew she would be angry if she found out. But he had so much hoped.

"I asked him not to say anything," Billy finally admits. "There was no need. But Tommy is who he is. And I suppose that if you were determined enough to go out to Canada to learn about him, you'd find out sooner or later."

"Did Donny and Tad know?"

"No. Only Tommy and Nigel. Tommy told me after the war was over. For some reason, Jimmy didn't want it widely known. Perhaps he thought it wasn't a good idea to have too many married men on a crew. We already had Nigel. But, who knows? Jimmy may have had other reasons. I don't know how to be more honest with you."

"Why did he tell Tommy?"

"Barbara, you've got to understand that this was a long time ago and it was wartime. Things happen then. I don't know that your father and Tommy were that close, or at least closer than the rest of us. I can't say more, but Jimmy must have had good reason to tell Nigel and Tommy and not to tell the others."

Now where is he going? She is not going to be put off. She waits for him to continue.

"Barbara, Tommy told me that Jimmy got married just before we joined the squadron. So it must have been after we were at the HCU. He told Tommy that he'd met her while he was in training with Coastal Command down on the south coast. That was before we made up the crew in Cornwall. He married her after Nigel's wedding and she never came up to Leaton. Jimmy seemed to want it that way."

"Then why did Tommy imply to me that Jimmy had been married for some time. At least while he was with my mother."

"As I said, Barbara, Tommy is who he is. He can be thoughtless. Some people are like that."

"But Jimmy didn't tell you all, did he? So how long had he been planning to get married?" Barbara's voice is sharp with the expectation of what she may hear next. Was he engaged to someone else when he was with her mother? What does that say about the man that had been described to her as honourable and steady? Has everyone been lying?

"I can't answer those questions, Barbara. He knew her before we crewed up, that's all I know."

Barbara's thoughts come in jumbled clutches. What can she live with? It's as basic as that. Can she live with the idea that this man made promises to different women that he had no intention of keeping? No. So how can she rationalize his actions? Donny told her not to. But she feels compelled to find some explanation. She realizes that she can live with idea that he was following his conscience and his sense of duty. That at least would allow her to maintain the picture of the man she has created in her mind. But if this is what she finds, then she must close the book with that picture intact and never again go back to open it.

"Was she pregnant?"

Her voice is stiff and she clutches the phone tightly. Why else would he have married her so quickly and so quietly?

This time Jimmy doesn't hesitate. "Yes, Barbara. I need to be honest with you. You have a sister or rather a half-sister."

"How old is she?"

"I'd have to go and check, Barbara. But does that matter?"

"Does she know about me?" Barbara recognizes the feeling. It is the same sick need to know that Marilyn felt when she was told about her cancer. When Marilyn talked to her doctor, she retreated into clinical professionalism. Barbara is doing the same thing. She imagines the worst. Is she now going to have to deal with someone who will accuse her of trying to steal her father? Barbara feels an irrational need to protect her parents, to feel responsible for them. She is defensive and angry.

"No. But then no one knew about you until a few months ago. I didn't see the point in calling her right away. We talk now and then about the crew because her mother wasn't able to. I don't think she's ready to hear something like this. She's idealistic about him. He was human, like the rest of us, and crews didn't come back. It was live for today and no one could blame us. Anybody who lived then wouldn't be upset or surprised. These things happened and they'd know what it was like. But I think she would be upset."

And I'm not? Barbara thinks. But she controls her composure and simply thanks him. She knows he didn't want to tell her. He must have thought he could keep both daughters from knowing. But when things are meant to be out in the world, they have a way of leaking through the barriers set up to contain them.

Barbara hangs up the phone and tries to sort things out. She feels exposed and vulnerable. Has her searching for this man made her ridiculous? Did Billy and Tommy pity her and secretly wonder when she was going to get what she deserved. Does her sister look like him too? Does she have the same blue eyes? But he belongs to someone else. That thought goes screaming through her mind. He isn't hers.

She takes the underground over to Sheridan's flat with her head still spinning. Just being in his neighbourhood helps to soothe her. She loves the view from his spacious flat. Long walls of glass overlook the rise and fall of the river's tides. The black and steel of the kitchen match the checkered tiles of the vestibule and the soft, deep carpet of the living room. Sheridan called in a professional decorator who used beiges and browns to set off an eclectic collection of paintings of London chosen without mind to period or style. Sheridan loves the city in all its ages and from all viewpoints. She settled into his home and felt it welcome her.

"What happened?" Sheridan asks when she uses her key. He's been waiting for her and kisses her as she steps in.

"Tommy was fine. He's got quite a place. He told me what he knew. But he also told me something else."

"Come and sit down," Sheridan says. "How about a sherry?"

"I could use one."

"So tell me what happened."

He hands her the glass and she takes a deep swallow of its musky sweetness.

"He was married."

"Who was married?"

"My father." She tries to keep her voice from becoming a wail.

"Start at the beginning, Babs, I'm having trouble following you." He pulls his chair around to look directly at her. She takes a deep breath and recounts the day.

"I got over to Tommy's and spoke with him and his wife, May. They apparently met at Nigel's wedding. Then Tommy told me about what happened at the Heavy Conversion Unit where he and the engineer were assigned to the crew. He doesn't know why Jimmy didn't get out of the aircraft. It seems as big a mystery to him and it does to me."

"All right," says Sheridan, "what's the part that's upset you?"

"Jimmy was married."

"Married to whom?"

"Someone he met in training. And there's another daughter."

"So you have sister?" Sheridan laughs with relief. "And you're upset about it? I think that's wonderful."

"But you don't understand." Now her voice has become a wail despite her best intentions. "She doesn't know about me and they don't want to tell her because they're afraid she'll be upset."

"Well, she will be if she's anything like you. You're upset aren't you?"

She looks at him in surprise. The idea that the daughters might be alike is uncharted territory. In fact the whole idea of a sister hasn't registered beyond the fact that it is a problem.

"Are you so sure that he was seeing them at the same time?" he asks.

She shakes her head. She's not sure of anything.

"Why don't we try to work this out? Do you know when he met her?"

"Billy said that he met her while he was being trained at Coastal Command. That would have to be in 1942 while he was training as a wireless operator."

"So when was that in relation to the forming of the crew?"
"It was before. He had to spend a year getting experience in a ground station."
"All right. So that was before the crew were formed."
"Yes."
"So what did he do after Coastal Command?"
"He went to the Operational Training unit at Cornwall."
"What happened there?"
"They formed up as a crew and learned to fly together."
"Cornwall was not where he was in Coastal Command, right?"
She nods.
"So," Sheridan continues trimphantly, "The crew did not meet this lady, whoever she is. They would have if she'd been in Cornwall. That's where he met your mother, right?"
She nods uncertainly.
"So your father and the woman, whoever she is—let's call her X—met and saw each other while your father was in the early part of his training. What do you know about his life before that?"
"He told my mother that his wife and father had been killed in the London bombing."
"So he's alone. He's lost his family. He's probably deeply shocked and vulnerable. He needs a friend. He meets a girl. They have a romance. Then he goes off to Cornwall to the Operational Training Unit. There he meets your mother and perhaps keeps in touch with X. Or perhaps not. But they're apart now and maybe he thought the relationship was over. You've said he wasn't given to talking about himself so he wouldn't have told his crew. How long was he in Cornwall?"
"About two months, I think."
"Where did he go after that?"
"They were posted to a conversion unit near York."
"So," Sheridan continues, "let's assume that X finds out that she's expecting a child and she writes to him. Give her a month or so to be sure and that could be about the time the crew were getting ready to leave Cornwall and you were already started. It's close but possible. By that time, as you say, the crew had been posted to York. Maybe he didn't have leave due him. In that case, he'd need to wait. Did he tell anyone where he was going?"
"They said he didn't tell them. After Nigel's wedding, he said something about going down to the coast. That was all they knew."
"Well, continue the thought," Sheridan says. "Jimmy, wanting to do his duty—that's what you said about him, right?—might want to head down to

marry X and give the child his name. Your mother was married and didn't want anything from him. He couldn't do anything much for you but he could for the other child. So what's so wrong about that? Seems to me the chap did all he could."

"That does make sense. But how would I ever know that it's true?"

"If my guess is right, she'll be a couple of months older than you. But I'm wondering, Babs, if any of that matters. He created a beautiful, generally level-headed daughter and I'm grateful to him."

She polishes off the sherry and manages a smile. Then she leans across to him and give him a lingering kiss. His moustache is damp.

"Now what was all the fuss about?" Sheridan asks.

"I suppose I had such high expectations that I didn't know how to deal with this."

"You were disappointed, Babs, but you'll have to admit that you also judged. Remember what Orffen says about that in the play?"

She nods and whispers her lines: "Our soul-serpent hisses the words I judge, and then turns to bite our hearts."

"I don't know what any of us would have done in wartime," Sheridan says. "I've been proud of how you've looked for your father. The first thing I ever noticed about you was your courage. You stood by your mother. You took on a difficult acting role and grew into it. Without the head wife, the play could have been bleak. You brought hope into all that blackness and you held your own with Maggie. Has she ever told you how proud she is of you? Then you remade yourself and came out of your shell. No one else I know would have gone out to Canada as you did. I'm sure your father would be proud of you as well. But you know, Babs, when you go digging into the past, you have to be ready to deal with what comes up."

"Wouldn't you if it had been your father?"

"I've got my own regrets," he says. "My father was in the army and was sent over to Asia. He was a prisoner of war, held by the Japanese. Things such as survival take precedence, and I think we need compassion when we look back on them. War changes things."

He reaches out and takes her hand. She feels a surge of love for him and hopes that her sister has the same type of companion to help her if she ever learns about Barbara.

"I wish I knew how to deal with it if she finds out and is angry," she says.

"She'll have to deal with the situation the same way you have. She'll have to deal with life as it is and not as she would like it to be. I imagine that she will be hurt and upset. That's only human. But I hope that over time you both can see that this is a tremendous gift he's left you."

"A gift?"

"He didn't have much life to share with you so he gave you each other. I think that's special."

"When I was in Canada, Donny and Tad told me not to judge the past. But you have to, don't you? If you're to learn from it?"

He leans toward her and lays his hand on her arm. "You can judge the reasons and the motives. You can ask who's been hurt. That's where the learning comes from. But that's also the limit of it." He sits back in his chair. "So who's been hurt here?"

"Me. My sister and her mother, if they knew."

"Intentionally?"

She searches for a response to his question but cannot find one. There was no premeditated desire to hurt. She understands that the universe does not require her judgement, only her acceptance.

"No," she finally admits.

"Then what you are dealing with is thoughtlessness. Last time I looked, that was not a crime."

"Sheridan," she says playfully, "what has made you so wise?"

He looks at her sadly. "I had to learn compassion the same way as everyone else. It comes through experience. When my father came home from the war he was unpredictable. We were afraid of him. I didn't know him at all. I'd been born after he left, so he came back a stranger. I stayed away from him as much as I could as I was growing up. I once told my mother not to tell him when I was in a school play because I thought he'd come and embarrass me. I suppose he cared. He had a funny way of showing it. I remember one time he tried to put his arm around me. He was awkward about it and I pulled away. Maybe I contributed to his depresssion. I don't know. But then there was his drinking. After we'd gone to bed, we'd hear our mother talking softly to him, calming him. She loved him despite it all. He had a suitcase under the bed that we were forbidden to touch. After he died, we opened it up and found his military records.

He'd been in a prison camp up on the border between Burma and Thailand. Do you remember the Alec Guiness film, *The Bridge on the River Kwai*? That's where he was. It was mosquito infested. They were starving and beaten. Everyone was sick with dysentery or cholera or malaria and God knows what else. They died by the scores. I went over to Bangkok a few years ago and took a tour up there to get a sense of it. There's a museum and memorial. The Australians had suffered staggering losses there. I came away with a much greater understanding about what he'd been through. But by then he was dead and I couldn't ask him anything. There's not a day that I regret not sitting down with him. If I hadn't been so quick to dismiss him, I might have understood who he was and what he had been through."

"But you couldn't know."

She thinks for a moment about what it must have been like for her father in the dark pitching plane, with the flak pounding the fuselage, and the cannon shells from the night fighter shredding the controls. So who did he hurt if he found friendship and warmth? From Sheridan's perspective, she would have to say no one.

"He was my father and it was my business to know. The families had sent messages to be displayed in that museum. I remember one distinctly. It was from the family of a teenage boy. 'He was a good lad,' his father had written, 'we miss him.' I think that we owe it to the older generations to try to understand before we judge. You've got a chance here that I didn't. Don't waste it."

"Donny said they were ordinary people asked to do extraordinary things."

"He's right."

"But it's still a mess."

"Babs, close your eyes for a moment and put yourself in his place. Go on. Close your eyes."

She sits back in the chair and does as he asks.

"Now picture yourself at the squadron. What do you remember about this woman you were with in Cornwall."

"She was married, she had a sick child, she was a nurse, she worked in a hotel. I saw her there when I was in training. I was lonely. We enjoyed each other's company. We used to spend time together talking, but it was a friendship. Then one day she told me her son was dead and she wanted to have another child right away."

"All right," Sheridan says. "Keep going. Did you think there was a future to the relationship?"

"No. She was taking care of her mother. She was going to move away. I wasn't sure she would even tell me when she had the baby."

Her eyes are wide open now and she is staring at Sheridan.

"Keep going," he says.

"There's no future. Even if she tries to tell me when the child is born, I could already be dead, or I could be dead the next day. There's nothing I can do. I have the knowledge that perhaps I've left a part of me behind to show I lived. Maybe if she has the baby and maybe if I'm alive I'll hear because I gave her my squadron address. But I as well may never hear. And when her husband comes back, if he does, he may well demand that the child be his. I don't have the time to wait to see how things turn out."

"Now," Sheridan continues, "let's say you knew someone from before. Someone who wasn't married and doesn't have the baggage the other woman did. She's about your age and a nice young woman because why would you bother with someone who wasn't nice? You liked her but thought that the romance was over, that maybe it wasn't fair to her to get married when you could be killed the next day. You thought you were free and the break had been clean. Then let's say she contacts you to say she's found out she's pregnant."

"There's no question. I'd marry her to give the child a name. Why wouldn't I? This is one child I can officially acknowledge. Maybe I can feel that I have a had chance at life. It's something to look forward to. I have to trust the other woman to take care of her child. I can do something about this one."

Sheridan smiles. "Keep going. What is your day-to-day life like in the air force?"

"Very uncertain. Aircraft don't come back. People get killed. You never know what's going to happen. You can't worry about tomorrow."

"So are you still angry?" Sheridan tilts his head appraisingly and looks at her.

She shakes her head in return.

"He couldn't afford the time to wait and see what happened."

She gets up from her chair and pulls Sheridan to his feet to hold him close.

"If it's not true," she whispers, "can we just pretend it is?"

He strokes her hair and nuzzles her cheek. He feels her tremble.

"If that will make you happy."

"Have I told you that you're wonderful?" she whispers and looks up into his face.

"Not nearly enough," he replies and kisses her gently on the cheek.

18
The Game of Tank, August 1943

Jimmy kept looking at his watch and looking out at the entrance gate. The crew had reported to the squadron all except for Nigel. Jimmy arrived before lunch, Tad and the others came in before supper. The hours kept ticking down, but no sign of Nigel. Jimmy knew that he and Lettuce had planned a few days in the Lake Country for their honeymoon and then were going to Tunbridge to see his father. Nigel had wanted Jimmy to come with them to Tunbridge.

"Not on your life," Jimmy'd said. "Honeymooners don't need company."

Jimmy remembered the precious two days when he and Rose had slipped away for theirs. They'd left his dad to mind the flat. The landlady said she'd look in on him. But his dad didn't like that idea. He said that the woman had designs on him. Jimmy knew he'd have come along if they'd asked. But Jimmy didn't want his dad tapping on their bedroom door in the middle of the night to inquire plaintively if they were all right because he'd heard strange noises. He did that enough after Jimmy and Rose got back. His dad didn't sleep much. He prowled about at night in his carpet slippers and tattered tartan dressing gown. Jimmy wondered if his dad had was looking for his dead wife.

"It's my dad that I'm worried about," Nigel said. "He's been acting strangely even for him."

Nigel seemed to be almost begging him to come. But Jimmy said he had other things he had to do and couldn't be persuaded. He hadn't liked Nigel's father and couldn't see spending more time with him. He hoped for Nigel's sake that the old man would not start up again on the subject of comparative honour between fighter and bomber squadrons. It wasn't fair and he knew that Nigel would be upset. Jimmy drifted off to sleep, hoping that Nigel was all right. When he woke, Nigel still wasn't there and didn't show up until after breakfast. Jimmy came back from the mess to find him sitting on the edge of an empty bed with his head in his hands and his kit on the floor beside him. His face was grey and he looked rumpled and unhappy.

"Are you all right?" Jimmy asked.

"Had a pisser. Spent the night in the guardhouse. They said I should sleep there because I hadn't reported to the duty officer yet. I wasn't that bad when I got there, just looked a mess."

"But you don't drink that much," Jimmy said quietly, unsure of what else to offer. He could never remember Nigel drinking more than he did.

"Obviously," Nigel said. "Made a right charley of myself, because I couldn't do it right."

"How are you feeling?" Jimmy said foolishly.

"Like I deserve, I suppose. Feel like something threw me up. My tongue feels like felt. You've never been drunk, have you?"

Jimmy shook his head. "Can't say that I have."

"Tell me why again."

"If I drink more than one or two beers, it all lands on the floor. Usually I don't have the money for more."

"God," Nigel said as he rubbed his temples and closed his eyes, "I wish I'd vomited after a couple of drinks. Would have to be better than I feel now. Where's everyone?"

"In the mess having breakfast."

"I can't think of food right now. I need to wash up."

"I'd say so," Jimmy smiled. "You look like you fell in a ditch."

"Probably did at some point. I walked part way from York. Miracle I got here. No lights. No signposts. First time here. Wouldn't have made it if I hadn't hitched a ride."

"Why didn't you stay in York? There's a reception centre there at the station. You could have called here in the morning."

"I wanted to report here on time. More or less."

"We'd been worried about you. I began to think you might not make it."

"No fear. Wouldn't let you fellows down, would I? I wouldn't make you fly with another pilot. Oh God, we're not on Ops tonight are we?"

"I don't know," Jimmy replied honestly. "Nothing's been posted yet."

Nigel groaned again and his stomach made an ominous rumble.

"I'll need a night to get rid of this headache."

"You gonna be all right?" Jimmy persisted.

"Right as rain, Old Chap. As soon as I get some sleep."

"How was the honeymoon?"

Jimmy didn't know what else to say. It was best in his experience to change the subject and get on with it. In Nigel's position he wouldn't have appreciated someone trying to provide moral guidance. Jimmy didn't feel prepared to do that anyway.

"Splendid. Lettuce is a splendid girl so that's no surprise. We walked along the lakes and went on picnics. The war was far away. Never should have gone to Tunbridge, though."

The door banged open as the rest of the crew came back from the mess. They all stopped short when they saw Nigel and the condition of his uniform.

"My god," said George, "did Lettuce throw you out already?"

"This is what happens when you walk in the dark. Particularly if you're not seeing straight to begin with," Nigel explained.

"You?" said George in mock horror. "Now I'd expect it from Donny here. But not you. Keep this up and I'll have to give you lessons on how to hold your liquor, Mate."

"Yes," said Tommy. "By all means listen to George. You'll end up like a windsock at the end of the airfield."

"Now, you've done it. You've attacked Australia's honour. We know how to hold our liquor and can teach you Limeys a thing or two about it."

"I think we'll concede that one to you," Tommy said acidly. "Remember, you can always be replaced by a toothache."

George threw up his large hands in laughter. "Watch it Mate. Remember, I know where you live."

"I don't know, George," said Billy entering the fray for the first time. "I think Canada can give you a run for the money. I'd set Donny up against you any day."

"Nah," said George. "You're stirring. He's a piker, but."

"Hold on, chaps," said Nigel. "I'll award the prize to anyone who has a good cure for a hangover. My head feels like it's splitting."

"So what did you drink?" George asks. "Different remedies for different things. Take one hair of the dog that bit you."

"I hate to think about it. I dropped Lettuce and the car off at her home yesterday and then went to the pub down by her station. People stood me to drinks and I was feeling no pain by the time I caught the train to York. Then I walked around and stopped in at Betty's to see if I could get a lift. There were no taxis or a bus so I started walking from York to Leaton."

"You walked here in the dark with your kit? My hat's off to you, Mate. Maybe you Limeys are tougher than I've given you credit for."

"Not all the way. A lorry picked me up after a while and dropped me at a place called The Three Martyrs. Someone there gave me a lift. I don't know how far I walked. I think I left York about seven. I'm not sure. They said they wrote me in at the guard house about 2200."

"That was pretty good in the dark," Tommy pointed out.

"A couple of lorries passed me before the one that picked me up. They either didn't see me or thought I was a spy. But here I am."

"Anyone got aspirins for the man? You know, I cured some of my better hangovers by having another drink."

"George, if you drank anywhere near as much as you claim," Jimmy said, "you'd be a walking advertisement for pickled livers. You like to play the fool."

"Don't say that," George moaned, "or you'll ruin my reputation."

By teatime, Nigel was more or less recovered. They sat in the NAAFI and talked about their various leaves. Fortunately for Nigel, that night the squadron stood down. Donny and George described how they had been caught outside in an air raid in London and couldn't find a shelter. They had vivid descriptions of the city's smells and sounds as it was bombed. "A pair of fools," they said a warden called them when he spotted them. "But since you're here, you can pitch in."

Tommy smiled slightly when asked about his tennis game. "I lost," he admitted, "but there were biking and hiking and I could do those."

Tad said that he and Margie had walked around the moors and gone up to take a look at Hadrian's Wall.

Billy had gone home to see the family and said he'd learned that his girlfriend, Martha, had got a job in the Leaton NAAFI. "We'll be seeing her here, all right," he said. The others told him that he would have to behave himself. He didn't look convinced.

When asked, Jimmy said he'd gone down to take a look at where he was in training on the coast. "Nice place," he said, "except the beaches all had barbed wire and the piers had big sections out. I suppose that was to stop the Germans from tying up alongside and unloading troops."

"What did you do there?" George asked. He expected to hear about bars and girls.

"I walked for the most part," Jimmy said. "Did a lot of walking."

George looked disappointed. "Gotta do better than that, Mate. Don't you know there's a war on?"

Next day, they were on the battle order and the guessing game began about where they would be going. Nigel seemed to be taking things well, considering that he had been given a good dressing down for reporting to his squadron in unprofessional condition. A black eye for his crew, he was told and he abjectly apologized. But he hadn't been AWOL and had a good record so far, so this time etc. etc.

"What's the petrol load look like?" Nigel asked George.

"Maybe Holland or France," said George. "But I wouldn't take bets."

They weren't expecting to be sent into the Ruhr on their first Op. General knowledge said that new or "sprog" crews would be given milk runs for their first couple of Ops. That was to break them in. Once they had some Op time under their belts so to speak, the real stuff began. Many crews went down on that third one when the real fireworks began.

The general knowledge turned out to be right about new crews and milk runs. Nigel's crew was sent to France for the first two Ops and after that they got some time off. Nobody ventured outside Leaton this time. The Three Martyrs had a few rooms for rent and Letitia drove Nigel's car up and took one. She and Nigel were the hub that drew in the others. The crew had a favourite table in a dark corner near the fire. On an evening when the squadron stood down, the place was packed. Nellie, the owner, would sling out the beers, washing the glasses in water that was as dark as the walls, floors, and furniture. It was a wonder that no one got sick. Perhaps the combination of washing water and beer sanitized the glasses.

The evening before what was to be their third Op, the crew gathered as usual at the pub. It was crowded at the table since Letitia had come down from her room, Tad had brought Margie, and Billy had brought Martha. Things got off to a boisterous start but nobody else in the pub took notice. That was the good thing about Nellie. She liked aircrews. She said she would always have beer for them and the noise was simply a bonus.

"I hear you went down to London," Margie said to Donny.

It was the first time that the crew had brought their girls and she hadn't heard the stories.

"Me and George," Donny agreed.

"What was it like?"

"Headed for the Strand Palace and did some pub crawling," Donny said. "We saw some sights. Managed to get tickets to The Windmill. Even ran into some chaps I knew from home."

"And I hear you got caught outside in an air raid. That must have been an experience."

Donny furrowed his forehead and took a moment to reply. He glanced over at George. But George looked studiedly at the glass in front of him.

"Yes, we got caught in a raid." Donny didn't seem inclined to go much further but then started up again. "We kept looking for a shelter but it was hard to find one in the dark and we finally stumbled into a boarded up shop front. Wasn't much we could do. A bomb fell somewhere near and a wall across the road fell down. We could see our way clear then because of the flames. A couple more bombs fell a little further away."

Donny looked over at George, but the Australian was being uncharacteristically quiet.

"And you stayed there?" Margie persisted.

"We decided it wasn't a good place to be because things kept exploding and sending glass all around, so we got out of the shop front and ran down the road. The All Clear hadn't sounded and the smoke was choking. I remember that we covered our heads with our arms, or at least I did. No idea where we were running. Finally we stopped when a warden yelled at us. There'd been a direct hit on a shelter he said. They needed help bringing out the wounded and the bodies. That's where we spent the rest of the night."

Donny didn't continue and George remained silent. Tommy broke the silence.

"I wonder where our bombs fall."

"Probably a mile from the target and right in the middle of a pasture," George said. "French cows are not giving milk on account of us."

"As the bomb aimer, that's not on my account," Tad said indignantly.

Tommy looked unimpressed. "How do you know where they fall? One crater's the same as another unless you're on the ground."

Conversation ceased at Tommy's comment. Everyone remembered that Tommy's home was now one of a series of craters stretching across London. Jimmy looked uncomfortable as well. He was remembering the terrible walk along his bombed-out street.

Nigel saw the danger quickly. What could follow would either be futile justifications based on who had started what, or a creeping depression. The job had to be done. The job was theirs. The subject should not have been broached. There was an unspoken agreement not to talk about consequence and meaning. The conversation must be changed.

"Billy, did you tell Martha what happened the last time you played Tank?" he asked.

The air lightened and George picked up the invitation to create a diversion. "The time we all had to chip in for the damage?"

"What's Tank?" Lettuce asked.

"Nigel didn't tell you?" Donny said with amazement. "It's like a child's game, if you can call it a game, that gets played in the sergeant's mess. It's like sooty feet on the ceiling, something to let off some steam. Billy, you're the one who does this insane thing the most, so you explain it."

"It's something like rugby," Billy said. "Except the goals are beer glasses." Billy glanced at Martha and seemed disinclined to go further.

"All right," said Donny, "you have to picture this. The room divides into A flight and B flight and they pile their empties up in layers on a table on each side. When they're piled high enough, those are the goals. The idea is to knock down the opponents' pile. But the player allowed to knock the glasses off sits on the shoulders of the team. So you're trying to knock the other scorer down as well as get your own person over to the other side's table. Billy is the scorer for B flight because he's the smallest."

"As you can imagine," Tommy said drily, "furniture and glasses get broken and the damage gets put on the bills of everyone there."

"Does anyone get hurt?" Martha asked.

"Cuts and bruises," George explained. "No one wants a replacement crew member so there's just shoving and pushing. This game is almost reserved for when an Op has been cancelled last minute and there's energy to let off. It's something like bombing. Get to the target, do some damage, and get home safe."

"Do the rest of you play this?" Letitia asked.

"I did it once," George said. "Don't think anyone else here has. Made me think of Australia Rules football back home, but it wasn't the same. No motive to kill like there is when we play the Kiwis."

"Then it's not rough enough?" Martha wasn't sure how she felt about Billy's pranks. But didn't he know that now she worked at the NAAFI she was bound to hear the stories? She'd been among the first to hear about the night that Nigel spent in the guardhouse.

George laughed again. Laughter was George's defiance of life. If you could laugh, you could survive anything.

A man wearing the double pilot wings and carrying beers passed by their table. His crew was set up on the other side of the fireplace and making their own noise. Nigel nodded at him as he passed.

"Member of another crew," Nigel explained to Lettuce.

Lettuce looked around the table. "Have you met many of the other crews in the squadron?"

"Not many," Donny replied. "I've spoken to some of the other navigators when we're briefed. But it's mainly this gang I see. God help me."

"And don't think we don't have to put with you," George threw back at him. "Anyone tell you that you snore like an express train?"

"No I don't."

"Too right you do. I have to put a pillow over my head to get some sleep."

"I'll back George up with that one," Jimmy laughed. "You sound like an express train."

"Woo woo," said Donny.

The table broke out in laughter.

"No," said George, "it more like achoo hiss, achoo hiss."

"But that's a steam engine," replied Donny. "Surely I'm a diesel."

George stood up at the end of the table and spread out his arms. "We don't have diesels in Australia so let's stick to aircraft. Aircrew ought to go roar, roar." He waved his arms up and down imitating the banking of an aircraft.

"Nah," yelled Tad. "That's the Lancs that do that."

The crew at the other table erupted in laughter and there was scattered applause in the room. George turned round and bowed. "This feels almost as good as getting back from an Op," he said.

"Good for you, but how am I going to sleep after being insulted like this?" Donny tried to sound indignant.

"It's all right, Mate," George replied, "You're not the only one. There are a few others I could name. The place sounds like a farm at night."

Nigel leaned back to put his arm around his wife. He knew where he preferred to sleep and came to The Three Martyrs whenever he could.

"Wouldn't know about that," Tad said.

"I bet you wouldn't," Donny said, "over there in the rarified air of the officers' quarters."

"Officers snore and need showers like anyone else."

"Never mind the snores," Nigel interrupted, "We're celebrating tonight. It's our anniversary. Lettuce and I have been married for four weeks."

"Congratulations, Skipper and Lettuce. We wish you many more." Tad raised his glass amidst the hear-hears from the rest of the crew. "And how is married life? Should the rest of us jump in?" Tad gave a sidelong smile at Margie.

"Highly recommended," Nigel laughed. "As long as it's with Lettuce. But that's too bad for you because she's taken."

"Well," said Tad, "Donny's got his Noreen. Billy has Martha here. Tommy has—well, who does Tommy have?" Tad looked expectantly at Tommy who had been sitting quietly at the other end of the table.

"Her name is May," Tommy said. He had decided to ask May up for the next time they had time off. Usually he slipped off to see her on his own. But he's feeling more secure with her and it is time. He's even put her into his records to be notified if anything happens to him. "So Tommy has May," Tad continued. "I have Margie—at least I hope I do. And that leaves George and Jimmy. Why are you on your own tonight?"

"The night's not over, Mate," George said.

Jimmy smiled and said nothing.

"Didn't you meet someone down at Cornwall?" Donny asked Jimmy. "Down at the hotel?"

"Just someone to talk to," Jimmy said evasively. "That was it."

"But that's how it starts," George said with a great gust of laughter. "It's supposed to go somewhere from there, Mate."

"I didn't know you'd met someone," Nigel said. But that wasn't so surprising as Lettuce had come down to Cornwall and taken all his infrequent and precious off-duty time.

"I didn't. I'd go down to the hotel now and then when I was by myself. Mostly I was with you lot."

"George, how did you get to be with this lot?" Margie asked. "Australia seems such a long way away."

"It's that all right. And different from here, I have to say. For one thing we see the sun."

"Now you've got him started," Tommy groaned. "You're about to get the travel guide."

"You watch it," George said. "I told you I know where you live. So how did I get in with this lot, you asked."

"Blind luck if I say so," Nigel quipped. "Best crew in the squadron."

"Won't argue with you there," George said. "Dad had a farm up in Toowomba, but I was mad for engines. Motorcycles were it as far as I was concerned. Bit like Jimmy here and his cars. I wasn't much for school. Soon as I could, I got out and started working for a garage. Then the war came. Off I went to join the RAAF. They took me but said I should train as ground crew because I knew about engines. First year over here, I was an erk. Then the Halifaxes came and they needed flight engineers. I asked if I could qualify and got sent to Wales for training. And so here I am. I haven't met another Australian engineer since I've been here, so you could say I'm unique."

"No one would say anything else about you," Donny said.

"I'll take that as a compliment, Mate."

"Drink up, chaps, getting to be time," Nellie called out from the bar.

After the women had gone home and the crew had driven erratically back to the base, Nigel came over to Jimmy and asked if they could talk. There was nowhere to be alone, so they walked out and sat in Nigel's car. It was chilly, but Jimmy didn't complain. He waited for Nigel to tell him whatever it was.

"You never asked me about the night I slept in the guard house," Nigel said slowly.

"It wasn't my business." Jimmy had learned some time ago not to ask about things unless he was willing to deal with what he was told. He'd kept that as a principle for his life. Ask about things, and you may have to deal with them.

"I'd like to tell you."

"There's no need," Jimmy began.

"No, I want to tell you. You're my friend. I need to tell someone. And I want to ask you for something."

Jimmy waited quietly. He didn't need confidences but he wouldn't avoid a sincere request. That was the Baldock motto: "We stand Firm." Problem was, his dad used to say, that when it translates into the Baldock women they are stubborn as hell.

"Day before the wedding, Dad got a telegram about my brother. It said he was missing. Plane gone down in the channel. Dad kept expecting to get a call. Hello, everyone, they picked me up I'm safe. But it didn't come. He told me that Peter couldn't make it. I didn't hear he was missing until Lettuce and I got to Tunbridge. Dad tells me with this accusing look that said how could you be so happy with your brother missing, except that I hadn't known. After that we sat around the house looking at one another. No one knew what to say or how to act. Dad sat staring out into the garden. After a while, he got out the photo albums and started looking at old pictures. That's when I knew he'd given up. Don't you worry, I tried to tell him. There's still hope. But he looked through me with dead eyes. The day we left, he got the letter from my brother's Squadron Wing Commander. It was the usual. Great chap, well liked, will be missed. The things they always say. And he was listed as presumed dead. I went up to my dad and tried to put my arm round him. The look he gave me told me he had lost the only person who mattered. We packed up our bags and we left. Then I drove Lettuce home and I came on up here."

"Did he say anything to you about it?" Jimmy asked.

Jimmy could imagine the joy he would have felt to see Rose or his dad. He wouldn't have asked questions. But then Jimmy had not liked the cold, upright man he had met at the wedding.

"Not much," Nigel replied. "Not anything I could help with."

"Forgive me if you don't want to say," Jimmy said hesitantly, "but what made you want to get drunk?"

Nigel stared moodily through the car window. He shrugged his shoulders as if he had been asked to spell an easy word that he had somehow forgotten. When he spoke, his voice was modulated levelly as if he was determined to project a calm indifference. But his body was tense and in the moonlight, Jimmy could see that the hand Nigel had rested on the steering wheel was trembling.

"My father told me that it should have been me."

Jimmy sat for a moment considering those cruel words. He hadn't liked the man. But perhaps it was that he was dealing with loss of his older son. Perhaps that might explain some of it. That had to be it. No one could be that callous. Surely the man would come round in time.

"People say things that they regret later."

"Wish I had your faith in people, Old Chap." Nigel removed his hand from the steering wheel and thrust it into his jacket pocket. "I've always envied your ability to handle things. You don't let things boil inside you."

"I wish that was true."

"Well, I've never seen it. If I were in trouble, you're the one I would want with me."

"Nigel, there's something I haven't told you that I'd like to tell someone."

"Shoot, Old Chap."

Jimmy considered for a moment the additional burden he was placing on Nigel after what he had just heard. But there was no one else he could trust.

"When I went down to the coast, I didn't tell you where I was going. But I went there to get married. I didn't want to say anything for a number of reasons. And I don't want the crew to know yet. Her name is Ann and she's expecting a child."

"Well, that's good news, isn't it? I'd have thought so. I hope Lettuce gets pregnant."

"Ann is a good kid. She doesn't have family like Lettuce does. I told her to stay down there so she'd have help. Her parents are there."

"That sounds like a good thing," Nigel agreed.

"But I'm worried that if something happens to me, I'd like to be sure she's all right. That the child's all right. So I wanted to ask if you'd be willing to keep an eye on her if I don't make it back."

"I'd be delighted, and I hope you'll do the same for me. I can't ask my dad. That's what I was going to ask you. If I don't get back, would you see that Lettuce is all right?"

"I'd be glad to. But remember what we said at Oxford? We're going to make it."

"Yes, Old Man. You're not going to do anything ridiculously noble, and I'm going to believe that this all makes sense."

Jimmy smiled. Oxford seemed another lifetime. In those dreadful months of basic training in Blackpool when he had to deal with the finality of his loss, it was Nigel's friendship that broke through his numbness. He'd felt included when Nigel said he'd met a super girl and rattled on about her. But then Nigel left and Jimmy went to wireless school and then to Coastal Command. He'd met Ann when he was down there on the coast. He saw her in a canteen and was startled because she looked like Rose. She wore her hair in the same tight little curls around her ears and when she smiled her face broke into dimples like Rose's. He kept looking at her until she noticed him. Then she asked his name and chatted brightly about inconsequential things. She liked the cinema. She liked to walk on the Downs. After a number of times when he said nothing, she asked him if he'd take her to a dance. And so they began a friendship. He took her out for long walks or, when the weather got cold, to the cinema. They sat and talked. She was eighteen. She lived at home and wanted to be a teacher. He was happy for her company, but he never touched her. If she was surprised, she never said. But one night when he took her home, she turned on the doorstep and kissed him. He knew he was going to Cornwall to an Operational Training Unit by then and didn't want to mislead her. But one evening when her parents were gone out, he made love to her. It was the first time he'd touched a woman since Rose's death. He gave her his address when she saw him off at the station. It was there that she told him that she loved him. He kissed her on the cheek and fought down his guilty feelings. In his heart he felt he had been unfaithful to his Rose.

"Ann's very young," Jimmy said slowly. "She'll have to stop work in a while. But she'll have the allowance from my pay, so she should be all right if anything happens."

"Can I make a suggestion though," Nigel said thoughtfully. "I'd tell someone else on the crew so you've got double coverage, so to speak. Pilots are like sea captains, they tend to go down with the ship."

"Who would you suggest?" Jimmy recognized the wisdom of what Nigel was proposing, but he was doubtful about whom to ask.

"Well, George is going back to Australia and Tad and Donny to Canada, so they aren't going to be able to do it. That leaves Billy and Tommy."

"Not Billy. I think he's too young to understand. Maybe Tommy. I never said before, but I was bombed out like him. The night that I came back from Oxford when we were tested. I feel bad about not telling you. You're the best friend I've ever had. But I couldn't bring myself to talk about it. At first, it didn't seem real. Then it was too hard."

"I'm so sorry to hear that," Nigel replied. "I had no idea. But I understand."

"I lost my dad and my wife, Rose, and the baby she was expecting. It leveled the house. There was nothing left. That's why I want to take care of Ann."

Jimmy stared stolidly ahead. Now that he had told Nigel, he was amazed by what he'd done. Perhaps it was that he was ready to talk at last. Perhaps the memories were containing themselves into something he could deal with. But he could not talk about anything further. Not about Marilyn. He was not sure even how to think about that. Now that he had told Nigel about Rose and his father, something inside him started to break free. He found himself experiencing again the awful smells and heat of the flames of his bombed house, and the horror of the emptiness that he had tried for so long to keep hidden. He felt his eyes begin to sting. He tried to control his feelings but now the door was open. As he sat next to Nigel, he felt the tears roll unchecked down his cheek and onto the dark blue of his uniform.

19
Ordinary Men Doing Extraordinary Things, September 1943

They filed into the Nissen hut that the squadron used as the briefing room. Tables were set in rows across the room with the numbers of the aircrew attached to them. In front was the raised stage where the section leaders would give their briefing. The room was a buzz of conversation and scraping chairs. The air quickly became thick from the cigarette smoke curling up to the arched ceiling and hot from the press of bodies.

Everyone was tense but dealing with it in his own way. Some were lounging in their chairs, giving the impression, or at least trying to, of nonchalance. These were the crews who had completed six or more Operations. The senior crews were the most nervous. They were the survivors who were close to completing their tour and being sent down for six months' rest. They hadn't thought about their chances before because it all seemed too remote. Now that it was within reach, they had something to lose. Newer crews looked slightly dazed. Squadron talk said that if you survived the first three Ops, you were good for seven more.

The navigators and bomb aimers had been briefed before and were carefully making marks on a set of navigation maps laid out on the tables in front of them. They did not look up. The others were left to their own thoughts until the larger briefing started. Nigel watched the coils of cigarette smoke merge on the ceiling. He was quelling the butterflies in his stomach. Billy fidgeted as usual. He drummed his fingers on the table, caught himself, and shrugged his shoulders. He had developed a spot on his face overnight and was trying not to scratch it. George sat back in his chair with his large hands clasped behind his head. He was among the tallest men in the squadron and was feeling glad as he always did that he'd be standing at his engineer's panel, not cramped into a gun turret. Jimmy was thinking about Ann. He'd received a letter from her. She had stopped being sick in the mornings and wanted to come up to Leaton. He couldn't think why she shouldn't except for his own previous reluctance. When he got back from this Op, he'd write her and tell her to come up. He hadn't heard from Marilyn and believed now that he wouldn't. He was married now. It was time to move on with his life. Tommy stared at the large covered map hanging from the ceiling at the front of the room. What was on the map had been the target of speculation all day. Once the cover was removed, they all would know where they were going. Sometimes the unveiling would be met with groans or not-agains from the crew who had not already had their sectional briefings, particularly if the target was somewhere in the Ruhr Valley, Happy Valley as it was called because of the intense flak and searchlights.

The crews stood to attention when the Wing Commander entered and were told to be seated when he reached the front. The crews respected the Wingco. He'd flown many Ops and knew what he was doing. He'd won the DFC for bringing back a crippled aircraft with only the wounded bomb aimer to help him. He was a distinguished looking man with a restrained Southern England voice. He knew both bombers and their crews. Given to few words by nature, he had a quietly dismissive attitude toward those who gave orders without the experience to back them up. He easily won loyalty because he supported his crews against the bullshit that came their way. On the other hand, it was also well known what he would do to crews who were what he called "bloody stupid." Until the order had come from HQ Bomber Command, High Wycombe, he flew the Ops himself. Somewhere along the line, Bomber Command got tired of losing commanders and restricted him.

"Good evening," the Wingco said and the men sat down. Then he went to the map and pulled the cover to one side. The crews leaned forward and carefully studied it. A black tape went in a zigzag rectangle with several turning points from Yorkshire east over the North Sea, down into Germany and then back over Holland.

"Hannover is our target for tonight," the Wingco said. But everyone could see the point furthest east where the line began to turn southwest back toward England.

"It's a combined effort," he continued. "4 group has 312 aircraft going including the Pathfinders. Your target is the industrial area where there has been considerable build up since we were last there. 958 Squadron will be on the first and second waves. H-hour is at 0200. The first wave is over target from 0200 to 0203. The attack will be in three waves of three minutes each for a total over the target of nine minutes. The second wave is from 0203 to 0206. Be sure to watch out for the other traffic about. 6 Group is sending a diversionary group to Essen. So be on the look out for them."

The Wingco then sat down and left the stage to the Intelligence Officer. The IO had a diffident, thoughtful air. Because of his grey-streaked dark hair, the crews called him the Badger after that most quintessential of British animals. It fitted him. Badgers were generally wary but capable of a good bare of the teeth when needed. He had been a teacher before the war, and he tended to speak to the men as he did to his prep school boys.

"A good show tonight will give German war production a bloody nose. We need to stop the factories from supplying parts. There's a residential area around the target so bombing accuracy is needed to get the job done. Beside the coastal flak batteries watch out for flak ships along the coast. We've had several reports about them. The main defences you'll deal with on the way to the target will be at Bremen but expect heavy flak and night fighters around Hannover as well. On the way back, you'll be passing near Osnabruck and Munster and both can be expected to put up some flak. Then there'll be usual coastal batteries between Amsterdam and Rotterdam."

The Meteorological Officer followed. He was a tall thin man with thick glasses and a perpetually harried look. If anything, he looked defensive, something like a cricket player with an alarming inability to protect his wicket. Indeed, the weather forecast would be met with sceptical humour. Most crews believed that they'd know the weather when they saw it. But, who knew, he might be right? Tad listened intently to this information. He needed to know whether he'd be able to see the target and whether the camera could record where the bombs fell. With 10/10 or full cloud cover, the bomb aimer had to align his bombsight on the Pathfinder "Wanganui" sky markers, over the reflected glow of the illuminated target area. Donny also needed to know the predicted wind direction and velocity since it affected navigation.

"There's a front about sixty miles west of the target area that should not be a factor by the time you get there. Winds are expected to pick up after midnight, which should push the cloud cover over to the east. For take-off, it should be broken cloud with visibility of about one to two miles and you can expect a tail wind of about 30-40 knots. Over the North Sea you should see broken cloud with tops about 10,000 feet and cloud bottoms at 6,000. Over the target, it's predicted to be 8/10 cloud. It should be clear for the way home with winds decreasing to 20-30 knots, with cloud over Yorkshire and visibility one to two miles. The freezing level is 3,000 feet. The temperature tonight will be minus 30-Fahrenheit degrees at 20,000 feet. There will be thin cloud up top, so visibility will be good once you are out of the clouds."

Some crews groaned. Good visibility meant they'd be silhouetted against the sky for the enemy night fighters.

The Navigation Leader came next. He was regular RAF and known to be no-nonsense. He was short and dark and had a tendency to avoid eye contact. He spoke in a clipped Welsh accent and very rapidly as his eyes slid away to the side. He used a pointer to follow the tape on the map.

"We will be taking off on runway 26 tonight. We'll be turning due east at 1000 feet. We'll open up as we cross the North Sea and rise to 18,000 feet."

His pointer traced their way across the sea, indicated the turn points, and then took them over the German coastline. He stabbed at the map where they could expect that things would not go down well with the enemy.

"Here we level off and cross the enemy coast. We turn to the southeast. Then we climb again and turn starboard to make a gentle descent into the target area for the level bomb run. Don't forget to stick to your bombing heights. We are among the lowest tonight."

A few more groans. In the congestion over the target area, higher aircraft could drop bombs on those flying below. Several Halifaxes had limped home with large holes through their fuselages. It was the Stirlings, though, that got the worse of it because they couldn't fly as high.

"After bombing, increase your speed to 180 and proceed southwest for the short leg before turning northwest. We will cross the enemy coast south of Amsterdam at 12,000 feet and hold that at the speed of 185 over the channel. Once over our coastline south of Great Yarmouth, we have a rapid descent to 8000 feet. We'll hold 8,000 feet straight up to York and then descend down to bases. As the Met Officer told you, you will probably have 8/10 over target. This should make more difficult for the searchlights but there will be night fighters about."

The Bombing Leader followed. Because his nose hooked prominently down to his chin, this was the first and perhaps the only thing that people noticed about him. But he had a cheerful outlook that suggested he would be equally at home in a lorry driving produce up to Covent Garden market or driving an express train through the night on its way up to Waverly Station. His eyes were shrewd and his face deeply lined. He was called Punch behind his back, from the Punch and Judy show.

"Don't forget to enter the time in the navigation log when you release the bombs. Drop any unreleased bombs live on Germany. If you have early return or hang-ups, jettison your bombs fifty miles from Flamborough Head. Enter the time in the engineer's log and look out for shipping. The Pathfinders will drop red and yellow markers tonight six minutes before H-Hour. The Master Bomber will advise you of the colours to aim for. Switch on your bombsights well before the target."

The Gunnery Leader ended out the briefing. He was a small, compact man, promoted to Flight Lieutenant for his capacity and competence. He was known to having shot down five enemy fighters and was well respected by the gunners.

"Keep your eyes peeled tonight," he said. "Remember that moonlight has a light and a dark side. Enemy fighters will come from the dark side. Remember also that enemy fighters can fire at you vertically. They are going to stay below and in back of you. Watch out also for any new form of aircraft or tactic. We want to know about it if you see anything."

Then it was time for the Wingco to give the pep talk before dispersing the crews.

"The lorries for your aircraft will leave at 2130. The first aircraft takes off at 2235. The raid opens at 0200 and you should be back in good time for breakfast. Remember to empty your pockets before you go out to your aircraft. And remember, all you give the enemy is your name, rank, and number. It's an important target for tonight. There are numerous factories there that can support the German war effort. Let's have a good, accurate run. See you in the morning."

Nigel's crew stood up with the others and went over to their lockers in the building. They were issued their escape packs and parachutes. They emptied their pockets and gave up their personal things for safekeeping in numbered drawstring bags. Then they milled around outside waiting for the pilots to complete their special briefing and for the lorries to take them to their aircraft.

"G for George, M for Mother," the driver of the aircrew lorry called.

The two crews climbed in and rode silently out to the aircraft. The M for Mother crew got off first. Nigel and the others got off at G for George. The ground crew was rolling out the starter trolley. Their sergeant came up to Nigel.

"All ready for inspection," the man said. He walked with Nigel around the aircraft while Nigel did his pilot's inspection of the tail, trim tabs, and wing flaps.

The crew threw in their parachute packs and sat on an empty bomb trolley.

"Looks good. Thank you, sergeant." Nigel signed off on the Form 700.

Tad came out from under the aircraft where he had been looking up into the bomb bay.

"One two-thousand pound and rest incendiaries," he told Nigel.

Donny lit the first of his two pre-flight cigarettes. Strictly no smoking in the aircraft because of the fuel. Tad lit one too. He was an occasional smoker who now and then cadged a smoke from Donny. Billy never had smoked. Without lighting up to distract him, he found it difficult to sit still. He kept running his hands across the soft stubble on his chin and fingering some adolescent bumps.

Jimmy was relaxed even though he'd stopped smoking some time ago. He said he didn't want to develop the habit. He was thinking for the future that it all costs money. "You'd better have some vice," George once chided him. "You've got to die of something, Mate. Might as well be happy."

Tommy smoked a pipe. He thought it made him look more sophisticated. He'd also started a moustache for the same reason. "Wormy straws," George called the effort. Tommy had got Nigel started on the pipe. He was trying, but he wasn't good at keeping it lit and all the tamping and tapping was frustrating him.

"Getting to be time," Nigel said as he saw the signal flare. They relieved themselves on the grass and climbed into the aircraft. Beneath them, the ground crews attached the trolley and the engines were ready to be started. Nigel went through his regular routine of checks. Then he used the intercom to contact the crew. They had each completed their own checks. The crewmembers not needed for take-off were in their positions. Tad came up from the nose and sat in the pull-down chair. They edged out onto the perimeter track and turned onto the runway.

The light flashed green. Nigel gripped the control column and released the brakes. The Halifax roared down the runway and rose into the sky. They turned in a slow turn to port on the first leg of the flight plan. Tad went down into the bomb aimer's position. Donny followed and snapped on the small light over his table. He set course from base as they flew over the airfield. Tommy and Billy went to their turrets.

"Navigator, confirm course please," asked Nigel.

"Course 101, 1000 feet. Speed 170."

"Roger, set course 101."

The aircraft climbed over Yorkshire, across Flamborough Head, and out over the dark North Sea. All navigational lamps were turned off.

"Rear Gunner. Request permission to test guns."

"Go ahead, Billy" Nigel replied.

The rattle of the four .303 machineguns from the rear didn't sound over the noise of the engines. The guns in the mid-upper turret were tested in turn.

"Skipper, prepare to alter course starboard onto 110, five minutes." Then "Starboard 110. Speed 160. Start to climb to bombing height."

"Eight thousand feet. Check oxygen," Nigel said to George. "I'll let you know when we reach ten thousand."

"Reporting variable winds of 30-40 knots over target," Jimmy broke in.

"Preparing to switch fuel tanks," George said after a few minutes.

Then they were over the enemy coast and could see faint flashes of guns and flak from the shore batteries reflected against the clouds. The cloud cover was thick enough that the ground batteries were having trouble finding the aircraft. None of the flak came close.

"Gunners. Keep your eyes peeled for night fighters."

"Roger, Skipper," both replied.

"Skipper, prepare to alter course starboard in five minutes." Then when the moment came "Turn now."

They were a hundred miles from the target when there was an explosion ahead. They watched as a flaming Hali spiraled down. Then another.

"Fighter. Corkscrew port. *Go!*"

Nigel rammed the aircraft into a twisting turn. Bullet holes tore through the aircraft's thin skin. The plane jumped. At first it seemed they might not have sustained serious damage, but then the port inner engine exploded into flames.

"Cutting fuel to the port inner." George said. He pressed the engine's fire extinguisher and feathered the propeller. "Still on fire," he said. "Fuel tank's ruptured."

"I'll dive to try to put it out." Nigel put the nose down and they rapidly dropped several thousand feet. The smell of the petrol seeped into the aircraft.

"Corkscrew starboard. *Go!*"

The night fighter was following them to assure itself of the kill.

Nigel threw the aircraft into another violent turning dive. The guns in both turrets rattled. The night fighter's cannon raked the aircraft again. This time the shells ripped open the side of the aircraft and blew out the perspex bubble over the upper turret. The starboard outer engine erupted into flames and the wing began a vibration that shook the entire aircraft. The Halifax wanted to plunge and began to lose altitude. Nigel fought the sluggish controls and released the bombs.

"We're done for. Bale out, bale out," he said abruptly. "I'll hold her level as long as I can. Good luck."

Donny clipped on his parachute and went out through the escape hatch in the floor at the foot of the steps. Tad followed him. George handed Nigel his parachute and went down the steps from the engineer's position and dropped out next. Billy swung his turret and kicked himself free. He fell backwards from the aircraft. After a few moments, Tommy stumbled down the steps next to Nigel and jumped. Nigel felt relieved. He assumed that everyone was out.

Down below Nigel, Jimmy had heard the words *bale out* over the intercom and automatically reached for his parachute. He turned his seat sideways and watched Donny slip through the hatch. Tad went next in a matter of seconds. George followed.

Jimmy moved forward to go and realized that he had not disconnected his headphones from the wireless set. He had to fight the pitching of the plane to untangle them and pull out the cord. When he turned around to go he saw someone coming down the steps. He could see only the legs. He assumed that it was Nigel, but it wasn't. He recognized Tommy. This wasn't Tommy's regular escape route. Something must be wrong. Where was Nigel?

Jimmy waited the seconds it took for Tommy to clear through the hatch and went up two steps to see if Nigel had escaped. But Nigel was in his seat, fighting with the control column. Nigel looked at him and gestured fiercely for Jimmy to go back down the steps and get out of the aircraft. Instead Jimmy came up the last steps and reached over to help Nigel engage the autopilot. He didn't think about risk to himself. This was his skipper. This was his friend. Every ounce of Baldock stubbornness ran through his veins. He would not leave Nigel. Nigel shook his head emphatically and again pointed down the steps. He didn't want Jimmy's sacrifice. He'd committed himself to keep on flying while there was any of his crew on board. Jimmy pointed down the stairs and took Nigel's arm. But the pitching of the plane made even simple tasks like getting out of the pilot's seat next to impossible. Then the Halifax finally seemed to give up.

Only a few seconds had elapsed between the time that Jimmy had come up the steps and when the aircraft nosed sharply down and turned viciously to starboard. The rate of spin pinned Jimmy and Nigel in their places. Then a violent explosion tore off the wing and Jimmy shut his eyes. He felt the centrifugal force pull the skin away from his cheekbones. He clutched blindly for something to hold onto before there was blackness.

The wounded Halifax spiraled down the remaining few thousand feet, carrying its pilot and wireless operator, until with a rending crash the Hercules engines drove themselves eight feet into the ground, the petrol tanks caught fire, the ammunition exploded, and everything was reduced to mangled metal. A large black cloud erupted from the wreckage and stained the sky. The grass and shrubbery at the crash site burned in a black circle around the fuselage until the leaking fuel was done.

And above in the dark, the bomber stream flew on its way.

20

Expensive French Perfume

Barbara stands in the Commonwealth Graves section within a large cemetery in Germany, thinking about the steps that inevitably brought both her and her father to this place. The irony does not escape her. She is meeting her father for the first time, even though it is a headstone that stands as proxy for him.

She reaches forward and places yellow roses on the grass in front of his stone. It is one of a set of matched white slabs extending across the grass in straight lines. There is no holder for the flowers, so she wonders if leaving flowers is not usual or expected. The roses look forlorn and she knows that they will soon shrivel in the sun. But the impulse behind laying them on the grass is too sincere for her to feel it inappropriate.

She kneels before the stone and runs her fingers over the chiseled letters. The slab commemorates a young flyer, an ordinary man called upon to do extraordinary things. Neatly cut into the stone is the RAF insignia on the top, then his number and rank, his name, his age, then Wireless Operator, and the date when he was shot down. It stands almost touching the gravestone of the pilot, Nigel Broadbent. She's been told that when the headstones are this close together, it means that they couldn't be separated when the time came to move the remains to this permanent home. Nigel's says simply 'In God's Keeping.' She guesses that Letitia chose this inscription because each grave says something different. She wonders what Letitia has told her son about his father. He must be around her age. She hopes that one day he comes looking for her.

The skies are a pale summer blue right now, and the cemetery is peaceful. In the distance an elderly couple walks along a pathway. Their clothes are cut in a European fashion. The woman is carrying flowers wrapped in green paper. They don't come anywhere near her. Barbara assumes they are visiting civilian graves, perhaps even those of people killed in the bombing. It is all circular and ironic.

The Commonwealth War Graves Commission section is off by itself. It has always seemed to her—and more so now—that these peaceful cemeteries are a strangely ordered and personal way to remember something as terrible and impersonal as war. The Commission has erected a large stone Celtic cross that looms above rich green grass and shining rows of identical headstones. It reminds her vaguely of the crosses in market towns in England except that in the centre of the cross, echoing its shape, is a sword.

Barbara cannot stay long. She flew over from London this morning and came straight to the cemetery. The flight was nothing like the one to Canada, a few minutes in the air rather than hours. She had a taxi bring her to the cemetery and ordered it to come back for her. She knows that it will not be long before it pulls up at the iron entrance gates. Then she will fly home and go from Heathrow Airport's cavernous hallways directly to the theatre. This moment alone with the grave is an interlude, her equivalent of a moment's silence to consider things she never had the chance to know. The messages in the visitors' book at the stone shelter say things like "Well, Uncle Jack, I finally made it," "Good bye, Dad, am finally able to say it now," and "We miss you at the family do's, Chris, you're always with us, love Sis." The years have done little to dampen loss. She imagines an entire generation named for lost fathers, friends, and uncles.

She would like to think that her father would be proud of her. She knows her mother would. Marilyn would be happy to know that she has a permanent relationship at last. Sheridan and she have already established those little agreements that committed couples make. Like who turns off the lights and checks the front door locks. Who deals with the tradesmen or the missing newspaper. Who cooks and what it is safe to tease one another about. She's met his sister and taken him to see the place where she scattered Marilyn's ashes near her brother's grave in Cornwall. Marilyn would have liked Sheridan, and she might even have behaved herself when she was with him.

Barbara sits on the low wall around the graves. Her thoughts go to her half-sister. Billy phoned a couple of weeks ago to say that he had finally worked up the courage to tell her about Barbara. She too had idealized Jimmy but in her case she had a lifetime's worth of shattered dreams to deal with. Barbara got a letter from her, a long, disjointed flow of thoughts that began with suspicion and angry denial before finally veering into curiosity. They've started an awkward exchange trying to figure out how much they have inherited from their father and what their relationship should be. It has been hard since her mother, Jimmy's wife, Ann, is still alive. Barbara hopes that one day when both are ready, they can meet and tie together the lost threads of their father's life. But not now. Not while there are people alive who can be hurt. Not while neither has come to terms with the idea of sharing him nor the reasons that led him to start a child with a woman with whom there could be no future.

She had imagined that her father's family would welcome her with open arms, feeling that some unexpected part of him had been returned. She has been deeply disturbed to realize that she is instead an inconvenience. She must put that down to her own naïvite. Life is not like the theatre where there is resolution in a matter of hours. In the real world, there are no necessary reconciliation and no necessary justice. You have to make your choice and simply hope the outcome is something you can live with. Her mother protected her from all this. Barbara now understands her mother's extraordinary strength and courage. She hopes she can live up to it.

Much of her new insight is her growing maturity. She is ashamed now of what she sees as her callow self-righteousness. She had no right to demand that her parents be perfect, and she shudders at her adolescent treatment of her mother. But even this understanding is merely the promise of what is left to do. She is wise enough to understand that she has dealt intellectually with the loss of her parents. The real work, the emotional part, has only just begun. Sheridan was absolutely right: truth has consequences. Truth is the easy part. Dealing with it takes a lifetime.

While the what next? of her life is slowly becoming clearer, it's the past that has refused to stay in focus. She can see now that she was stuck somewhere during the movement out of childhood when she allowed her life to be governed by her mother's choices. Even if she didn't realize then what was happening, the damage was the same. She has never made her own choices and taken the responsibility for them. There was always someone else to blame. Now it is different. Her mother lived her life. Barbara must do the same. And she should bear only those burdens that are really hers. As a whole human being, she cannot be expected to apologize for her beginnings. The past is complex and it presents no single vantage point from which to assess its impact. It is as impossible to judge the past absolutely as it is to judge an individual human being.

This new knowledge has spilled over into Barbara's work. She recognizes the truth of what Sheridan told her at Maggie's party. She is on the stage to be believed. To be human. This means that she must be honest with herself and with the audience. She could not be before because she could not resolve the issues with her mother and, as it turned out, with the past.

Still, she cannot blame herself entirely. She hadn't known. She finds it hard to separate her mother from the idea of locks and secrets. It was the perfect metaphor for her. For all the outward chatter of her life, Marilyn lived inside herself. If she had been an aristocrat, people would have said she was eccentric. In her world, she was merely silent. But there comes a time when locks spring open and secrets fall out. She protected her daughter because she did the same thing Barbara did. She judged herself. To keep her secret, she forced on her child a lifetime's resentment of a man she thought had abandoned her. That was preferable to the truth for Marilyn. But it was too high a price for a child to pay. If Barbara's life was to be her mother's atonement for losing her son, then Barbara's success could never be enough. Nothing could have assuaged Marilyn's guilt. It took her death to set them free.

Looking back on her search for her father, Barbara no longer feels the need to judge. Donny told her that was the way to look at the past. It should not be judged except by those who were there and even then it shouldn't be. He was in some respects talking about himself and the bombing that the young aircrews were asked to do. But it applies as well to those who lived and survived those years. What happened was caused by the war. Her mother lost a child and desperately needed to replace her loss. Her father helped a grieving and desperate woman, probably wanting to leave something of himself behind as well. But even if it were the case that Marilyn was beautiful and lonely and he was good looking and frightened, it is not her business. She has never been asked to lay down her life for others. She has never been bombed. She hopes that she would do her duty with as much endurance and grace as they did.

But the effects of war endure. When it was done the aircrews had to find ways to live with memory and loss. Tad and Donny had one another and their enduring friendship. Even then, Donny is defensive and Tad deals with the guilt of his own survival. Tommy turned anger with the war into anger with his crew. Perhaps that's easier for him to deal with. Billy has never left the past. He finds his comfort in ensuring that their sacrifice is not forgotten. George has let geographical distance become his shield. How homesick he must have been for Australia when the cold rain swept across the Yorkshire moors. What it must have cost him to be the heart beat of the crew. Laugh in the face of it, he told them. Barbara hopes he found his peace out there in his green mountains.

She walks along the graves, reading out the names and their ages when they died. She imagines that there is a story behind every one. Parents who lost their only son. Wives and girlfriends left behind to grieve and in many cases raise children by themselves. Fellow crewmembers who survived as prisoners of war but who came home with their deeply buried secrets. She knows that she will never know what happened on her father's flight. Whatever held him back inside the aircraft meant that she would never know him. But it doesn't mean that he has to be forgotten. With her sister and her mother, the survivors of the crew, and Barbara herself, there are eight people who miss him. Not such a bad record to leave behind.

She walks across the sweet-smelling grass to where the pathway leads out to the town. She stops at the boundary of the graves' section and looks back. By finding her father, she has found compassion. It wasn't what she expected when she started her search, but this discovery has changed her perception of herself and of her work. The characters she is asked to play can be no more black and white than she is. They have their depths and secrets that need to be respected. Maggie is right to look for the humanity beneath even the most tortured and unsympathetic characters. She shudders at how she behaved in her RADA classes. No wonder they said she was too detached. She was trying to play live human beings while ignoring the turmoil and the confusions of existence. How arrogant. She will never make that mistake again. When she is on stage, she will try for the voice of ordinary people asked to do extraordinary things. She sees now that her best roles will be those where she portrays a woman struggling to emerge and understand. She can picture that first hopeful flicker, the stumble toward might be possible, the stretch of soul with the first deep breaths of unaccustomed air, the awkward emergence into another reality, and the acceptance that the transformation is not guaranteed to bring happiness or peace of mind. She has been perfectly cast as the head wife because that is what the role demands. Sheridan must have seen that quality in her when he chose her. She just didn't know it.

Not long after she talked with Tommy, she told Sheridan that Maggie's role is not for her. Not at this time, at least. She can play Lily adequately but not distinctly because she has nothing to bring to her. She asked him if she could stay with the London cast for now and go with him to the New York production in her same role as Head Wife. The Americans should allow it, she argued, since she won the Olivier for it. She told him that a role will open for her one day that will be hers alone—one that she can create and shape to who she is. And then perhaps there will be greatness. Sheridan said he would respect her wishes. She could not be sure, but it seemed to her that he was proud.

She walks toward the bustling town outside the cemetery gates. She knows she will come back and will always place yellow roses on the grave of the man she never knew but missed all her life. At the airport shop, after the taxi has threaded its way through the narrow streets that make European cities both quaint and dangerous, she goes to the airport's shopping arcade. Just before boarding the flight back to London, she buys a large bottle of French perfume. She smiles as she does so because she knows exactly how she plans to use it.

Epilogue

Entertainment News UK
February 2006

Theatre Couple Win Double Lawrence Olivier Awards

    Well-known West End theatre couple **Sheridan Mann and Barbara MacDonald** took home paired Lawrence Olivier Awards last night for their work on Richard Orffen's *The Last Coming*. Mann won for best direction and MacDonald for actress of the year in a drama. This is the fourth Olivier for Mann and the third for MacDonald. She previously won as best actress in a supporting role in *Yesterday's Lies* by Orffen, and actress of the year in Walter Berg's *Transformations*. Mann won previously for Orffen's *Yesterday's Lies* and *The Sunday Madness*, and Steven Benedict's *I Bet My Life*. Mann and MacDonald will leave *The Last Coming* at the end of May. They will then spend several months in Canada where Mann will direct his wife in repertory for the Stratford Shakespeare Festival in Ontario. The couple will visit Canadian family before opening *The Last Coming* at the Helen Hayes Theatre in New York in December. Accompanying them will be their son, Jimmy B. Mann. Their daughter, Marilyn Mann, will remain in London where she is starring in the revival of *Oklahoma!* at The Theatre Royal Drury Lane.

978-0-595-41505-2
0-595-41505-9